A Text Book Of

PRACTICAL ZOOLOGY
(PAPER III)

For

S.Y.B.Sc. Practical Zoology, Semester III
As Per New Revised Syllabus of Pune University, June 2014

Prin. Dr. Kishore R. Pawar
M.Sc., Ph.D.
Karmaveer Shantarambapu Kondaji Wavare,
Arts, Sci. & Com. College, CIDCO,
NASHIK – 422008.

Dr. Ashok E. Desai
M.Sc., Ph.D.
Reader in Zoology, P.G. Deptt. of Zoology,
K.T.H.M. College,
NASHIK – 422002.

NIRALI PRAKASHAN
ADVANCEMENT OF KNOWLEDGE

N2271

Practical Zoology (Paper - III) **ISBN 978-93-5164-020-2**

Fourth Edition : June 2017

© : **Authors**

Published By : (−ve)

NIRALI PRAKASHAN

Abhyudaya Pragati, 1312, Shivaji Nagar,
Off J.M. Road, PUNE – 411005
Tel - (020) 25512336/37/39, Fax - (020) 25511379
Email : niralipune@pragationline.com

☞ **DISTRIBUTION CENTRES**

PUNE

Nirali Prakashan : 119, Budhwar Peth, Jogeshwari Mandir Lane, Pune 411002, Maharashtra
Tel : (020) 2445 2044, 66022708, Fax : (020) 2445 1538
Email : bookorder@pragationline.com, niralilocal@pragationline.com

Nirali Prakashan : S. No. 28/27, Dhyari, Near Pari Company, Pune 411041
Tel : (020) 24690204 Fax : (020) 24690316
Email : dhyari@pragationline.com, bookorder@pragationline.com

MUMBAI

Nirali Prakashan : 385, S.V.P. Road, Rasdhara Co-op. Hsg. Society Ltd.,
Girgaum, Mumbai 400004, Maharashtra
Tel : (022) 2385 6339 / 2386 9976, Fax : (022) 2386 9976
Email : niralimumbai@pragationline.com

☞ **DISTRIBUTION BRANCHES**

JALGAON

Nirali Prakashan : 34, V. V. Golani Market, Navi Peth, Jalgaon 425001,
Maharashtra, Tel : (0257) 222 0395, Mob : 94234 91860

KOLHAPUR

Nirali Prakashan : New Mahadvar Road, Kedar Plaza, 1st Floor Opp. IDBI Bank
Kolhapur 416 012, Maharashtra. Mob : 9850046155

NAGPUR

Pratibha Book Distributors : Above Maratha Mandir, Shop No. 3, First Floor,
Rani Jhanshi Square, Sitabuldi, Nagpur 440012, Maharashtra
Tel : (0712) 254 7129

DELHI

Nirali Prakashan : 4593/21, Basement, Aggarwal Lane 15, Ansari Road, Daryaganj
Near Times of India Building, New Delhi 110002
Mob : 08505972553

BENGALURU

Pragati Book House : House No. 1, Sanjeevappa Lane, Avenue Road Cross,
Opp. Rice Church, Bengaluru – 560002.
Tel : (080) 64513344, 64513355,Mob : 9880582331, 9845021552
Email:bharatsavla@yahoo.com

CHENNAI

Pragati Books : 9/1, Montieth Road, Behind Taas Mahal, Egmore,
Chennai 600008 Tamil Nadu, Tel : (044) 6518 3535,
Mob : 94440 01782 / 98450 21552 / 98805 82331,
Email : bharatsavla@yahoo.com

niralipune@pragationline.com | www.pragationline.com

Also find us on www.facebook.com/niralibooks

Preface ...

The authors are indeed very happy to present this book **'A Text Book of Practical Zoology'** for the students of S.Y.B.Sc. of Pune University. Learning of any science subject is incomplete without experiments and demonstrations. Hence, theoretical and practical training has given equal importance in the syllabus of undergraduate and postgraduate students. The subject Zoology is an interesting and live subject of life sciences in which more emphasis is given on practical studies. Along with classical zoology, number of applied zoology courses are included in the syllabus of S.Y.B.Sc. class. Teaching and learning becomes more and more meaningful if field exercursions, Visits to Fishery, Sericulture, Apiculture, Agriculture University or Agriculture Farm or Sea Shore units are arranged. Close observations, handling of the animals, Study of the various animals in their natural habitats, their life-cycle etc. are the most effective methods of study of Zoology. Along with the laboratory studies field studies are most important for thorough understanding of the subject.

Now-a-days, number of students are being attracted by the subject Zoology, but they are being denied of the facilities. Therefore, spacious and well equipped laboratories are essential. Laboratory is the place of good interactions among teachers and students which ultimately creates more and more interest of the subject in the students. There are number of reference and text books on the subject however, the practical books or laboratory manuals are very limited. There was long left demand from students and teachers for the text books on Practical Zoology.

The present Practical Text Book has been written to meet the needs of S.Y.B.Sc. Zoology students. The book describes the procedure of dissection, important mountings, different systems and museum specimens along with suitable illustrations. The life cycle of important animals, equipments, preparation of different solutions, principles of colorimetry and chromatography are also well described. The Practical Syllabus is considerably very vast and it is very difficult for the students to collect the information from several books. The present book covers entire syllabus in a simple and lucid language with neat, clear line drawing illustrations. Emphasis has been given on the important characters and comments which are given pointwise to facilitate the students remembering and writing the same spotting at the time of practical examination. The authors sincerely feel that this Practical Text Book will fullfil the needs of the students.

The authors are thankful to Dr. Vasantrao Pawar, Secretary, M.V.P. Samaj, for his constant inspiration and encouragement. The authors are grateful to Shri. Dineshbhai Furia, Shri. Jignesh Furia, Shri. M. P. Munde and the staff of Nirali Prakashan for the prompt publication of this book.

Suggestions for improvement of the book shall be highly appreciated from teachers and students.

July, 2014

Prin. Dr. Kishore R. Pawar
Dr. Ashok E. Desai

Syllabus and Contents ...

ZY-223: PRACTICAL COURSE

Class Mammals – Rabbit, Mungoose, Kangaroo

Practical 16. Identification of Poisonous and non- poisonous snakes with the help of identification key with two examples of each (D)   **16.1 - 16.7**

Practical 17. Study of modifications of beaks and feet in birds (Museum specimen) (D)

    (a)   Beaks: tearing and piercing, fruit eating, mud probing, fish catching, wood chiseling and flower probing.

    (b)   Feet: perching, raptorial, climbing, swimming, running.   **17.1 - 17.4**

Practical 18. Study of external characters and digestive system of Scoliodon (E) **18.1 - 18.4**

Practical 19. Study of brain of Scoliodon (E)   **19.1 - 19.3**

Practical 20. (a) Temporary preparation of placoid scales from Scoliodon (E)   **20.1 - 20.4**

    (b) Study of cranial nerves, eye ball muscles of Scoliodon (D)

    Study of Membranous labyrinth of Scoliodon (D)

Practical 21. (a) Study of life cycle of Honey bee (D)   **21.1 - 21.9**

    (b) Study of mouth parts, thoracic appendages (legs and wings)

    and sting apparatus of Honey bee (E)

Practical 22. Study of various bee keeping equipments (D)   **22.1 - 22.8**

Practical 23. Study of: (a) bee products, (b) bee pests, (c) bee enemies (D)   **23.1 - 23.8**

Practical 24. (a) Study of life cycle of *Bombyx mori* (D)   **24.1 - 24.8**

    (b) Study of any five equipments in Sericulture (D)

Practical 25. Compulsory submission of field visit report along with at least five Photographs/sketches of insect pest/fishes/any animal corresponding to theory courses   **25.1 - 25.1**

Practical 26. Compulsory study tour/visit to sea coast/fishery institute/sericulture farm/ apiculture institute / agricultural farm.   **26.1 - 26.4**

•   **Practical Skeleton Paper**   **P.1 - P.1**

***

Practical **1** ...

Aim:

To study the classification with reasons of the Phylum Arthropoda: Scorpion, Crab, Cockroach, Head louse, Centipede, Peripatus [D].

PHYLUM – ARTHROPODA

Arthropoda means 'jointed legs' (Greek; arthros = jointed; Podos = foot). Therefore, jointed legs is the most important characteristic structure of this phylum.

1.1 General Characters

(1) The animals are bilaterally symmetrical and metamerically segmented.

(2) The body is covered externally by thick, tough, non-living, organic chitinous exoskeleton.

(3) Exoskeleton is cast off periodically and this process is called ecdysis or moulting. It is essential for the growth of the animal.

(4) The appendages are jointed and they are modified as gills, jaws, legs etc. for various functions.

(5) They are triploblastic animals but true coelom is reduced in adult and represented by excretory and reproductive organs.

(6) Respiration may occur throughout the body surface but generally takes place by special structures like gills, tracheae and book lungs.

(7) Circulatory system is of open type i.e. the blood flows in spaces or sinuses comprising haemocoel instead of blood vessels.

(8) True nephridia are absent. Excretion occurs by green glands or by malpighian tubules.

(9) Nervous system is of annelidan type.

(10) Compound eyes are present.

(11) Sexes are usually separate and often there is distinct sexual dimorphism.

(12) Fertilization is generally internal. Development includes larval forms which undergo varying degree of metamorphosis to become adults. Parental care is often well marked.

1.2 Phylum Arthropoda is divided into Six Classes

1.2.1 Class - Onychophora

(1) These are terrestrial, air-breathing primitive worm like animals.
(2) They possess claws (Onychos = claw and Phoros = bearing).
(3) The animal possesses a single pair of antennae, eyes and jaws.
(4) Many pairs of stumpy legs are present which are not joined.
(5) Body shows no distinct external segmentation.
(6) *Peripatus* the representative of this sub-phylum is the connecting link between phylum Annelida and Arthropoda.

Example: *Peripatus.*

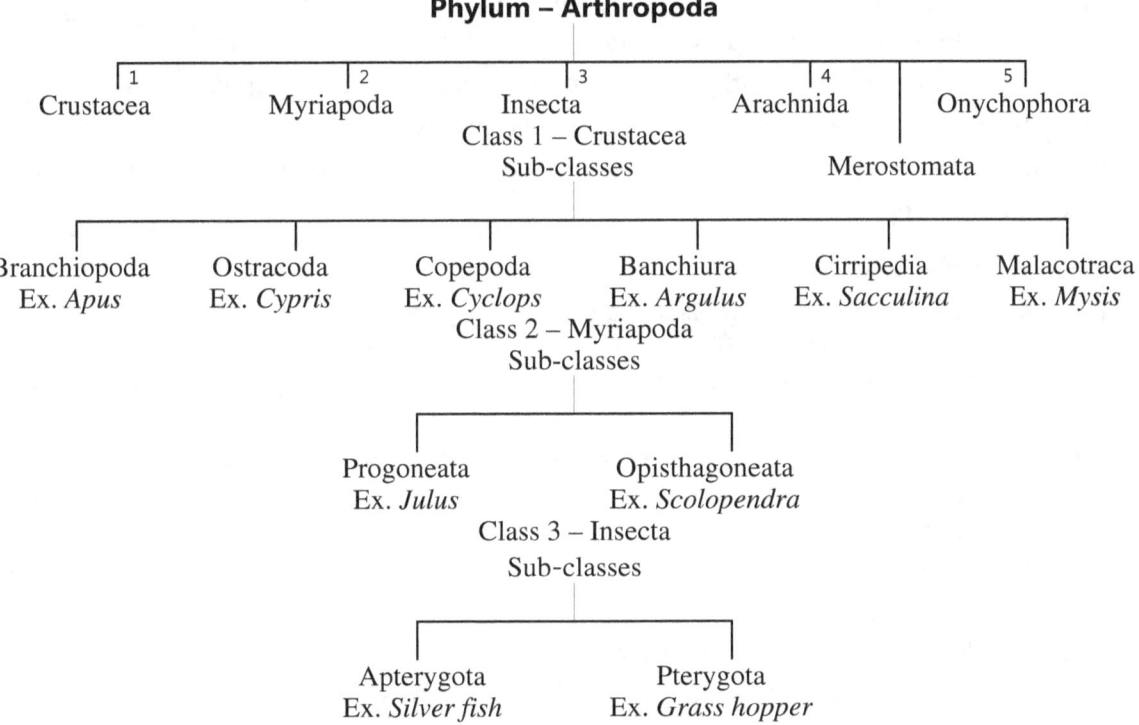

Subpylum-Chelicerata

(1) These animals lack both antennae and mandibles.
(2) Body is usually divided into two parts: anterior unsegmented prosoma or cephalothorax and posterior segmented opisthosoma or abdomen.
(3) Prosoma has six pairs of appendages, one pair of chelicerae, one pair of pedipalpi and four pairs of legs.
(4) Animals show respiration by gills, book lungs or tracheae.
(5) Coxal glands or malpighian tubules are the excretory organs.
(6) Sexes are separate. Males are smaller than females.
(7) Animals are terrestrial and predaceous.

This subphylum includes two important classes: **Merostomata** and **Arachnida**.

1.2.2 Class-Merostomata

(1) They are aquatic and marine chelicerates, with branchial respiration.

(2) Body shows two parts: anterior cephalothorax or prosoma and posterior abdomen or opisthosoma. Abdomen is again divisible into meso and metasoma.

(3) The cephalothorax is covered by a broad, horse-shoe shaped unsegmented carapace and dorsally it bears pair of lateral compound eyes and pair of median simple eyes.

(4) On ventral side cephalothorax carries one pair of chelicerae and five pairs of similar joined walking legs.

(5) Antennae are absent.

(6) Mesosoma bears six pairs of appendages of which first pair forms genital operculum and remaining five pairs of appendages bear book-gills.

(7) Metasoma is reduced, without any appendages but possesses spike like telson.

(8) Malpighian tubules are absent but coxal glands are excretory organs.

(9) Sexes are separate. Fertilization is external and development includes trillobite larva.

Example: *Limulus* (king crab).

1.2.3 Class-Arachnida

(1) Mostly terrestrial, solitary, air-breathing arthropods.

(2) Free living, predaceous or parasitic.

(3) No head, body divisible into prosoma (cephalothorax) and opisthosoma (abdomen).

(4) The cephalothorax bears simple and sessile eyes and six pairs of joined appendages. Of these one pair is of chelicerae, one pair pedipalpi and four pairs of walking legs.

(5) Antennae and mandibles are absent.

(6) Abdomen is without appendages.

(7) Cuticle is with sensory hairs or scales.

(8) Mouth parts and digestive tract are adapted for sucking.

(9) Respiration by tracheae or book-lungs or both. In aquatic forms it cutaneous or by book gills.

(10) Excretion takes place by Malpighian tubules or coxal glands or both.

(11) Sexes are separate and sexual dimorphism is inconspicuous. Males are smaller than females.

(12) Fertilization is internal. Oviparous and few viviparous. Development is direct.

Examples: *Palamnaeus, Buthus* (Scorpions), *Spiders, Ticks and Mites.*

Subphylum-Pantopoda (Pycnogonida):

(1) Aquatic, marine, small spider like animals.

(2) Body has single cephalic somite and 3 or 4 trunk somites and abdomen is rudimentary.

(3)   They bear one pair of chelicere, one pair of palps, one pair of ovigerous legs and 4 to 6 pairs of long walking legs.

(4)   Long porboscis bears mouth.

(5)   Two pairs of eyes are present.

Examples: Sea spiders (*Nymphon, Pycnogonum*).

Subphylum-Mandibulata:

(1)   The animals are terrestrial: freshwater or marine.

(2)   Body is divisible either in two parts (cephalothorax and abdomen) or three parts (head, trunk and abdomen).

(3)   One or two pairs of antennae, one or two pairs of maxillae and three or more pairs of walking legs are present.

(4)   Gills or tracheae are respiratory organs.

(5)   Malpighian tubules and coxal glands are excretory organs.

(6)   Sexes are usually separate and development includes larval stage.

Subphylum mandibulata includes three important classes:

Crustacea, Myriapoda and **Insecta**.

1.2.4 Class - Crustacea

(1)   They are aquatic, marine and freshwater.

(2)   Some are parasitic or sedentary.

(3)   They have variously shaped bodies with three divisions; head, thorax and abdomen.

(4)   Exoskeleton is made up of thick protective, chitinous cuticle strengthened by impregnation with calcium salts, hence crustacea.

(5)   The thorax may fuse partly or wholly with head to form cephalothorax, which is partly or entirely covered by exoskeletal shield called carapace from dorsal side.

(6)   Head bears pair of stalked compound eyes.

(7)   Jointed appendages vary in number but there are two pairs of antennae, one pair of mandibles and two pairs of maxillae on head and one pair of appendages on each segment of thorax and abdomen.

(8)   First pair of antennae are uniramous but remaining all appendages are biramous. The appendages are variously modified as jaws, legs, fins, gills or accessory reproductive organs.

(9)   Respiration by gills or pseudotracheae or by body surface.

(10)   Excretion by green glands malpighian tubules are absent.

(11)   Mostly, unisexual except cirripedia. Sexual dimorphism is common. Generally, females carry the eggs.

(12)   Some groups like **Brachiopoda** and **ostracoda** show Parthenogenesis.

(13)   Development includes more or less of metamorphosis and is accompanied by free living larva nauplius.

Examples: *Lepas, Daphnia, Cypris, Cyclops, Palaemon, Lobster, Crab*.

1.2.5 Class-Myriapoda

(1) They are terrestrial, air breathing.

(2) Body elongated vermiform with distinct head and trunk has number of segments.

(3) Many jointed pair of antennae are present, pair of mandibles and maxillae are present.

(4) The body is segmented and bears one or two pairs of jointed legs.

(5) Respiration by spiracles and tracheae.

(6) Malpighian tubules are excretory organs.

(7) Sexes are separate, single gonad with paired gonoducts.

Examples: *Spirobolus* (millipede), *Scolopendra* (Centipede).

1.2.6 Class-Insecta

(1) Mostly terrestrial, aerial, air breathing animal. Rarely aquatic.

(2) Body is divided into three distinct regions - head, thorax and abdomen.

(3) The head is formed by fusion of six segments and bears a pair of antennae, a pair of compound eyes, few simple eyes or ocelli, a pair of mandibles, two pairs of maxillae.

(4) The mouth parts are variously adapted for chewing, biting, piercing, sucking, lapping or siphoning etc.

(5) The thorax consists of three segments and bears three pairs of jointed legs (hence hexapoda), two or one pair of wings present dorso-laterally. Some insects are wingless.

(6) The abdomen consists of 7 to 11 segments and lacks appendages but genitalia are present at the end.

(7) Salivary glands are present but liver is absent.

(8) Respiration by tracheae opening out by paired segmental spiracles.

(9) Heart is tubular muscular and 8 chambered situated in the abdomen

(10) Excretion occurs by two to many malpighian tubules attached to the anterior end of the hind gut.

(11) Nervous system is of the annelidan type.

(12) Sense organs are well developed.

(13) Sexes are separate, sexual dimorphism is distinct.

(14) Gonads are composed of numerous tubules or follicles.

(15) Fertilization is internal. Development usually occurs with some sort of metamorphosis. Parthenogenesis takes place in some forms.

Examples: *Mantis, Gryllotalpa*, Dragonfly, Grass hopper, *Pediculus* (Louse), Butterfly, Moth, Honey bee, Beetle.

1.3 Palamnaeus (Scorpion)

Classification:

Phylum – Arthropoda	–	Jointed appendages metamerically segmented, triploblastic body, cavity-haemocoel
Class – Arachnida	–	Air breathng, terrestrial; Body divisible into two regions prosoma and opisthosoma, four pairs of legs.
Order – Scorpionidea	–	Body is divisible into prosoma, mesosoma and metasoma, respiration by four pairs of book lungs.
Genus	–	*Palamnaeus*

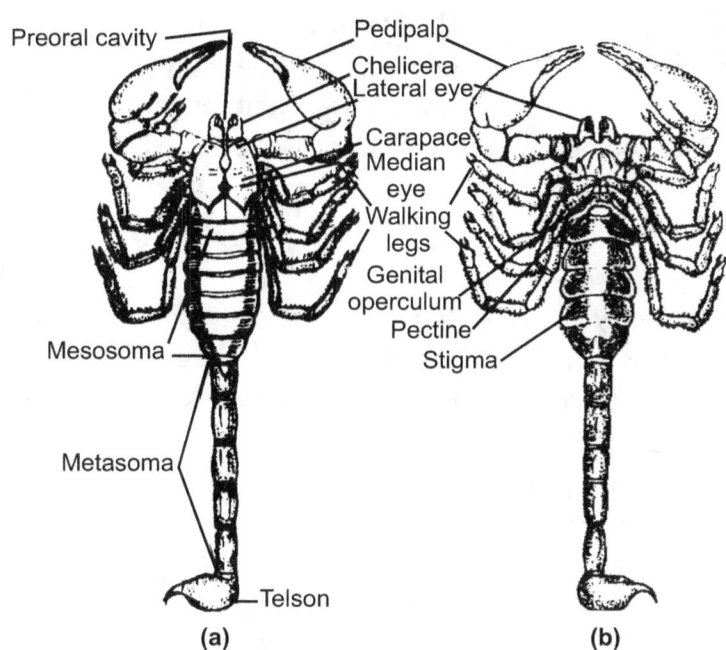

Fig. 1.1: *Palamnaeus bengalensis*. (a) - Dorsal view; (b) - Ventral view

Characters:

(1) It is nocturnal animal found under stones, bark of trees, burrows in tropical and subtropical regions.

(2) Body consists of 3 parts, anterior prosoma (cephalothorax), middle mesosoma and posterior metasoma.

(3) Cephalothorax or prosoma is formd by 6 segments and it possess a pair of median eyes; 2-5 pairs of lateral eyes and 6 pairs of walking legs.

(4) There are 7 segments in mesosoma. Genital opening in present on the sternum of first segment. Pair of pectines are on the second segment and sterna of 3rd, 4th, 5th and 6th segments bear laterally a pair of stigmata, which are the openings of stigmata.

(5) Metasoma consists of 5 segments but without appendages.

(6) The sting is present on last segment of metasome. Sting has ampulla and spine.

(7) The book lungs are the respiratory organs.

(8) Sexes are separate and gonads are like network.

(9) It is viviparous animal.

(10) Scorpions are harmful to mankind because sting causes severe pain, fever and sometimes it proves fatal.

1.4 Carcinus (Crab)

Phylum – *Arthropoda*   –   Jointed appendages, metamerically segmented, triploblastic, body cavity-haemocoel

Class – *Crustacea*   –   Thick exoskeleton; head fused with thorax to form cephalothorax

Subclass – *Malacostraca*   –   Thorax comprises 8 segments and abdomen 6 or 7; Abdomen devoid of caudal style, eyes usually stalked.

Order   –   Decapoda

Genus   –   *Carcinus*

Species   –   *meanus*

Characters:

1. Carcinus commonly known as crab.

2. Cephalothorax is large, broader and covered with carapace.

3. Abdomen is greatly reduced and hard. Abdomen is bent and fits into a groove in the thoracic sterna.

4. Antennules and eye stalks lodged in sockets of carapace.

5. Throacic legs (pereopods) five pairs, well developed. First pair is chelate.

6. Uropod is absent.

7. Flattened paddle on the fifth pair of walking legs.

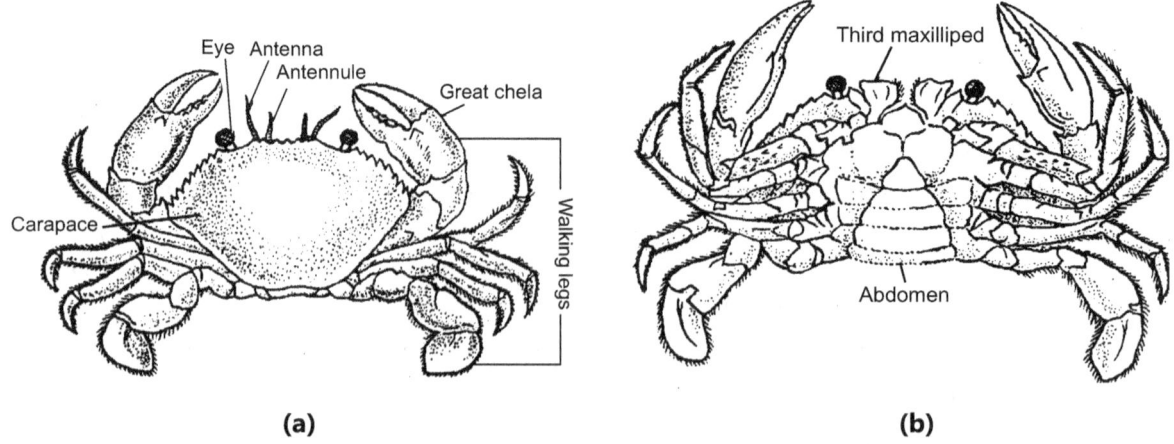

(a)   (b)

Fig. 1.2: Crab (*Carcinus maenus*). (a) Dorsal view, (b) Ventral view

1.5 *Periplaneta* (Cockroach)

Phylum – Arthropoda	–	Jointed appendages; metamerically segmented; body cavity is haemocoel; triploblastic.
Class – Insecta	–	Body is divisble into head, thorax and abdomen; three pairs of legs and two pairs of wings.
Subclass – Pterygota	–	Wing usually present; abdomen devoid of appendages except genitalia and cerci; metamorphosis simple or complex.
Division – Exopterygota	–	Young stages are known as nymphs; wings develop externally metamorphosis primitive or simple.
Order – Dictyoptera	–	Antennae filiform with numerous segments; mouth parts are mandibulate type, forewings are lethery and hindwings are membranous; eggs contained in ootheca.
Family – Blattidae	–	It includes about 35,000 species; ootheca divided into two rows of packets by longitudinal partition; similar legs with large flat coxae.
Genus – *Periplaneta*	–	Presence of wings in both the sexes.
Species - *americana*	–	Colour is light and size is large about 2.5 - 5 cm.

Characters:

1. Body is divisible into head, thorax and abdomen.
2. Three pairs of legs, therefore known as hexapoda.
3. Two pairs of wings, forewings are leathery and hindwings are membranous. Forewings form wing covers called *tegmina*.
4. Head bears a pair of compound eyes.
5. Spiracles and tracheae are the respiratory organs.
6. Antennae almost invariably filiform with numerous segments.
7. Mouthparts are of the chewing or mandibulate type.
8. Metamorphosis is gradual, without a pupal stage. Young stages are called nymphs.
9. Cerci many segmented.
10. Gizzard with powerful masticatory armature.
11. Head nearly or completely covered from above by large, shield like pronotum.
12. Eggs contained in ootheca.
13. *Periplaneta* is common household pest, and commonly called as ship cockroach or American cockroach.
14. Cockroach is nocturnal animal i.e. it comes out to feed at night.
15. It is omnivorous or scavengerous in its diet.
16. The adult cockroach is narrow, elongated, dorso-ventrally compressed and bilaterally symmetrical. It measures about from 30-40 mm in length and about 10-12 mm in width.

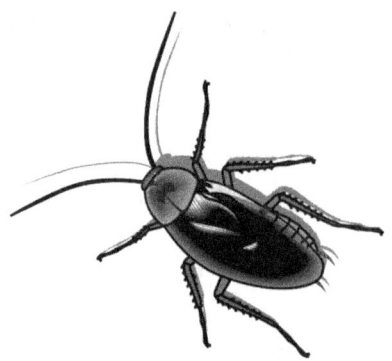

Fig. 1.3: *Periplaneta*

1.6 *Pediculus* (Human louse)

Phylum – Arthropoda	–	Jointed appendages; metamerically segmented; triploblastic; body cavity haemocoel.
Class – Insecta	–	Body divisible into head, thorax and abdomen; three pairs of legs; two pairs of wings; terrestrial or aquatic and air breathing.
Subclass – Pterygota	–	Wings present; metamorphosis is simple or complex. Abdominal appendages absent except genitalia and cerci.
Division – Exopterygota	–	Wings develop externally, young ones called numphs, metamorphosis is primitive or simple.
Order – Anoplura	–	Body flattened, elongated without wings; mouthparts piercing and sucking type; legs with single claw for grasping hairs, cerci are absent.

Genus – Pediculus
Species – humanus

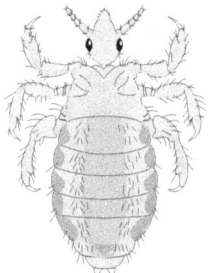

Fig. 1.4: *Pediculus*

Characters:

1. *Pediculus* is commonly known as human louse.
2. Body is divisible into head, thorax and abdomen. Head bears small paired compound eyes and a pair of five segmented antennae.
3. Mouth parts are piercing and sucking type.
4. Body is dorso-ventrally flattened and pale coloured.

5. Wings are absent.
6. Three pairs of legs, each leg bears a large curved claw adapted for clinging to the hairs.
7. Abdomen is nine segmented.
8. In male, posterior end of abdomen is turned upwards.

1.7 *Scolopendra* (Centipede)

Classification:

Phylum – Arthropoda	–	Triploblastic, body metamerically segmented, jointed appendages, body cavity is called haemocoel.
Class – Myriapoda	–	Terrestrial; air breathing; elongated body with many segments each bearing one or two pairs of legs.
Subclass – Opisthogoneta	–	Genital openings are situated at the posterior end of the body.
Order – Chilopoda	–	Numerous trunk segments, each bearing a single pair of legs; poison jaws present.
Genus	–	*Scolopendra*

Characters:

(1) It is also commonly called centipede.

(2) Body elongated, dorsoventraly flattened with many segments.

(3) Body is divisible into head and trunk.

(4) Head bears a pair of antennae, a pair of mandibles and two pairs of maxillae.

(5) There are 22 segments in trunk which are alike.

(6) Each segment from 2-22 possess one pair of walking legs.

(7) The first pair of legs curved, clawed and act as poison glands.

(8) Each legs has 7 segments, that last one ending in a single claw.

(9) Anus in the last body segment.

(10) It is carnivorous, feeds on insects, spiders, worms, slugs, etc.

(11) It occurs under stones, rotten legs and in houses in damp places.

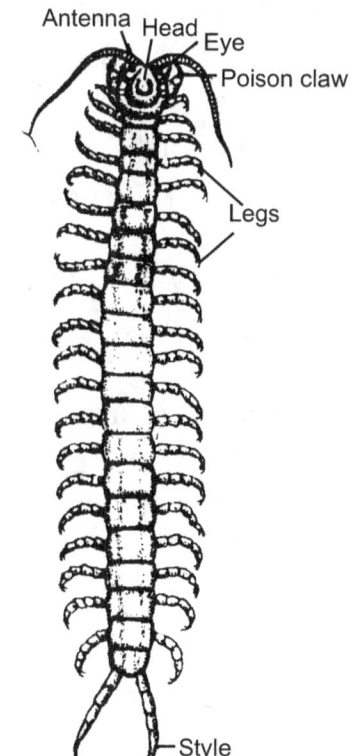

Fig. 1.5: *Scolopendra subspinipes*

1.8 *Peripatus*

Phylum – Arthopoda   –   Triploblastic, body metamerically segmented, jointed appendages, body cavity is called haemocoel.

Class – Onychophora   –   No external segmentation, appendages are not jointed but lobe like fleshy, pair of antennae, jaws and eyes are present on the head. Body slender. Slime glands are present. Connecting link between Annelida and Arthropoda.

Genus   –   *Peripatus*

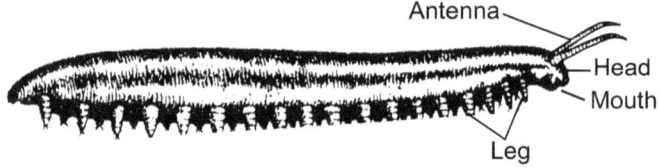

Fig. 1.6: *Peripatus capensis*

Characters:

(1) Body elongated, cylindrical, caterpillar like, soft and enclosed in a thin chitinous cuticle.

(2) Colouration varies from dark grey to brown but red and blue are not rare.

(3) The skin is velvety like with transverse wrinkles beering numerous small papillae armed with spines.

(4) Body divisible into an indistinct head and an elongated trunk.

(5) A pair of eyes, a pair of antennae, a pair of jaws, a pair of oral papillae are present on head.

(6) Mouth ventral on the anterior end.

(7) Trunk bears a series of paired short stumpy appendages which vary in number 14 to 43 pairs.

(8) Legs are stumpy, unjointed, ringed by ridges with tubercules and terminate in a foot bearing two curves claws.

(9) Slime glands open on the surface of oral papillae.

(10) Respiration by trachae.

(11) Carnivorous feeds on insects.

(12) It is a connecting link between Annelida and Arthropoda.

(13) *Peripatus* is nocturnal animal lives in crevices of rocks under bark, stones and leaves. It prefers *humid* habitat.

Practical **2**...

Aim:

To Study the Classification with the reasons of the following Phylum - Mollusca - Chiton, Snail, Bivalve, Dentalium, Octopus [D].

PHYLUM-MOLLUSCA

Mollusca means soft bodied animals (Latin, molluscs = soft). Aristotle first used this term for cuttle-fish. In latin soft nut enclosed in a thin shell is called mollusca. Thus, it is referring to the bivalve shell and soft bodied animal enclosed in the shell.

2.1 General Characters

(1) Molluscs are aquatic, mostly marine, some are freshwater and some terrestrial.

(2) The symmetry is bilateral, however, gastropods and cephalopods lose their bilateral symmetry and become asymmetrical due to torsion or spiral twisting.

(3) Body of the molluscs is soft, differentiated into four parts anterior head, dorsal visceral mass, ventral foot and mantle.

(4) Epidermis is single layered, generally ciliated with mucous glands.

(5) Muscular foot is present on ventral side which is locomotory organ and modified for creeping, swimming and burrowing.

(6) A thin, muscular, fleshy fold covers the dorsal body wall called mantle or pallium. The space enclosed by mantle is called mantle cavity.

(7) Shell is secreted by outer surface of mantle. Shell is hard, calcarious, and it may be bivalved, univalved, spiral or cone like, internal or external, reduced or even absent in some animals.

(8) Respiration by gills called ctenidia. Body surface, mantle or lungs are respiratory organs in terrestrial forms.

(9) Digestive system is complete. Buccal cavity contains a grasping organ, the radula with transverse rows of teeth.

(10) Circulatory system is of open type.

(11) Excretion is brought about by one or two pairs of sac-like kidneys.

(12) Nervous system consists of paired ganglia, cerebral, pleural, pedal, and visceral ganglia inter connected by commissures and connectives.

(13) Tentacles, eyes, statocysts and osphradia are the sense organs.

(14) Sexes are usually separate, some are hermaphrodite, fetilization is external or internal.

(15) Segmentation (cleavage) is spiral. Development may include **glochidium** or **veliger larva**.

The **phylum Mollusca** is divided into six classes: **Monoplacophora, Amphineura, Gastropoda, Scaphopoda, Pelecypoda** and **Cephalopoda**.

2.2 Class-Monoplacophora

(1) Marine and they are called living fossils.
(2) Body has bilateral symmetry and is covered by a spoon or cup shaped shell.
(3) Head bears tentacles.
(4) The disc like foot has a flat creeping sole.
(5) The visceral mass is divided into five segments each with a pair of shell muscles, gills, auricles, nephridia and gonads.
(6) Buccal cavity contains radula.
(7) Stomach contains a crystalline style.
(8) Nervous system lacks ganglia.
(9) Sexes are separate.

Example: *Neopilina*.

2.3 Class-Amphineura

(1) They are marine, bottom dwelling primitive molluscs.
(2) Body bilaterally symmetrical, vermiform, elongated and flattened.
(3) Head is not distinct, without tentacles and eyes.
(4) Foot is large, ventral, flattened and useful for creeping.
(5) Dorsal side of the body shows spicules or calcarious plates.
(6) Respiration by gills.
(7) Nervous system is primitive.
(8) Excretion by pair of kidneys.
(9) Sexes are separate or united.
(10) Fertilization is external and development includes a pelagic trochophore larva.

Examples: *Chiton, Neomenia, Chaetoderma*.

2.4 Class-Scaphopoda

(1) Body elongated, worm like and bilaterally symmetrical.
(2) Shell is tubular, curved and open at both the ends.
(3) Foot is conical and useful for digging.
(4) Head rudimentary and without eyes and true tentacles.
(5) Long, thread-like, prehensile, knobbed processes called **captacula** useful for capturing the food.
(6) Ctenidia or gills are absent.
(7) Respiration by mantle.
(8) Sexes are separate and life history includes a veliger larva.

Examples: *Dentalium* (Tusk shell) and *Siphonodentalium*.

2.5 Class-Gastropoda

(1)   Gastropoda includes marine, freshwater as well as terrestrial forms.

(2)   Body is asymmetrical due to torsion.

(3)   Head is distinct and bears tentacles and eyes.

(4)   Foot is ventral, large and flat useful for locomotion and attchment. It bears operculum for closing the shell aperture.

(5)   Shell is univalved and spiral, secreted by mantle.

(6)   Buccal cavity contains odontophore with radula having transverse rows of chitinous teeth.

(7)   Respiration by body surface or gills or lungs.

(8)   Circulatory system is open and lacunar, heart has one or two auricles and one ventricle.

(9)   The excretory system consists of a single kidney

(10)   Sexes are separate or united. Development may be direct or includes trochophore and veliger larval stages.

Examples: *Pila, Haliotis, Patella, Cypraea, Helix, Lymnea.*

2.6 Class-Pelecypoda

(1)   Majority of animals are marine, some are freshwater and generally lead sedentary or burrowing life.

(2)   Body is bilaterally symmetrical and laterally compressed.

(3)   Head is reduced without eyes and tentacles but bears a pair of labial palps.

(4)   Foot is ventral, large, muscular wedge shaped adapted for burrowing in sand and mud.

(5)   Shell consists of two (right and left) valves movably hinged dorsally and closed by one or two adductor muscles.

(6)   Mantle comprises two (left and right) lobes which are united dorsally but hanging free ventrally and enclosing spacious mantle cavity.

(7)   Inhalent and exhalent siphons are present for the entry and exit of water into and from the mantle cavity.

(8)   Respiration by ctenidia.

(9)   Alimentary canal is coiled tube without radula.

(10)   Circulatory system consists of sinuses and vessels, heart has two auricles and one ventricle enclosed in a pericardium.

(11)   Excretion by paired kidneys.

(12)   Sexes are separate. Development includes trochophore, veliger and glochidium larvae.

Examples: *Unio, Mytilus, Pecten, Pinctada (Oyster), Solen.*

2.7 Class-Cephalopoda

(1) They are marine, fast swimming, highly organised, predaceous animals.
(2) Bilaterally symmetrical body having head and trunk.
(3) Head is prominent and bears pair of eyes and mouth.
(4) Foot is partly modified into numerous sucker bearing arms or tentacles surrounding the mouth (hence cephalopoda). The tentacles may be 8 or 10.
(5) The trunk is uncoiled.
(6) Shell may be external and well-developed or internal and reduced or absent altogether.
(7) Mouth is provided with horny jaws and radula.
(8) Respiration by two pairs of ctenidia.
(9) Excretion by two pairs of kidneys.
(10) Sexes are separate.
(11) In male one arm is hectocotylized. Serves as a copulatory organ.
(12) Development is direct.

Examples: *Sepia, Loligo, Octopus, Nautilus.*

2.8 Study of Selected Animals from Phylum - Mollusca

2.8.1 *Chiton*

Phylum – Mollusca   –   Body soft, unsegmented, bilaterally symmetrical and consists of head, foot, mantle and visceral mass.

Class – Amphineura   –   Head reduced, no eyes and tentacles, mouth and anus terminal.

Sub-class – Polyplacophora –   Dorsal surface convex, ventral surface bears flat foot. 8 transverse shells.

Genus – *Chiton*

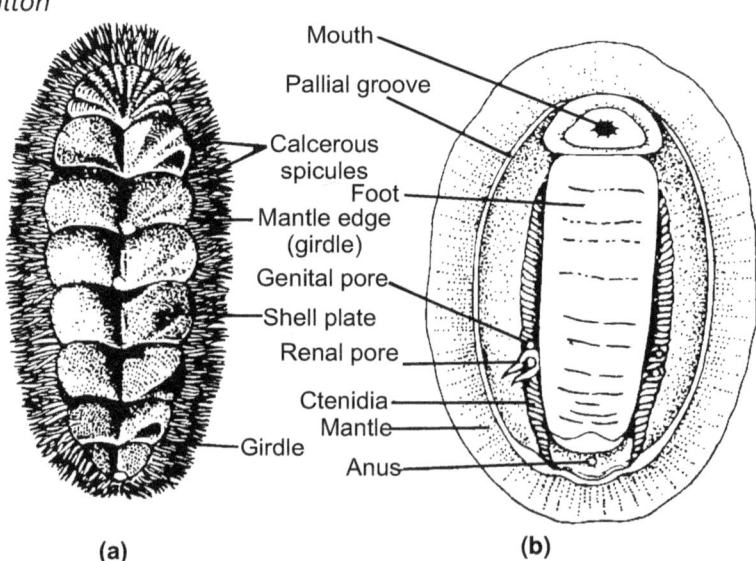

(a)   (b)

Fig. 2.1: *Chiton barnesi.* (a) - Dorsal view; (b) - Ventral view

Characters:

(1) Body is bilatreally symmetrical, elliptical, dorsoventrally flattened.

(2) Dorsal surface convex, ventral surface bears a flat foot.

(3) Eight pieces of transversely oriented shells on the dorsal surface.

(4) Head is small and not distinct. No eyes and tentacles.

(5) Foot is muscular, ventral and extending along the whole length of the body. Useful for locomotion and adhering to the substratum.

(6) Mouth and anus are terminal.

(7) Mantle covers the greater part of the body and partly covers the edges of the shell plates.

(8) Many pairs of bipectinate ctenidia (gills) are present on the either side of the body in the mantle groove.

(9) Sexes are separate and development includes trochophore larva.

(10) It is marine, sluggish animal found attached to the rock and feeds only on algae hence herbivorous.

2.8.2 *Pila* (Snail)

Phylum – *Mollusca*   –   Body unsegmented; bilaterally symmetrical and consists of head, foot, mantle and visceral mass.

Class – *Gastropods*   –   Body asymmetrical; spirally twisted shell in most cases it may be dextral or sinistral; torsion of visceral mass into 180°; visceral mass covered by mantle; foot large with creeping sole, kidney single.

Order – Mesogastropoda   –   Presence of operculum; siphion; single auricle; single gill and monopectinate, kidney single, osphradium single.

Genus – *Pila*

Species – *globosa*

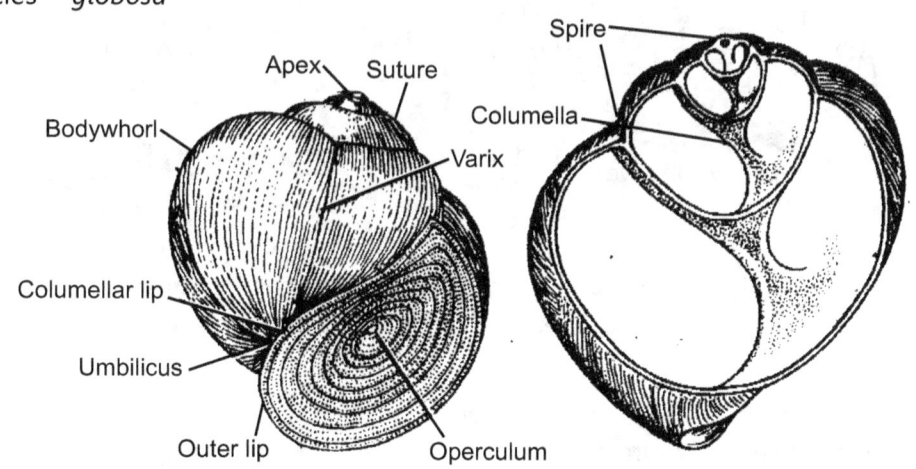

(a) An entire shell   (b) Half of the shell ground off

Fig. 2.2: *Pila globasa*

Characters:

1. Body enclosed in a thick, globular, dull yellow or brownish dextral shell.

2. Lines of growth present on the shell.

3. Head wall marked and bears a snout.

4. Tentacles are filamentous and two pairs.

5. One pair of stalked eyes.

6. Left pseudoepipodium large.

7. Foot triangular with a flat sole.

8. Visceral mass spirally twisted.

9. Respiratory organs ctenidium and pulmonary sac.

10. Shell surface is smooth and glossy.

11. Operculum calcareous.

2.8.3 *UNIO*

Classification:

Phylum – Mollusca   –   Characters same as *Aplysia*.

Class – Pelecypoda   –   Bivalved shell, body laterally compressed, head is not distinct.

Genus   –   *Unio*.

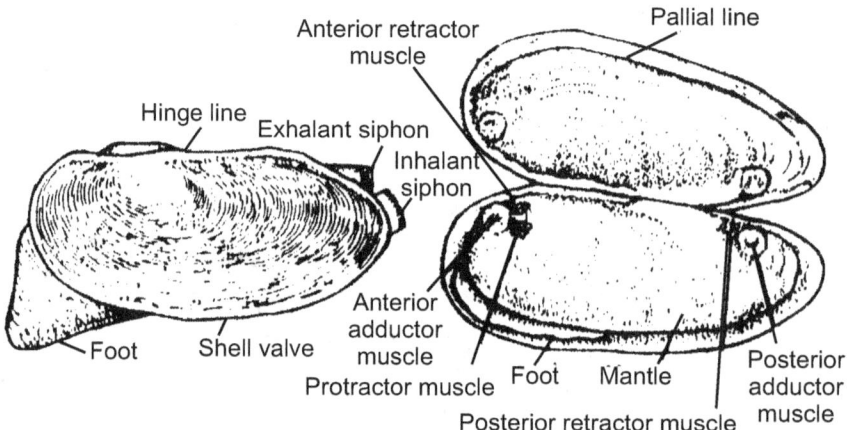

Fig. 2.3: Fresh water *mussel (Lamellidens marginalis)*
(a) An entire specimen; (b) Left valve of the shell open

Characters:

(1) It is also known as fresh water mussel.

(2) Body soft, bilaterally symmetrical and flattened, laterally compressed.

(3) Body is covered by bivalve shell which are equal and made up of calcium carbonate.

(4) Along the dorsal side both the valves of shell are joined together by hinge ligament.

(5) Umbo is located at the anterior end of the dorsal side.

(6) Closing and opening of the valves is done by anterior and posterior adductor muscles.

(7) Foot is large, muscular and wedge shaped useful for burrowing in sand or mud.

(8) At the posterior end of mantle inhalent and exhalent siphons are present.

(9) Two bipectinate gills, one on each side of the visceral mass are present.

(10) Sexes are separate, development includes glochidium larva.

2.8.4 *Dentalium*

Phylum – Mollusca   –   Body soft, unsegmented, bilaterally symmetrical and consists of head, foot, mantle and visceral mass.

Class – Scaphopoda   –   Elongated, tusk like cell, trilobed and protrusible, eyes, tentacles are absent.

Genus – *Dentalium*.

Characters:

(1) It is commonly called as tusk shell.

(2) Body elongated and bilaterally symmetrical, enclosed in a tubular shell.

(3) Shell opens at both the ends, it is delicate and curved tube.

(4) Head is vestigial, bearing mouth. Mouth is surrounded by a circlet of retractile tentacles, the captacula with succer-like ends.

(5) The foot is narrow, trilobed, conical, protrusible through the anterior opening of the shell. It is useful for burrowing the animal.

(6) Radula is well developed.

(7) No gills but respiration is by transverse folds in the lining of the mantle.

(8) No eyes and tentacles. Anus behind the base of the foot.

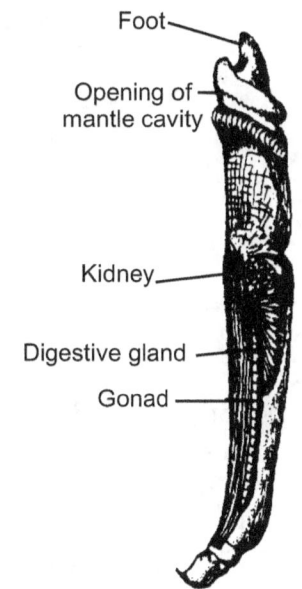

Fig. 2.4: *Dentalium vulgare*

(9) Sexes are separate and development includs Veliger larva.

(10) It is found in the sand and feed on the small organisms like foraminifera and diatoms.

2.8.5 *Octopus* (Indian Devil Fish)

Phylum – Mollusca	–	Body unsegmented, bilaterally symmetrical and consist of head, foot, mantle and visceral mass.
Class – Cephalopoda	–	Head well developed bears a pair of eyes; foot modified into oral arms and a siphon, mouth has a pair of horny jaws, odontophore well developed, presence of ink gland.
Order – Octopoda	–	Long non-retractile and oral arms 8 with sessile suckers, internal shell absent.

Genus – *Octopus*

Species – *macropus*

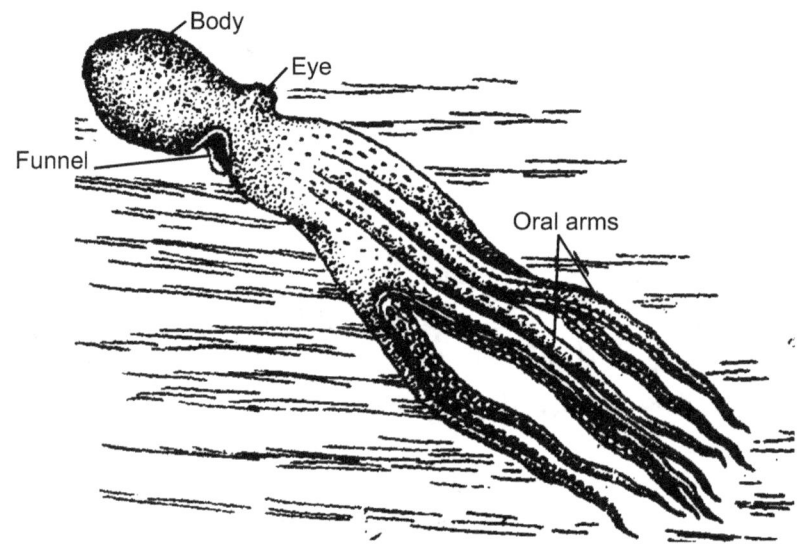

Fig. 2.5: *Octopus macropus*

Characters:

1. Body rounded and differentiated into head and visceral hump.
2. Head possesses 8-elongated arms with two rows of sessile, cupped sucker and a siphon.
3. Two large eyes are present.
4. Visceral mass globose, soft and fleshy.
5. Body sac-like, with conspicous white spots on reddish background.
6. Two rod-like vestiges of the shell present.
7. Female about 1.2 m and males about 1.3 m in length.
8. Males with left or right third are hectocotylized with spoon-shaped non-filamentous tip.

Practical **3**...

Aim:

To Study the Classification with the reasons of the Phylum Echinodermata: Star fish, Brittle star, Holothuria, Sea Urchin, Echinus [D].

PHYLUM-ECHINODERMATA

The name Echinodermata literally means 'spiny skinned animals'. Greek; echinus = spiny, derma = skin. The skin or test of these animals bears prominent spines.

3.1 General Characters

(1) Echinoderms are exclusively marine.

(2) They are gregarious, mostly free-living, slow-moving (creeping), some are pelagic and few are fixed.

(3) Animals show pentamerous radial symmetry and larvae show biradial symmetry.

(4) Body shape may be star-like, globular spherical, discoidal or elongated, flattened with oral and aboral surface.

(5) Ambulacral grooves are present on the body surface.

(6) Endoskeleton consists of closely fitted plates forming a shell or theca or test. These plates are hard and calcarious.

(7) Exoskeleton is made of movable calcarious spines.

(8) Body cavity or coelom is large, lined by ciliated peritoneum.

(9) Presence of water vascular or ambulacral system is the characteristic feature of echinoderms. Sieve plate like madreporite is present which is hydropore.

(10) Tube feet or podia are useful for locomotion, food capture and respiration.

(11) Respiration occurs through variety of structures such as papulae, (skin gills), peristomial gills, genital bursae and cloacal respiratory trees.

(12) Pedicellariae protect the delicate papulae or skin gills.

(13) Circulatory (haemal) system is reduced and lacunar. Heart is absent.

(14) Excretory system is wanting.

(15) Nervous system is primitive, lacks a brain, but consists of a circum oral ring and radial nerves.

(16) Sense organs are poorly developed and consist of statocysts, pigment eye-spots and tactile tentacles.

(17) Sexes are separate, no sexual dimorphism.

(18) Reproduction is entirely sexual, fertilization external.

(19) Development includes microscopic ciliated, transparent, free swimming larval stage.

(20) Some echinoderms reproduce asexually by transverse fission and some show autotomy by which lost body part can be regenerated.

Phylum Echinodermata is divided into two sub-phyla: **Eleutherozoa** and **Pelmatozoa.**

Subphylum-Eleutherozoa:

(1) They are free living without stem or stalk.

(2) The mouth lies on the surface facing downward and anus on aboral surface.

(3) Body is pentamerous.

(4) Tube feet or podia are locomotory as well as food gathering organs.

(5) Nervous system is located on oral surface.

This sub-phylum is divided into four classes: ***Asteroidea, Ophiuroidea, Echinoidea*** and ***Holothuroidea***.

3.2 Class-Asteroidea

(1) Free-living, slow-creeping and predaceous animals.

(2) The body is flattened, star shaped or pentagonal, radially symmetrical and differentiated into a central disc and arms.

(3) The arms are usually five in number but their number may vary up to 50.

(4) Oral and aboral surfaces are distinct.

(5) Endoskeleton consists of separate ossicles.

(6) The oral surface bears the mouth and five narrow open ambulacral grooves.

(7) Two to four rows of locomotory tube feet or podia are present in each ambulacral groove which are retractile and provided with terminal suckers.

(8) Respiration by papulae.

(9) Movable pincer-like spines called pedicellariae are present.

(10) Sexes are separate. Development includes either bipinnaria or brachiolaria larva.

Examples: ***Asterias*** (Sea-star), ***Pentaceros, Astropecten.***

3.3 Class-Ophiuroidea

(1) Body is flattened and star shaped.

(2) Arms are usually five, long slender cylindrical, joined and highly flexible.

(3) Ambulacral grooves are absent.

(4) Pedicellariae, skin gills and special sense organs are absent.

(5) Madreporite is present on oral surface.

(6) Tube feet are not locomotory but useful for respiration and touch.

(7) Locomotion is effected by slender arms.

(8) Sexes are separate. Development includes free-swimming larva pluteus.

Examples: *Ophiothrix* (Brittle star), *Astrophyton*, *Ophioderms*, *Goragonocephalus*.

3.4 Class-Echinoidea

(1) The body is globular, heart-shaped or disc like, without arms.

(2) Endoskeleton forms a shell or corona of close fitting, immovable calcarious ossicles.

(3) The outer surface of shell is covered by long, movable spines and are used in locomotion.

(4) Outer surface shows alternative 5 ambulacral and 5 interambulacral zones or areas.

(5) Oral and aboral sides are distinct, mouth is on oral side and aboral surface carries the anus and madreporite

(6) Ambulacral grooves are absent.

(7) Tube feet protrude in two rows on each ambulacral zones having ampullae and suckers and are used locomotory, respiratory and tactile organs.

(8) Pedicellariae are stalked and three jawed.

(9) Mouth has five teeth with elaborate system of ossicles, all forming the characteristic Aristotle's lantern.

(10) Sexes are separate. Development includes free swimming pluteus larva.

Examples: *Echinus* (Sea urchin), *Clypeaster* (Cake-urchin), *Echinocardium* (Heart-urchul).

3.5 Class-Holothuroidea

(1) Body is elongated, cylindrical and without arms.

(2) Endoskeleton is reduced to microscopic ossicles or spicules.

(3) Skin is soft, thin or leathery without spines and pedicellariae.

(4) Oral and aboral ends are distinct. Oral end is anterior and has the mouth surrounded by a ring of refractile, sometimes branched tentacles. These are modified tube feet and are often called buccal poidia.

(5) Aboral end is posterior and has the anus.

(6) Locomotory tubefeet usually present, occupying five ambulacral areas. Ambulacral grooves are absent.

(7) Alimentary canal is long coiled and cloaca usually having respiratory tree.

(8) Sexes are separate and development includes auricularia larva.

Examples: *Holothuria* (Sea-cucumber), *Thyone, Synapta, Stichopus.*

Subphylum-Pelmatozoa:

(1) Mostly extinct animals.

(2) In early life they are attached by aboral stalk supported by rows of calcarious ossicles.

(3) Oral surface is directed upwards and bears both mouth and anus.

(4) Tube feet are ciliated, food catching and without suckers. They function only as respiratory and tactile organs.

(5) Spines, madreporite and pedicellariae are absent.

(6) Main nervous system is aboral.

This subphylum includes a single living class namely, **Crinoidea.**

3.6 Class-Crinoidea

(1) Extinct or living forms, usually attached permanently or temporarily by a jointed stalk to the sea bottom. Many are free swimming and without stalk.

(2) Body is enclosed in a cup like theca, pentamerous with upwardly directed oral surface and downward aboral surface.

(3) The arms are long, slender usually five or ten in number branched with small alternating branches, the pinnules.

(4) Ambulacral grooves are ciliated radiate out from mouth on oral side of arms and pinnules to their tips.

(5) Calcarious endoskeleton is present.

(6) Tube feet are without ampullae and suckers, and are useful for excretory, respiratory and tactile function.

(7) Pedicellariae, spines and madreporite are absent.

(8) Sexes are separate, development includes doliolaria larva.

(9) Great power of regeneration is exhibited by these animals.

Examples: *Antedon* (Feather-star) *Sea-lily.*

PHYLUM - ECHINODERMATA

3.7 *Pentaceros* (Star fish)

Classification:

Phylum   – Echinodermata – Radially symmetrical, pentaradiate spiny skin, water vascular system is present.

Subphylum – Elentherozoa   – Free-living, mouth on the oral surface, anus on the aboral surface. Tube feet with suckers.

Class   – Asteroidea   – Star shaped body, oral surface directed downwards and aboral surface upwards, Ambulacral form groove provided with podia or tube feet.

Genus   – *Pentaceros*

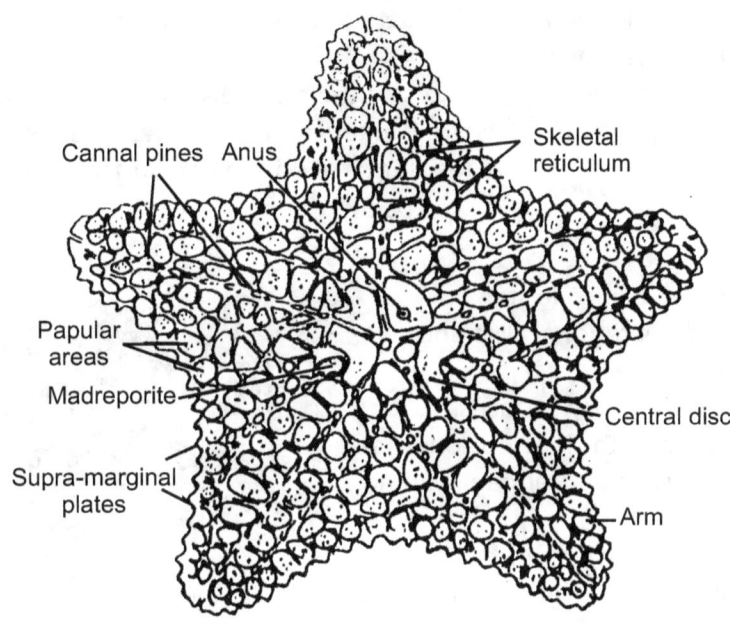

Fig. 3.1: *Oreastes (Pentaceros)*

Characters:

(1) It is also called as sea pentagon.

(2) Body is star shaped and thick. Five tappering arms are originated from the central disc which are not sharply demarcated from the disc.

(3) Central disc is large but arms are small hence it is called stellate.

(4) The body is covered by hard integument containing several plates and ossicles.

(5) The animal has two surfaces, upper flat aboral and lower oral which is convex.

(6) Mouth is five sided called actinostome and it is surrounded by a numerous peristome.

(7) Each arm has narrow ambulacral groove.

(8) On the each side of the ambulacral groove is a row of slender tube feet or podia.

(9) Tube feet are locomotry organs.

(10) Madreporite is present on the oral surface.

(11) There are many stout spines in irregular rows, large spines on the margin and marginal plates.

(12) On the aboral surface papullae are present between the spines.

(13) Stalked or sessile microscopic are present on both the surface of the body.

(14) Sexes are separate, development includes bipinnaria larva.

(15) It is marine animal, form on the sandy bottom and carnivorous. It is harmful to the pearl industry.

3.8 Brittle Star (Ophioderma)

Classification:

Phylum	– Echinodermata	–	Characters same as Brittle Star.
Sub-phylum	– Elentherozoa		
Class	– Ophiuroidea	–	Bases of the arms distinctly marked off from the disc. No ambulacra grooves, anus and intestine. Madreporite on the oral surface, bursa usually ten.
Genus		–	Ophioderma

Characters:

(1) It is also called as brittle star.

(2) Presence of pentagonal disc and five long arms.

(3) Oral and aboral body surfaces.

(4) Pentagonal mouth located on oral surface with several oral papillae and granules.

(5) Tube feet and anus are absent.

(6) Madreporite is located on oral surface.

(7) Arms are long, slender, cylinder and flexible with small spines.

(8) Sexes are separate.

(9) It is marine animal found in swallow water to a depth of 280 metres.

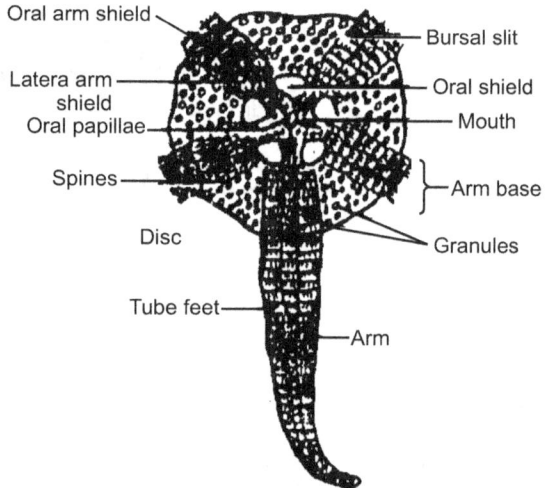

Fig. 3.2: *Ophioderma*. Disc and one arm in oral view

3.9 Holothuria

Classification:

Phylum	– Echinodermata	–	Characters same as Echinus.
Subphylum	– Elentherozoa		
Class	– Holothuroidea	–	Cylindrical body, elongated in oral-aboral axis; anus is absent, a circlet of long tentacles at the oral end.
Genus		–	Holothuria

Characters:

(1) Body is cylindrical with bilateral symmetry, bearing mouth and anus at opposite ends.

(2) Skin is soft, thin and without spines and pedicellariae.

(3) Circlet of long 20 to 30 tentacles at the oral end.

(4) Body bear numerous tube feet which are locomotry on the dorsal surface.

(5) Well developed respiratory tree.

(6) Madreporite is internal.

(7) Sexes are separate.

(8) Development includes auricularia larva.

(9) The sand containing organic food is taken in the mouth with the help of tentacles.

(10) *Holothuria* is marine found in shallow tropical and subtropical waters, on the sandy bottom.

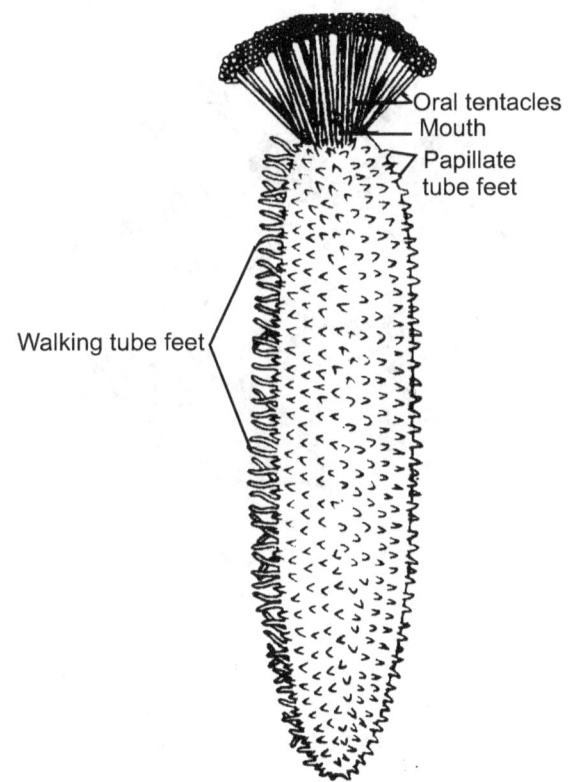

Fig. 3.3: *Holothuria nigra*

3.10 Echinus

Classification:

Phylum   – Echinodermata

Subphylum – Elentherozoa

Class   – Echinoidea   – Spherical body, enclosed in shell or test, Ambulacral grooves and anus are absent. Stalked pedicellariae with three jaws.

Genus   – *Echinus*

Characters:

(1) It is commonly known as sea urhcin.

(2) Body nearly spherical with flat oral and domed aboral surface.

(3) The body of the animal is enclosed in a rigid globular shell or corona which is formed by closely fitted calcarious plates.

(4) Whole surface of the test or shell except peristome and periproct covered by movable spines articulated to it.

(5) Three jawed pedicellariae and sphaeridia are present among the spines.

(6) Mouth is located in the centre of oral pole and it is surrounded by soft membrane called peristome. Through the mouth project five teeth of Aristotle's lantern.

(7) Tube feet are arranged in five double in the ambulacral areas.

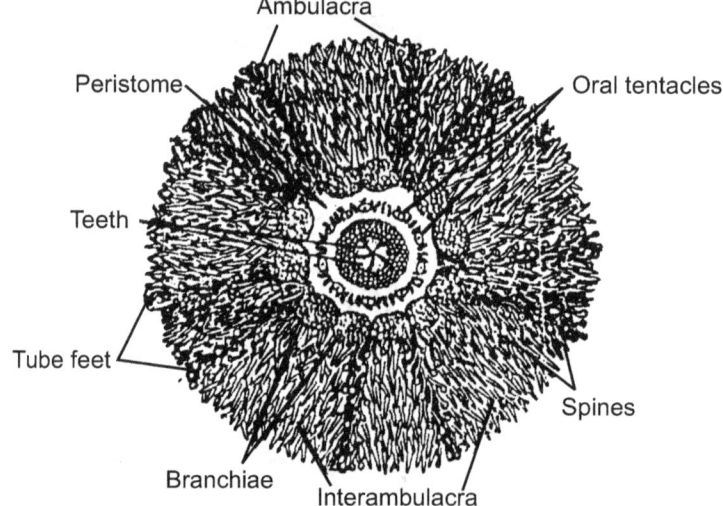

Fig. 3.4: *Echinus esculentus.* **Oral view**

(8) The surface of test is divided into alternating ambulacral and inter ambulacral areas.

(9) Sexes are separate. Development includes enchinopluteus larva.

(10) Macheporite and gonopore near the aboral anus.

(11) It is marine animal found in the sea in the rocky places.

Practical **4**...

Aim:

To study permanent slides of mouth parts of the following Insects:

(I) **Cockroach**

(II) **Mosquito**

(III) **Plant bug/Bed bug**

(IV) **Butterfly**

(V) **Honey bee**

(VI) **Housefly (D)**

The mandibles and maxillae, along with the labrum and hypopharynx form the mouth parts, useful for feeding. Insects show diverse modes of feeding and hence mouth parts are variously modified in different insect groups to suit their modes of feeding. The study of mouth parts of insects is important to control the insect pests.

Following are the main modifications which occur in different insects:

(1) Biting and chewing mouth parts (Cockroach).

(2) Chewing and lapping mouth parts (Honey bee).

(3) Piercing and sucking mouth parts (Plant bug/Bed bug and mosquito).

(4) Sponging and lapping mouth parts (Housefly).

(5) Siphoning mouth parts (Butterfly).

4.1 Biting and Chewing Mouth Parts (Cockroach)

These are the primitive mouth parts and from them all other types or mouth parts have evolved. They are also called as mandibulate type of mouth parts and are meant for pinching off, chewing up and swallowing the pieces of plant and animal tissues. Chewing type of mouth parts occur in **Cockroaches**, Grasshoppers, Crickets, Termites, Beetles, Dragon flies and Silver fish. These mouth parts consists of the following parts:

(a) Labrum: It is broad flap having variable shape and size hanging from the clypeus in front of other mouth parts. It forms the roof of the mouth cavity and show slight upward and downward movement. It has on its posterior (ventral) side a membranous swollen area, the *epipharynx* which bears taste buds.

(b) Mandibles: They are the pair of mandibles which are heavily sclerotized, triangular structures lying just behind the labrum. Each mandible bears teeth like denticles, which interlock while capturing the prey. The mandibles are moved by a pair of abductor and adductor muscles. The mandibles are useful for biting and chewing the food.

(c)   **Maxillae:** The maxillae are paired situated on the sides of the mouth behind the mandibles. They are regarded as the appendages of 5th head segment. Each maxilla consists of a basal two pieces, a proximal *cardo* and *distal stipes*. This portion is called *protopodite*. The inner endopodite has also two segments medial jaw like *lacinia* and lateral blunt *galea*. The outer exopodite or palp usually 5 segmented called *maxillary palp* functioning as a tactile organ. The lacinia and galea bear taste buds so they taste the quality of food. The maxillae are useful for holding the food material.

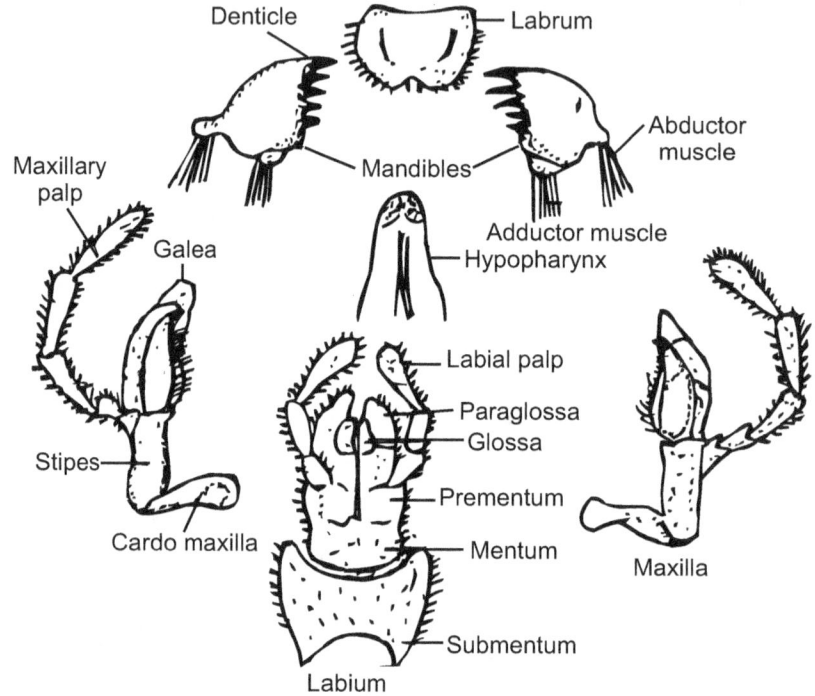

Fig. 4.1: Biting and Chewing (Mandibulate) Type of Mouth Parts

(d)   **Labium or Lower Lip:** This is also called second pair of maxillae, basically fused to form a broad plate divided by a transverse suture into two parts, the basal *postmentum* and the distal *prementum*. The postmentum may be divided further into a basal *submentum* and distal *mentum*. The prementum bears a pair of usually three jointed palps called *labial palps* laterally. In between the palp lie two *glossae* and *paraglossae*. They are commonly called *ligula*. The labial palps are sensory and help in testing the quality of food as they contain chemoreceptors. The glossae and paraglossae together prevent the loss of food particles while feeding. They also aid in pushing the masticated food into the preoral cavity. These organs are formed from the 6th head segment.

(e)   **Hypopharynx:** It is a short, median, tongue like appendage in the mouth cavity between the labium and mandibles. It is not muscular nor glandular but supported by few narrow sclerites. The common salivary duct opens into the base of the hypopharynx.

4.2 Piercing and Sucking Mouth Parts (Mosquito and Plant Bug / Bed Bug)

These mouth parts occur in **bugs**, aphids, scale insects, **mosquitoes**, fleas and some flies. They are used for sucking the sap or blood by piercing into plant or animal tissue.

(a) Mouth Parts of Mosquito: These mouth parts are used for piercing and sucking the blood from host. The labrum, mandibles, maxillae and hypopharynx form long, pointed stylets for piercing the host skin. The labrum is grooved ventrally. The hypopharynx encloses the salivary duct. The labrum, hypopharynx by getting closely applied together enclose the food channel for drawing blood. The labium forms a long hairy, dorsally grooved *proboscis* tipped with a pair of sensory *labellar* lobes representing the labial palps. It serves as a sheath for the stylets at rest but folds up as the stylets pierce the host tissue at the time of feeding. The mandibles are absent in the male. Maxillary palps are short and three jointed.

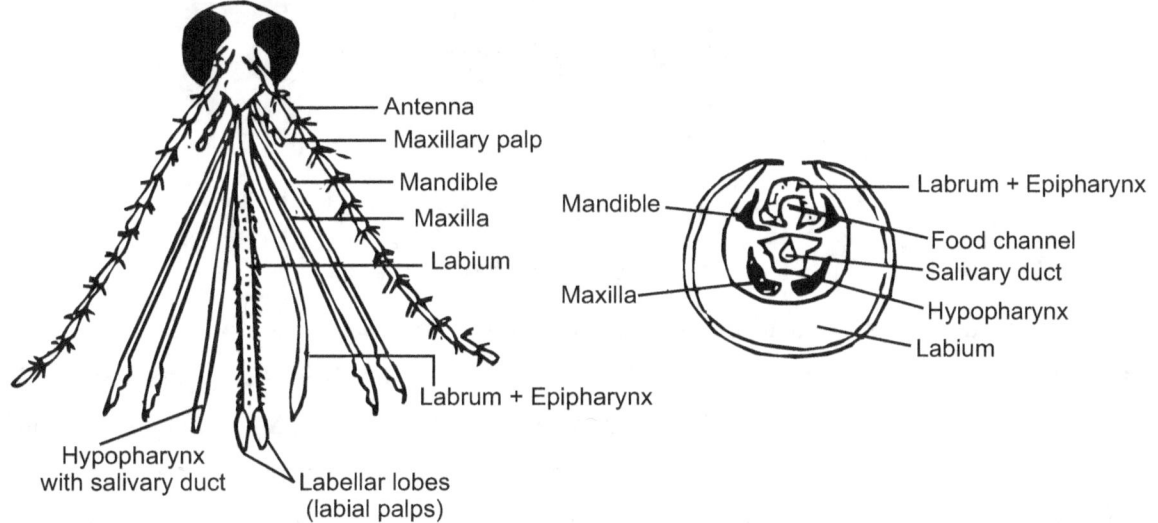

(a) Mouth Parts of Female *Culex*   **(b) T.S. of Mouth Parts of Mosquito**

Fig. 4.2: Piercing and Sucking Mouth Parts

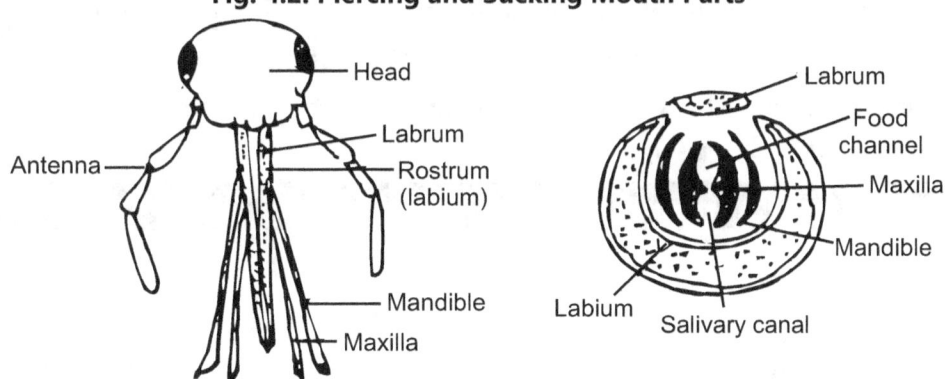

(a) Piercing and Sucking Mouth Parts of Bug   **(b) T.S. of Mouth Parts**

Fig. 4.3

(b) Mouth Parts of Bug: In the bugs, the labium forms usually a three *jointed rostrum* or *proboscis*. The mandibles and maxillae form four long, needle-like piercing stylets. The proboscis encloses the stylets. The hypopharynx is a short lobe within the base of the proboscis. The inner stylets in the proboscis i.e. maxillae fit together in such a way as to form the food and salivary channels. Maxillary and labial palps are absent.

4.3 Siphoning Mouth Parts (Butterfly)

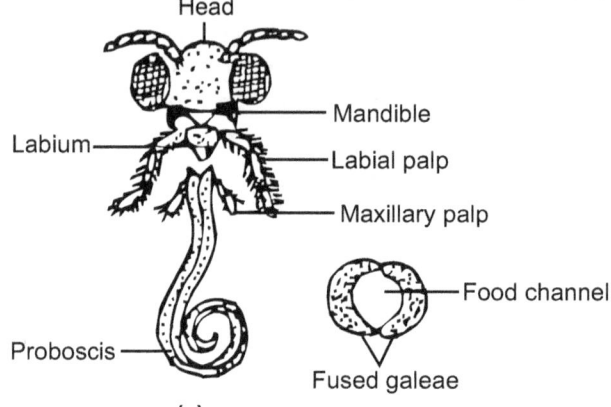

(a) Front View   (b) T.S. of Proboscis

Fig. 4.4: Mouth Parts of Butterfly

These mouth parts occur in **butterflies** and moths and these are modified for sucking the fluid nectar from the flowers and fruits. The mandibles and the labium are very much reduced. The labrum is merely a narrow transverse band. The maxillary palps are vestigial, but the galeae are very long and deeply grooved medially. When applied together the two galeae enclose a food channel and form as prominent proboscis, which is the main siphoning tube. When it is not in use, it is coiled like a watch spring under the head. At the time of feeding the proboscis remains uncoiled, inserted into flowers, fluid nectar is sucked by muscular pharynx which is present at the base of proboscis. The labium is reduced to a triangular plate bearing well developed three jointed labial palps. There are no hypopharynx and salivary channels are lacking.

4.4 Chewing and Lapping Mouth Parts (Honey Bee)

These type of mouth parts are found in some Hymenoptera (**bees** and **wasps**), particularly in worker bees. They are used for collecting nectar and pollen of flower and moulding wax. These mouth parts serve for both biting and licking. The labrum lies beneath the clypeus and fleshy epipharynx projects below the labrum. The mandibles are smooth and spatulate. The worker bees uses them in building the cells of the hive. The maxillae lack laciniae have vestigial palps and bear long blade like galea. The labium has elongated palps, reduced paraglossae and elongated curved glossae united to form a retractile tongue bearing a *honey-spoon* or *labellum* at the distal free end.

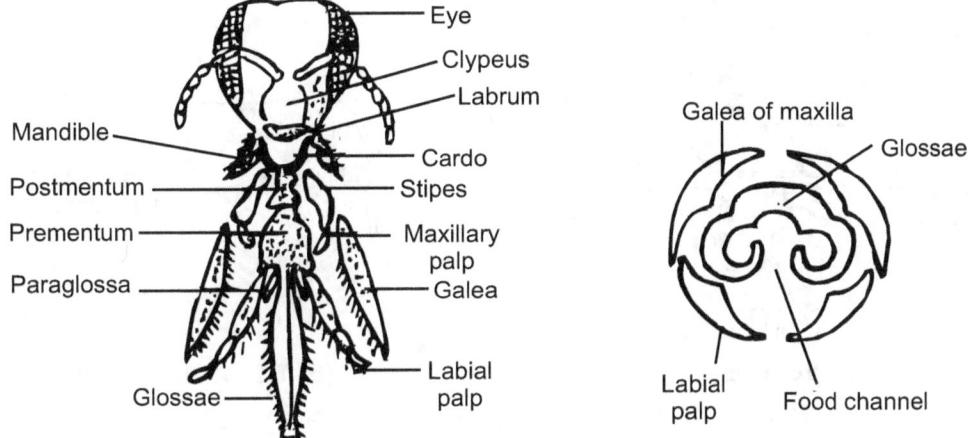

(a) **Mouth Parts of Worker Honey-bee**   (b) **T.S. of Mouth Parts**

Fig. 4.5: Labellum (Honey Spoon)

While feeding, galeae and labial palps are brought close together forming a long hollow proboscis, which can be inserted deeply into the corolla of a flower. Nectar is drawn up into the proboscis by black and forth movement of the tongue in it.

4.5 Sponging or Lapping Mouth Parts (Housefly)

These mouth parts are common in **houseflies**, blow flies, fruitflies. They are modified for sucking up the liquid food by salivary secretion. The mandibles are absent, while the maxillae are represented only by two maxillary palps each made up of a single piece. The labium is greatly modified to form so called proboscis which consists of three parts.

(i)   The proximal rostrum bearing maxillary palps.

(ii) The middle haustellum with a mid-dorsal groove, serving as the food passage and ventral plate like structure called theca.

(iii) The distal labellum (oral disc) or sucker. The labellum has two lobes or labellae on which innersides contain many cylindrical tubes called pseudo-tracheae. They converge into the mouth that leads into the food channel. The pseudo-tracheae soak the fluid food, which is then passed on to the food channel from where it is sucked up by muscular pharynx. The food channel is formed by labrum, epipharynx and hypopharynx.

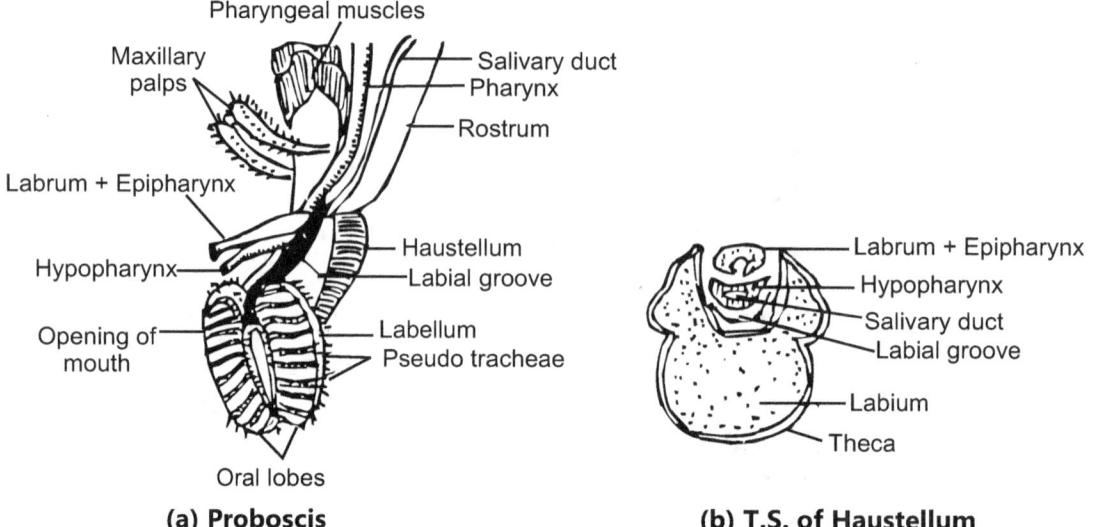

(a) Proboscis   **(b) T.S. of Haustellum**

Fig. 4.6: Mouth Parts of Housefly (Siphoning Type)

✱✱✱

Practical 5...

Aim:

To study the following animals with reference to shell and foot (D).

5.1 *Chiton*

Classification:

Phylum	–	Mollusca
Class	–	Amphineura
Order	–	Polyplacophora
Sub-order	–	Chitonina
Family	–	Chitonidae
Genus	–	*Chiton*

Shell:

The body of the *Chiton* is elliptical, bilaterally symmetrical and dorsoventrally compressed and consists of shell, foot, mantle and the visceral mass. The shell is made up of eight transverse, overlapping calcarious plates or valves, arranged in a longitudinal row. The shell forms a solid armour covering the dorsal surface. The name of the order *polyplacophora* is derived from the nature of the shell. The shell plates are movable upon one another and allow the animal to roll up like a wood louse. The first shell plate is called *cephalic* and the last or eighth plate is called *anal* and they are hemispherical in shape. The remaining shell plates are called *intermediate* shell plates which are rectangular and often keeled middorsally. The posterior edge of each plate overlaps the anterior edge of the next behind. Each shell plate is made up of two distinct layers. The upper layer or *tegmentum* which consists of organic conchiolin matrix impregnated with calcium carbonate.

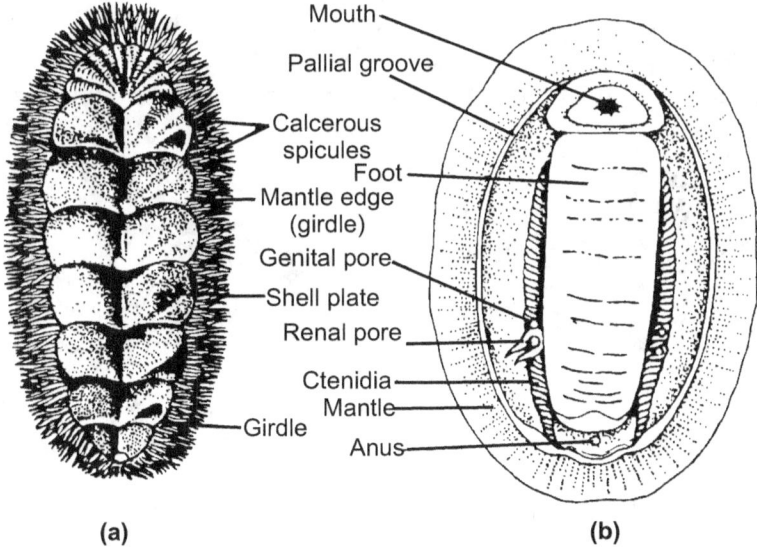

Fig. 5.1: *Chiton*. (a) – Dorsal View, (b) – Ventral View

This layer is perforated by numerous vertical canals containing sense organs and its upper exposed surface is sculptured. The lower thick and dense layer is called articulamentum consists of calcium carbonate only.

Foot:

The *chiton* has large, elliptical, muscular and sucker like ventral foot with a flat sole. The foot is abundantly supplied with slimy secretion and is adapted for creeping as well as clinging. *Chiton* is very sluggish animal moving by employing mucous and waves of muscular activity. If abundant food is available to one spot then the animal remains there for longer period. Foot is primarily useful for adhesion. The mantle girdle is also used for firm adhesion. When animal is disturbed, the girdle is lowered and clamped down tightly against the substratum. The inner margin of the girdle is then raised, thus creating a vacuum so the adhesion is improved. As a result, *chiton* is rarely disloged. These animals are generally found on smooth rock surfaces which provide better adhesion.

5.2 *Patella*

Classification:

Phylum	–	Mollusca
Class	–	Gastropoda
Subclass	–	Prosobranchia
Order	–	Archaeogastropoda
Genus	–	*Patella*

Patella is called true limpet. It is small, oval, sluggish and marine molluscs living between tide marks on rocky beaches. The shell is oval and which is raised like a miniature volcanic cone. Shell is single expanded whorl and assumes secondary symmetry in the adult looking like a Chinese hat. Shell has no operculum and mantle is lying below the shell. The outside of the shell show radiating ribs and lines of growth. The shell is madeup of organic matter called conchiolin matrix impregnated with calcium carbonate. The shell is secreted by mantle. The shells of the patella are used as decoration pieces. The narrow part where shell is pointed called apex.

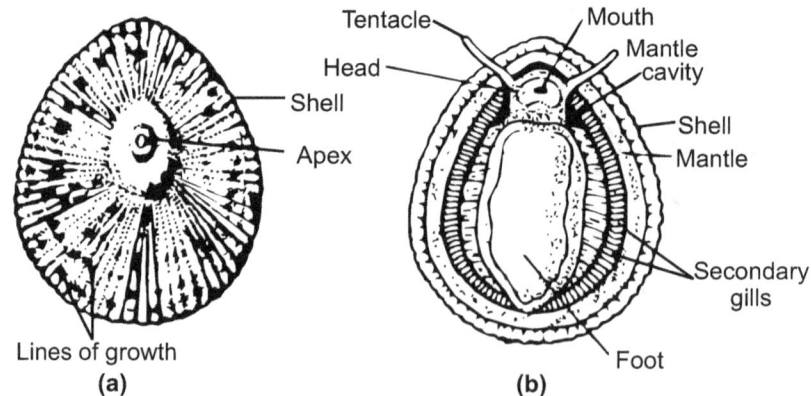

Fig. 5.2: *Patella*. (a) – Dorsal View and (b) – Ventral View

Foot:

The foot of the *Patella* is situated on the ventral side. It is broad and flat used for creeping and adhering. The foot has simple, elongated and undivided flat ventral creeping sole like ancestral molluscs. The foot of this animal acts passively as a hold fast organ to secure attachment or actively to produce movement. The foot of *Platella* is adapted for clinging and moving on rocky surfaces like *Chitons*. The animal is a sluggish, marine gastropod found attached to the rocks and feeding on minute algae. The foot contains unicellular and multicellular mucous secreting pedal glands. The mucous is useful for creeping movement in gastropods.

5.3 *Aplysia*

Classification:

Phylum	–	Mollusca
Class	–	Gastropoda
Subclass	–	Opisthobranchia
Order	–	Anaspidea
Genus	–	*Aplysia*

Aplysia is commonly called as sea-hare. In this animal, shell is also internal like *Sepia*. The body of the animal is soft, lumpy with a thin flexible, plate-like shell almost completely covered by mantle. The shell is somewhat round and exhibits lines of growth. The narrow part is called umbo.

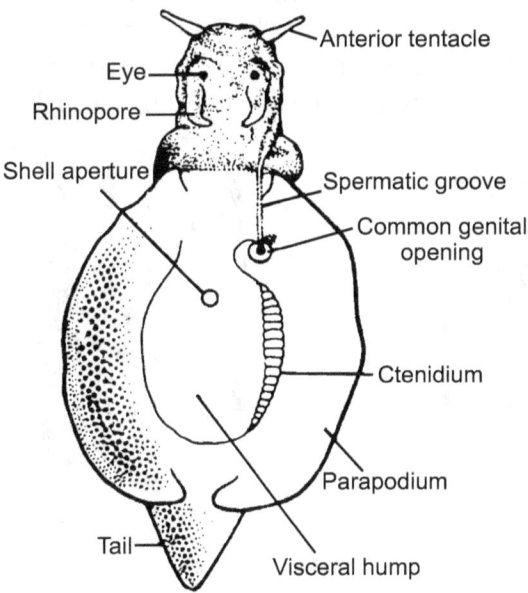

Fig. 5.3: *Apylsia*

In case of *Aplysia* the foot is broad, muscular and ventral and bears a pair of lateral fleshy outgrowths, the parapodia which are useful in swimming. The parapodia form the broad fins. These can be folded and united over the head forming a sac, through which water can be expelled forcibly like a jet. Swimming is achieved in short bursts by rhythmic waves which pass along the parapodia. Thus, for swimming purpose the parapodia are useful for the animal. It feeds mainly on sea weeds and found crowling in sea weeds. It is able to change its colour according to the colour of sea weeds.

5.4 *Sepia* (Cuttle Fish)

Classification:

Phylum	–	Mollusca
Class	–	Cephalopoda
Order	–	Coleoidea
Sub-order	–	Decapoda
Family	–	Sepiidae
Genus	–	*Sepia*

It is a marine mollusc living usually in shallow coastal waters. Body is divisible into head, coller and trunk. Head bears pair of large eyes and five pairs of arms surrounding the mouth.

Shell:

In most of the molluscs, the calcarious protective shell is external, but in case of *Sepia* the shell is internal and it is enclosed in the sac of mantle on the dorsal side. The shell is secreted by the mantle. The shell is flat, broad and oval in shape. The broader and rounded oval end of the shell is called *pro-ostracum* and the narrow, pointed abroal end is called *rostrum* which is projecting into spine. The shell is made up of calcarious material and provides rigidity to the trunk like an endoskeleton. The calcarious material is arranged in fine parallel layers called laminae, enclosing spaces containing fluid and gas. Due to this arrangement the light shell is useful as a hydrostatic organ or float. It also helps in maintaining equilibrium of the body. The shell is rather soft and spongy. These shells are used as bill sharpener as well as a source of calcium to caged birds.

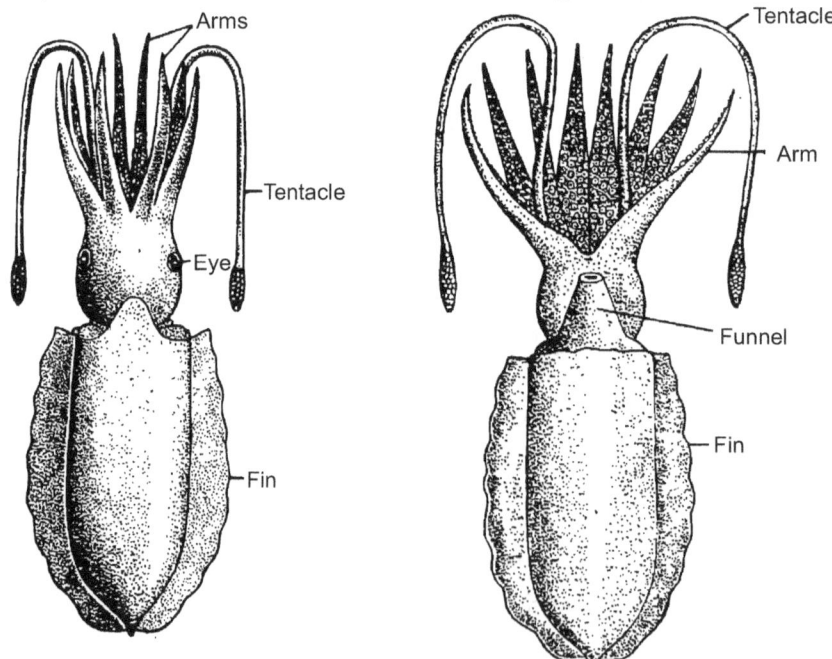

Fig. 5.4: *Sepia*

Foot:

In case of *Sepia*, the foot is modified into 10 arms, of which 8 arms are short and 2 are long. The eight smaller arms bear stalked suckers. The long two arms are called tentacles and provided with suckers only towards their free ends. The oral arms are useful for capturing the food.

5.5 *Dentalium*

Classification:

　　Phylum　　–　　Mollusca
　　Class　　　–　　Scaphopoda

Dentalium is commonly known as tusk shell because its shell resembles miniature elephant tusks so it is also called as elephant's tusk shell.

Shell:

The shell of the *Dentalium* is secreted by mantle. It is external, cylindrically tubular, slightly curved and tapering at posterior end. It has trumpet like shape. The shell is snowy-white with eight grooves running down the entire length. During life, the shell is buried somewhat obliquely in the mud with the wider anterior end lying deepest and the narrow posterior end of apex projecting above the surface of the mud. There is no operculum at the anterior or posterior end of the shell, but both the ends are open. The growth takes place at the larger anterior end. The shell is tubular and unchambered. The animal is situated in the shell and attached by muscles near the posterior end.

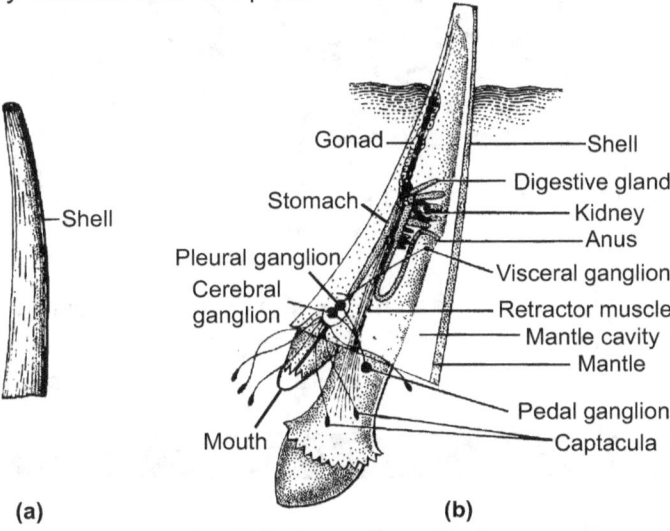

(a)　　　　　　　　　　　(b)
Fig. 5.5: *Dentalium* Shell

Foot:

It is highly muscular organ which protrudes from the broader anterior end of the shell. Foot is long, pointed, spade like and highly extensible. The free end of the foot is conical and trilobed carrying a wing like ridge or pleat on eitherside. The foot is well adapted for burrowing in the mud or sand. When gorged with blood the foot becomes fully extended. Then it plunges deep into the mud or sand and draws the animal by subsequent contractions.

5.6 *Mytilus*

Classification:

Phylum	–	Mollsuca
Class	–	Pelecypoda
Order	–	Filibranchiata
Genus	–	*Mytilus*

Mytilus is also called sea-mussel which is cosmopolitan and sedentary form found in between tide marks. This animal feeds on protozoans, diatoms and other organic detritus filtered from the sea water. They are attached to rocks, wood and even to one another.

The shell is equivalved and wedge shaped. It is pointed in front and rounded behind and the umbo is situated anteriorly. The two shell valves are united antero-dorsally by a hinge ligament. The outer surface of the shell valves show lines of growth which are concentric lines around the umbo as centre. The lines are running parallel to the free margin of the shell. The shell of the *Mytilus* is made up of the two valves hence called bivalve. The shell is made up of $CaCO_3$ and organic matrix conchiolin.

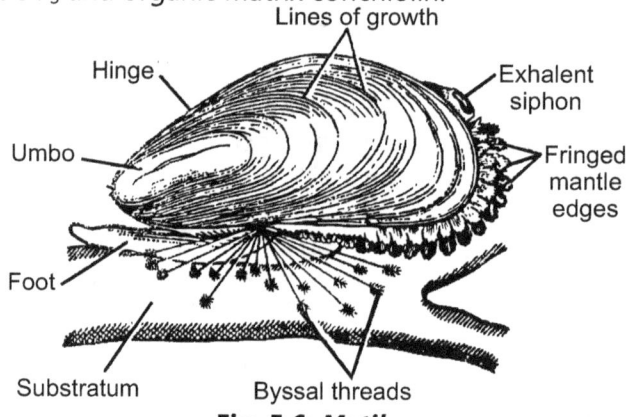

Fig. 5.6: *Mytilus*

Foot:

The foot of the animal is elongated and tongue shaped with ventral groove continuous with byssus pit. Instead of foot, a bunch of strong horny byssal threads protrude from between the two shell valves ventrally, which are useful for attachment to stones, rocks or substratum.

5.7 *Cypraea* (Cowrie)

Classification:

Phylum	–	Mollusca
Class	–	Gastropoda
Subclass	–	Prosobranchia
Order	–	Mesogastropoda
Genus	–	*Cypraea*

This animal is commonly called cowry. The shell is convolute, oval above and flattened below and consists of single whorl. The surface of the shell is smooth, polished and brightly coloured. The shell opening is long, narrow and serrated. The shells are conspicuous and prized by the collectors. The cowry shells are much used for ornaments, curios and mantle piece decorations. The foot of the animal is large and useful for locomotion. It is flat and large with the help of it animal can creep on the rocks, coral reef or sand.

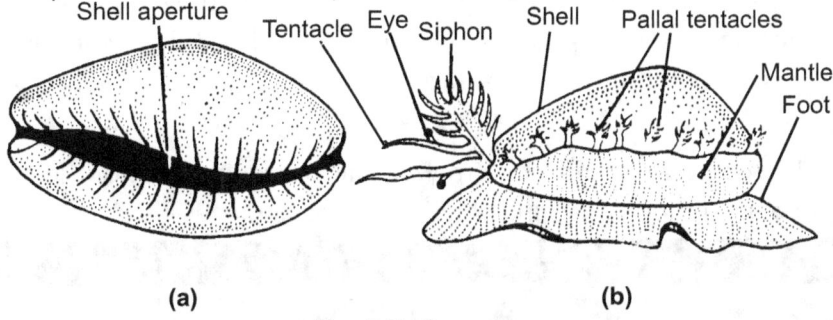

(a) **(b)**

Fig. 5.7: *Cypraea*

5.8 *Nautilus*

Classification:

Phylum	–	Mollusca
Class	–	Cephalopoda
Subclass	–	Nautiloidea
Genus	–	*Nautilus*

It is also called pearly *Nautilus* which lives on the bottom in deep water (550 metres). The unique feature of this animal is that it is the only living cephalopod possessing an external shell that can be used as house. The body is enclosed in a calcarious spirally coiled many chambered shell. The shell is about 25 cm in diameter. The texture of the shell is porcelain like white, the outer surface is brown with dark bands and the inner lining is pearly white. The animal lives in the outermost and largest chamber into which body can be withdrawn for protection.

The shell is divided internally by simple partitions or septa into a series of chambers of increasing size. The animal lives in the larger, outermost chamber. The remaining chambers are empty or filled with a gas. The innermost initial chamber lies in the centre. The septa are perforated in the middle and traversed by narrow tubular vascular prolongation of the visceral mass, the simphuncles.

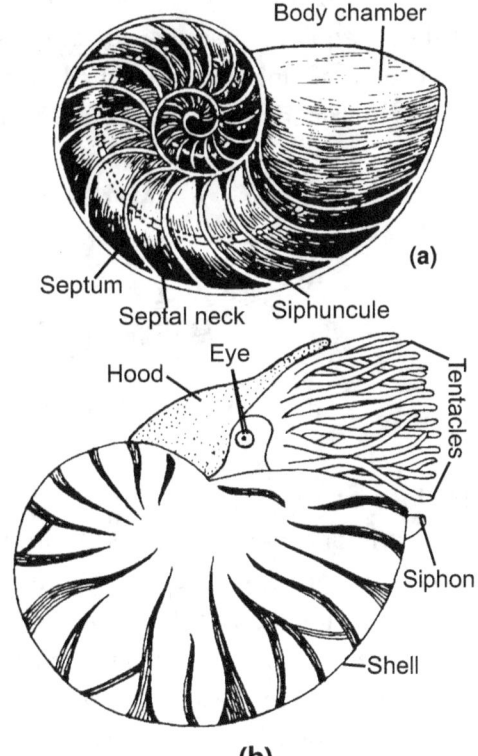

(b)

Fig. 5.8: *Nautilus.* **(a) Complete Shell, (b) Shell in Section**

Foot:

In *Nautilus*, also foot is no longer recognizable as a typical molluscan foot. In other cephalopods like *Sepia* and *Loligo*, foot is modified into 8 or 10 cephalic arms. The *Nautilus* do not show arms, instead, the pedal crown, round the head, is divided into lobes, each bearing numerous, short, prehensile tentacles which are strongly adhesive but without suckers.

This animal is gregarious and nocturnal crawling over the bottom in troops at night time in search of animal food consisting chiefly of crabs and shell-fish.

5.9 *Solen*

Classification:

Phylum	–	Mollusca
Class	–	Pelecypoda
Order	–	Eulamellibranchiata
Genus	–	*Solen*

It is called rezor shell or rezon clam which burrow in the sand about low tide mark. The shell of the *Solen* is thin, equivalve, long, narrow and straight with parallel margins. The flat umbo or point of union of the shell is placed terminally at the anterior end. The hinge ligament is elongated and external. In *Solen*, each shell valve has a single tooth.

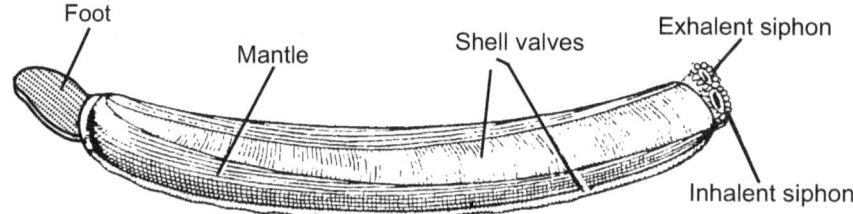

Fig. 5.9: *Solen*

Foot:

The foot of the *Solen* is burrowing organ which is enormously developed muscular organ. It is cylindrical and produced from the anterior end. The foot is some what pointed at the tip and is capable of swelling out with lightning rapidity and becoming stiff with inflowing blood. It becomes thin to a point and adapted to easy penetration into loose sand. It works like a probing finger into the sand and pulls the animal in. The animal not only bore into the sand but can swim backwards in jerks by suddenly withdrawing foot and thus squirting out water through the siphons. *Solen* is marine, burrowing animal found in the sand at low tide mark.

Practical 6...

Aim:

(a) Study of External Characters and Digestive System of Starfish (E).

Asterias is exclusively marine and lives on most sea-coasts. It prefers rocky areas for locomotion. Starfish is bottom dwelling hence called benthonic animal. It is carnivorous and voracious feeder.

Systematic Position:

Phylum	–	Echinodermata
Sub-phylum	–	Eleutherozoa
Class	–	Asteroidea
Order	–	Forcipulata
Family	–	Asteriidae
Genus	–	*Asterias*
Species	–	*rubens*

6.1 External Characters

Shape and Size:

The body of Starfish is star shaped, flattened in the oral, aboral axis and radially symmetrical, *pentamerous* in arrangement. It consists of a *central, pentagonal* disc from which radiate out five, elongated, tapering *arms*. The axes of the arms are known as *radii* and the regions of the central disc between the arms are termed as the *interradii*.

The body has an oral surface on which mouth is situated. This surface normally kept towards the substratum. The aboral surface is convex and covered with spines of various length. A minute opening is situated at centre called *anus*. This surface also bears *madreporite* at interradii position.

Colour:

Asteria is usually bright yellow, brown or orange coloured.

Oral Surface:

The surface normally kept towards the substratum is called oral or actinal surface. It bears mouth, ambulacral grooves, ambulacral spines, tube feet, eyes and tentacles.

(i) **Mouth:** It is a circular aperture situated at the centre of oral surface of the central disc. It is surrounded by peristomial membrane (peristome) and guarded by five groups of oral spines or mouth papilla.

(ii) **Ambulacral grooves:** From the five corners of *mouth* or *actinosome* radiate out five narrow grooves called ambulacral grooves; which runs along the middle of each arm upto its tip. Each groove shows two rows of tube feet.

(iii) **Ambulacral spines:** Each ambulacral groove is bordered and guarded from the lateral sides by 2 or 3 rows of movable calcarious *ambulacral spines.* These spines are capable of closing over the groove.

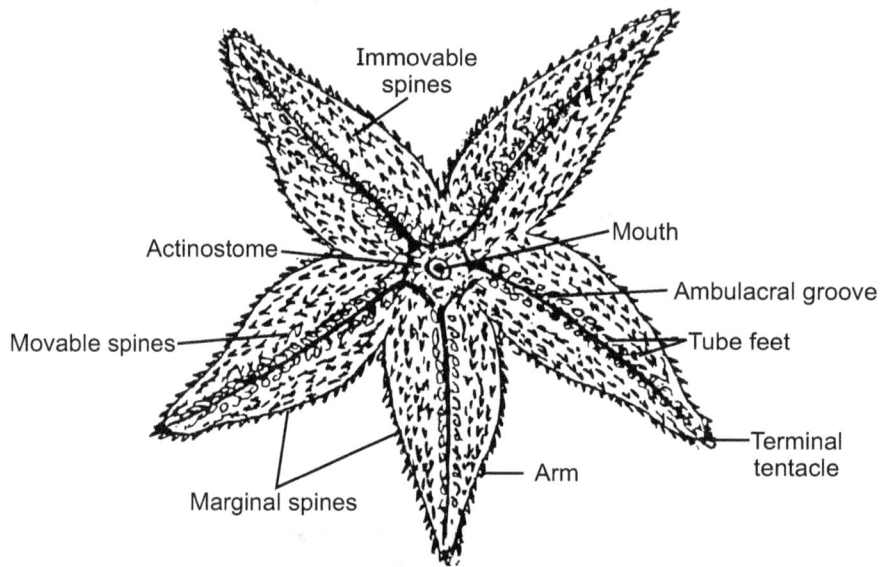

Fig. 6.1: *Asterias.* **Oral View**

(iv) **Tube feet or podia:** Each ambulacral groove contains two double row of soft, thin walled, extensible tubular structures called tube feet. Each tube feet has sucker disc; podium (middle) and ampulla (upper sac).

(v) **Eyes and Tentacles:** At the end of each ambulacral groove, there is a small, light sensitive, bright reddish pigmented spot called the *eyes*. Above the eye projects a median non-retractile process called the *tentacle* concerned with tactile and olfactory in function.

Aboral Surface:

The upper convex surface is called aboral or abactinal surface. It bears spines, dermal branchiae, anus, madreporite and pedicellariae.

(i) **Spines:** The entire aboral surface is covered by short, stout, blunt and immovable calcarious spines or tubercles.

(ii) **Dermal branchiae:** These are very small, soft, delicate, hollow, finger like membraneous rectractile process present between the ossicles of integument called dermal branchiae or gill or papula. Papula is a hollow evagination of body wall. The dermal branchiae are respiratory in function.

(iii) **Anus:** It is a small aperture, lies nearly in the centre of the aboral surface.

(iv) **Madreporite:** It is flat, round, small but conspicuous button like structure called madreporite. It is situated on aboral surface eccentrically. The two rays between which madreporite is present are called the *bivium* and three remaining rays *trivium.* The madreporite is a sieve like porous plate and leads to the stone canal of water vascular system.

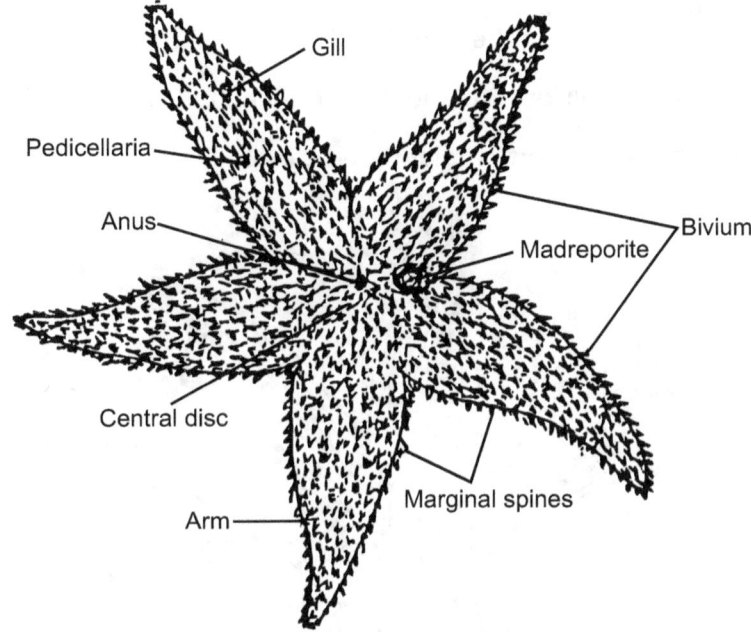

Fig. 6.2: *Asterias.* **Aboral View**

(v) **Pedicellariae:** Pedicellariae are modified spines that occur in the space between the spines all over the body. These are microscopic pincer-like or jaw like bodies. Each pedicellaria consists basal stalk which bears calcarious plates or ossicles and two jaws or valves. Pedicellariae are protection in functions.

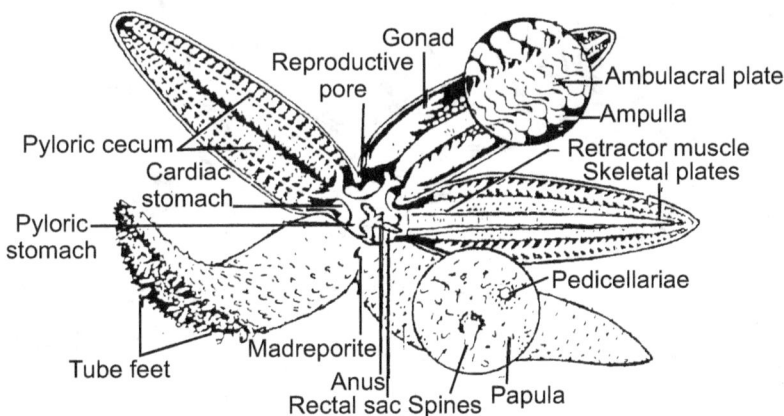

Fig. 6.3: *Asterias* **Showing Anatomy**

6.2 Digestive System of Starfish

Dissection Technique:

* Take a specimen, wash with tap water and place it in dissecting tray with the aboral surface towards upwards. Then put water to cover it.
* Make a 'O' cut on the dorsal wall of the trivium with sharp razor.
* Cut the dorsal wall transversely, close to the disc with scissor and remove it, without damaging the underlying structures.
* Cut the side of arm and remove the dorsal wall of arm.
* Keep madreporite and anus intact.
* After removal of body wall of disc and arm, the central portion and pyloric caeca of alimentary canal is exposed.
* The alimentary canal is a short, straight, vertical tube extending from oral to aboral surface.

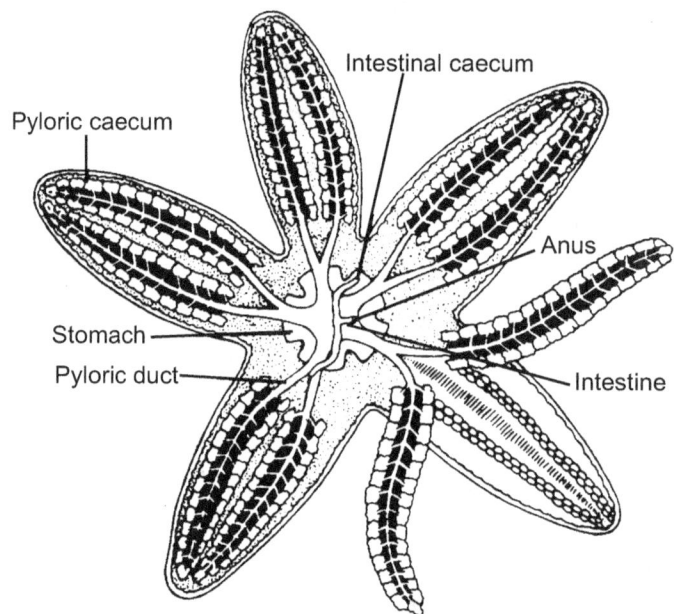

Fig. 6.4: (a) *Asterias*. Alimentary System. Aboral View

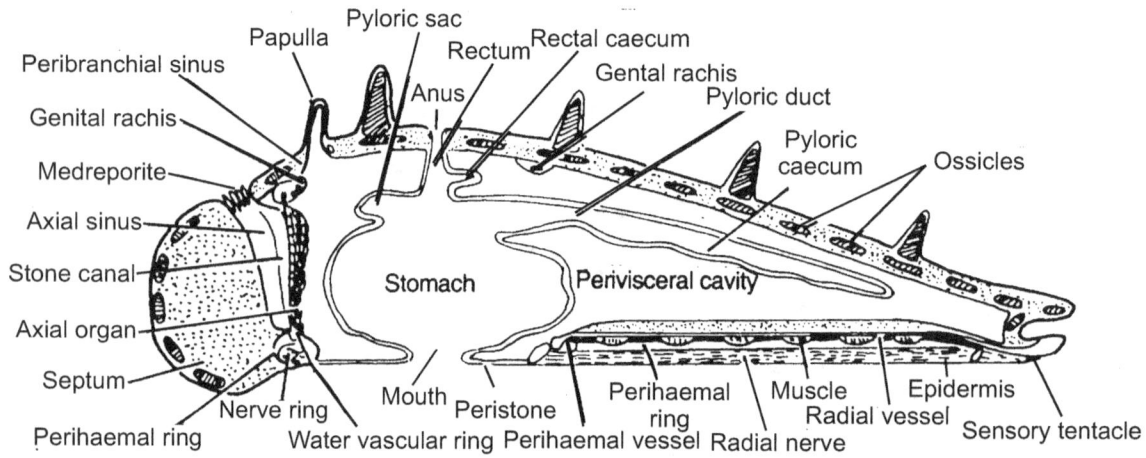

Fig. 6.4: (b) *Asterias*. Diagrammatic V.S. of Disc and arm to show Digestive System

Observe the parts of alimentary system. With the help of the following points, draw and label the diagram.

(i)   **Mouth:** A five-rayed aperture, present at the centre of the oral surface. It is also called the *actinosome*.

(ii)   **Oesophagus:** A short but wide tube connecting the mouth with the stomach.

(iii)   **Stomach:** It is divided into two by a horizontal constriction, the lower cardiac and the upper pyloric stomach. Stomach is largest part of alimentary canal.

     (a)   **Cardiac Stomach:** It is spacious, five lobed sac, occupy the greater part of the central disc. The wall of this is thin, muscular and highly folded. It can be completely everted through mouth by pressure of coelomic fluid.

     (b)   **Pyloric stomach:** It is smaller, pentagonal sac in communication with cardiac stomach dorsally. Each angle of the pyloric stomach is drawn out into a duct which enter in arm and branches to form a pair of large appendages called as *pyloric caeca* or hepatic caeca or gastric glands. Thus, there are five pairs of pyloric caeca, one pair in each arm.

(iv)   **Intestine:** A short, narrow tube runs from the pyloric stomach to end in anus. It gives off 2 or 3 little hollow diverticula called intestinal or rectal caeca before opening the anus. The rectal glands are brown in colour and probably excretory in function.

(v)   **Anus:** Intestine opens on the aboral surface by a small opening on the central disc called *anus*. It is slightly away from the centre.

(vi)   **Digestive glands:** Five pairs, long, brownish or greenish bodies. In each pyloric caecum, the hollow axis gives off laterally two series of small hollow branches, each terminating into a number of small bladder like pouches or lobules.

Digestive glands are concerned with the secretion of digestive juice containing proteases, amylases and lipases enzymes.

Practical **7**...

(A) Study of Water Vascular System of Starfish (E).

7.1 Dissection Technique

- Place a specimen in a dissecting tray.
- Remove the wall of central disc and one of the arm without disturbing the madreporite.
- Trace the water vascular system carefully.

7.2 Water Vascular System

The water vascular system or ambulacral system is a sort of hydraulic pressure mechanism and consists of madreporite, stone canal, ring canal, radial canals, Tiedeman's bodies, pollian vesicle, lateral canal and tube feet. This system concern with locomotion.

(i) Madreporite: A flat disc with radiating grooves at the bases of the bivium. It is hard, rounded, calcarious plate on the aboral surface. It leads to stone canal.

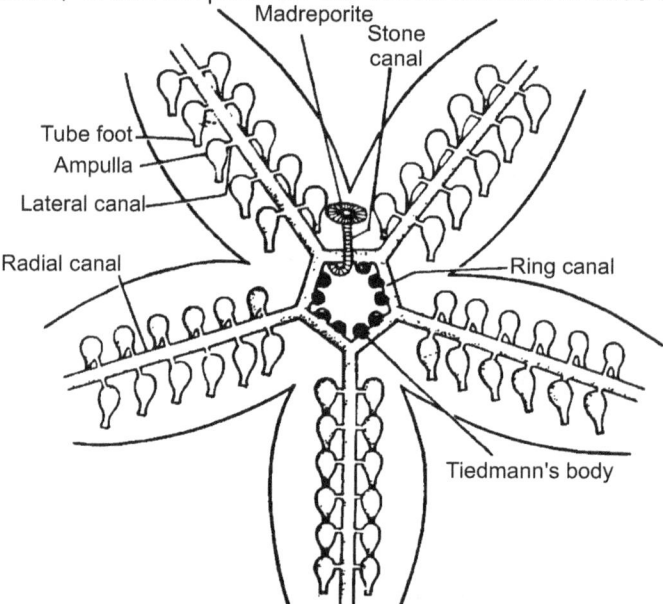

Fig. 7.1: *Asterias.* **Ambulacral System. Aboral View**

(ii) Stone Canal: A ampulla opens into a vertical 'S' shaped stone canal. It is a cylindrical tube, supported by calcarious rings. The stone canal runs downward from madreporite to join the ring canal.

(iii) Ring Canal: It is a wide, five sided or pentagonal, ring like canal situated around mouth. It lies just innerside of the peristomal ring.

(iv) Tiedmann's Bodies: The ring canal gives off inter-radially a pair of small vesicles on its inner side called recemose glands or Tiedmann's bodies. These are small, yellowish, rounded bodies. There are only nine Tiedmann's bodies, 10th being absent and its position is taken by stone canal. Tiedmann's bodies manufacture the amoebocytes which are phagocytic in function.

(v)   **Polian Vesicles:** The ring canal gives off in each inter-radius a large, thin walled, pear shaped sac called polian vesicle. There number is variable from 2 to 4. They are contractile structures which store water and suppose to regulate the pressure in water vascular system and manufacture amoeboid cells.

(vi) **Radial Canals:** Ring canal from its outer surface gives off five, long and ciliated radial canals into each arm. These canals runs upto the tip of the arm.

(vii) **Lateral Canals:** During the course of radial canal it gives off on either side a series of short, narrow, transverse branches called lateral or podial canals. They are arranged alternately long and short and open into the tube feet.

(viii) **Tube Feet:** There are two alternating rows of tube feet on either side in ambulacral groove of each arm. Each tube feet or podium is a hollow, elastic, thin walled sac like part is called *ampulla*, a middle *podium* and lower disc like structure called sucker.

The ambulacral system (water vascular system) mainly helps in locomotion, adherence to the substratum and plays an important role in the respiration.

***

Aim:

(B)   **Temporary Preparation of Gonads from Starfish (E).**

Asterias is unisexual animal. The male gonads (testes) and female gonads (ovaries) have similar form and structure but they differ in colour. The testis are pale grey while the ovaries are pink to orange in colour in fresh state.

Location:

There are pairs of gonads. Each pair is lie free laterally in the base of each arm between the pyloric caeca and the ampullae.

Method:

With the help of forcep pick up the gonads from above mentioned location on a slide, separate it with needles and mount in glycerine and observe under microscope.

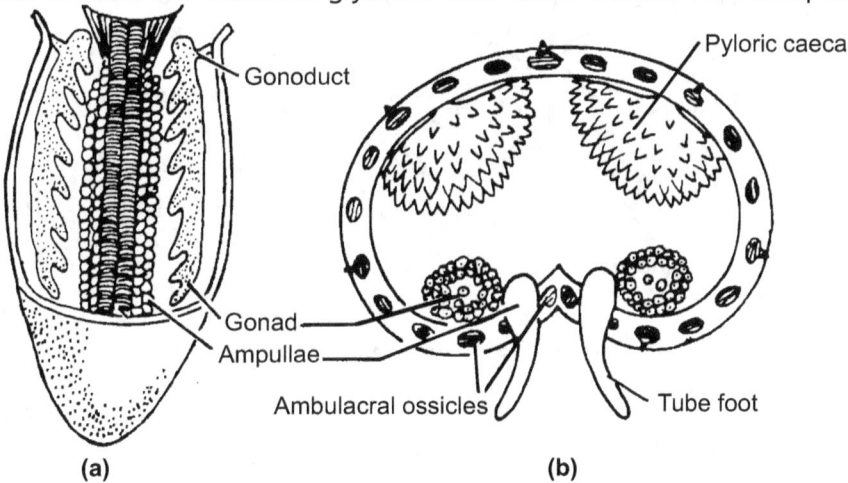

Fig. 7.2: *Asterias*. Gonads

Structure:

Each gonad is a branched structure consisting of masses of small rounded follicles like the bunches of grapes.

Practical **8**...

Aim:

> **(A) Study of Permanent Slides of T.S. of an Arm and Types of Pedicellariae [D].**

8.1 T.S. Passing through Arm of Starfish

T.S. of an arm of *Starfish* shows the following:

(i) The arm is covered by cuticle, ciliated epidermis and thick dermis.

(ii) The dermis contain numerous perihaemal spaces and ossicles.

(iii) Epidermis and dermis shows spines, pedicellariae and dermal branchiae.

(iv) In the T.S., the aboral surface appears thick and convex arch. While the oral surface is like an inverted 'V' shaped.

(v) The arm encloses a perivisceral coelom which contains a pair of pyloric caeca, each suspended by two longitudinal mesenteries from the aboral surface.

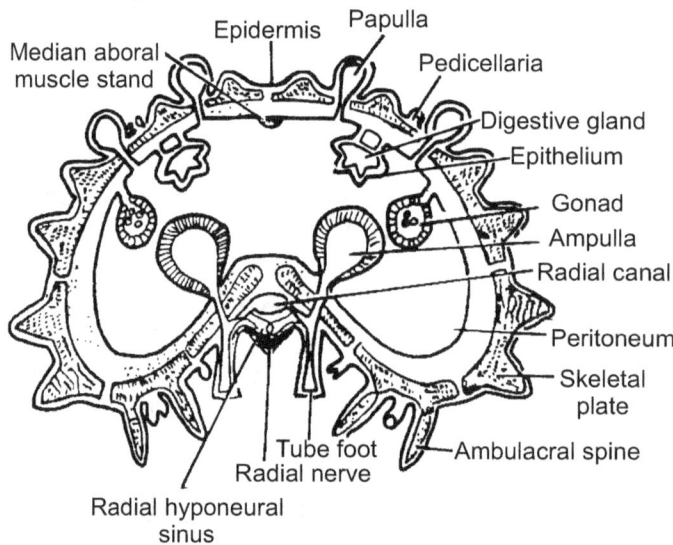

Fig. 8.1: *Asterias.* T.S. of an Arm

(vi) On the oral surface ambulacral groove is supported by two elongated ambulacral ossicles meeting at the summit of the groove.

(vii) Above the ambulacral groove runs a radial canal which is joined on each side by a podial branch to two ampullae called lateral water canals.

(viii) A radial hyponeural sinus is seen below the radial canal.

8.2 Types of Pedicillariae

The pedicellariae are the modified spines that occur in the space between the spines or in clumps around the bases of the spines all over the body. They are microscopic pincer-like or jaw-like bodies.

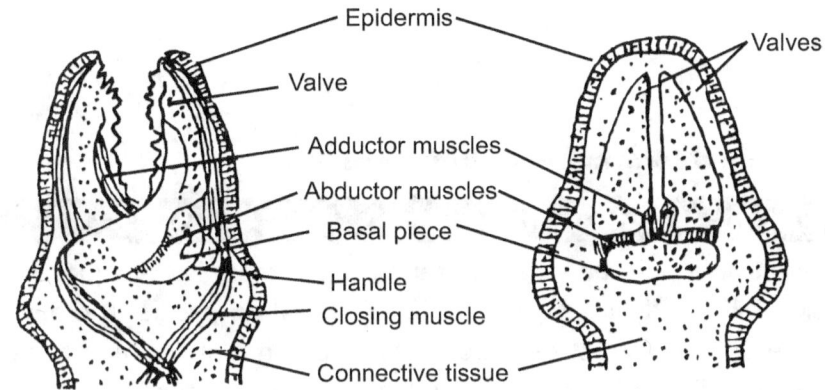

(a) **Crossed or Scissor type**   (b) **Straight or Forcep type**

Fig. 8.2: *Asterias:* **Pedicellariae**

Structure of Pedicellariae: The stalked or pedunculate type of pedicellariae are found in the genus *Asterias*. Each pedicellaria consists of a short, flexible and fleshy stalk, but there is no internal calcarious support. The stalk bears three calcarious plates or ossicles, a basilar plate at its top and two jaws or valves. The jaws are articulated with the basilar plate and serrated along their opposed edges. The pedicellariae having three calcarious pieces and a stalk are called forcipulate pedicellariae. They are covered with epidermis which is richly supplied with sensory and gland cells.

Types of Pedicellariae: There are two types of forcipulate pedunculate pedicellariae found in *Asterias*. These are forceps or straight type and scissors or crossed type.

(1) Forceps or Straight type: It is a simple type in which the two jaws are more or less straight and attached basally to the basal piece. When pedicellariae is closed the jaws remain parallel and meet throughout their length like a forceps. The jaws can be opened or closed by muscles. The two jaws are operated by two pairs of adductor muscles to close them and one pair of abductor muscles to open them.

(2) Scissors or Crossed type: These pedicellariae are relatively small and are arranged in rings round the white spines on the aboral surface. In this type, the basal ends of the two jaws are curved and cross each other like the mandibles of a cross bill, so that the basal piece is enclosed between their crossed portions. The movement of the jaws is effected by three pairs of adductor muscles and one pair of abductor muscles. The abductor muscles originate on opposite ends of the basal ossicle and insert on the neighbouring crossed parts of the jaws. An elastic ligament is present in the stalk which bifurcates for attachment to the outer surface of the basal end of each jaw. This type of pedicellariae functions like a pair of scissors. Sessile pedicellariae also occur on the body of *Asterias*.

Functions of Pedicellariae: The pedicellariae perform different functions. They are useful for the protection of delicate skin, gills or papulae and keep the body surface free from debris and foreign organisms. They also serve as defensive and offensive organs. In some starfishes the pedicellariae are said to help in capture of small prey. They are also sensitive to contact.

Aim:

(B) Study of Larval Forms in Echinodermata

8.3 Larval Forms in Echinodermata

In echinoderms although the sexes are separate but there is no sexual dimorphism. The gametes are released directly in sea water where fertilization occurs. The development may be direct or indirect. In the direct development there is no larval stage but in the indirect development different kinds of free swimming larval forms are found.

8.3.1 Bipinnaria Larva

(i)   This is the free living larval stage of *Asteroidae*.

(ii)   Bilaterally symmetrical and somewhat angular in shape.

(iii)   The anterior end of larva is enlarged to form a pre-oral lobe. The ciliated border of the pre-oral lobe is called pre-oral band which encircles the mouth. The pre-oral band separates completely from the rest of the longitudinal band or post-oral band.

(iv)   The larva develops three lobes on either side of the body which are bordered by post-ciliary band.

(v)   The larva shows the mouth, oesophagus, stomach and intestine.

(vi)   The larva is free-swimming.

(vii)   The bipinnaria larva changes into the next larval stage called brachiolaria larva.

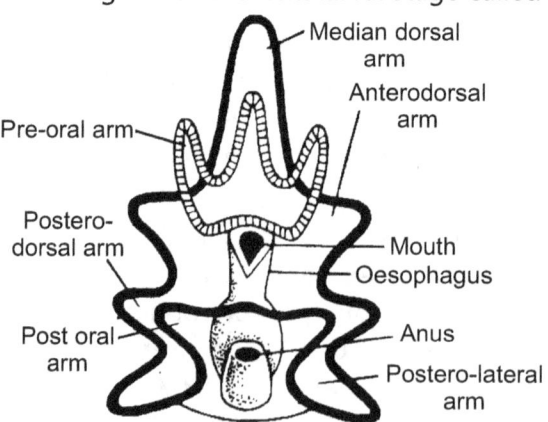

Fig. 8.3: Bipinnaria Larva

8.3.2 Brachiolaria Larva

At the time of the changing of the bipinnaria into the brachiolaria, three additional arms are formed in the preoral lobe. These are called brochiolor arms of these one is median and two are laterals. These arms contain coelomic extensions and adhesive cells at their tips. An adhesive glandular region is found at their bases. It acts like a sucker. The appearance of sucker markes the beginning of metamorphosis.

The bilaterally symmetrical larva gradually metamorphoses into the radially symmetrically adult. After about 6 or 7 weeks the brachiolaria settles down on some solid object or to the bottom where it remains temporarily attached by its fixing processes. The anterior end of the larva degenerates side aboral. The adult arms appear as extensions of the body. Internally, the entire digestive tract degenerate. All these parts are formed new and in a position conciding with the adult radial symmetry. The somatocoel forms the major part of the coelom. The left axohydrocoel forms the water vascular system and the hydrocoels develop five pairs of projections, two in each of the developing arms. These projections represent the cavity and coelomic lining of first pair of podia in each arm. As about this time, sea star is not more than 1 mm in diameter.

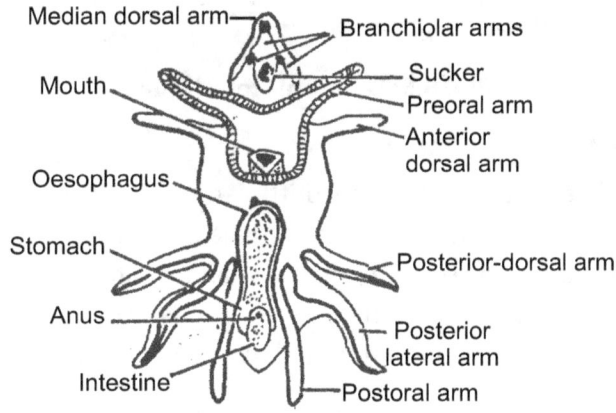

Fig. 8.4: Brachiolaria larva

8.3.3 Echinopluteus

In Echinoidea, free swimming, microscopic *echinopluteus larva* is formed after gastrulation in about 7-30 days. The gastrula becomes somewhat cone-shaped and gradually develops into echinopluteus. The invaginated part of stomodaeum becomes connected with the archenteron and the gut is differentiated into mouth, oesophagus, stomach and intestine. The blastopore forms the anus. It bears six pairs of arms called preoral, anterio-lateral, anterio-dorsal, post-oral, postero-dorsal and postero-lateral. The postero-lateral arms are very short and directed outwards or backwards. In some cases, the anterio-dorsal arms may not develop. Thus, there may be 5 or 4 pairs of arms in place of six pairs. The ends of these arms are pigmented and the skeleton is made up of calcareous rods, present in arms. These rods are originated from spicules secreted by mesenchyme. These rods may be thorny or simple or fenestrated or branched. The locomotion is performed by ciliated bands. In some cases the bands become thickened and known as epaulettes. In Arbacia and Cidaris, the ciliated lobes are formed between the bases of the arms which are known as vibratile lobes, auricular lobes or auricles.

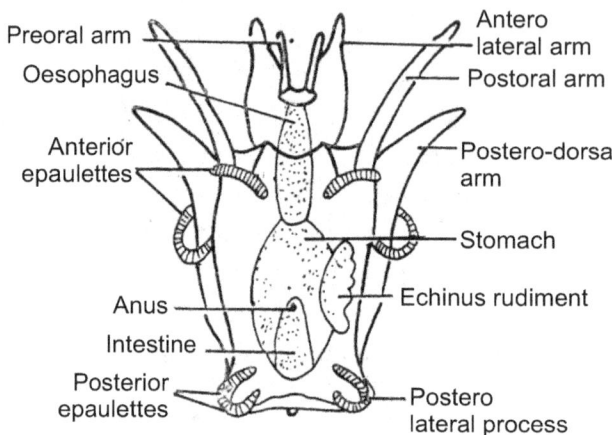

Fig. 8.5: Echinopluteus larva

8.3.4 Ophiopluteus

The pluteus larva is also formed in the brittle stars and it is called ophiopluteus. It is similar to echinopluteus but the number of arms is less in ophiopluteus. Its postero-lateral arms are formed first. The postero-lateral, postoral and posterodorsal arms are developed respectively on 4th, 10th and 18th days. The ciliated bands accompany the arms edges. The coelomic chamber and archenteron are found in larva.

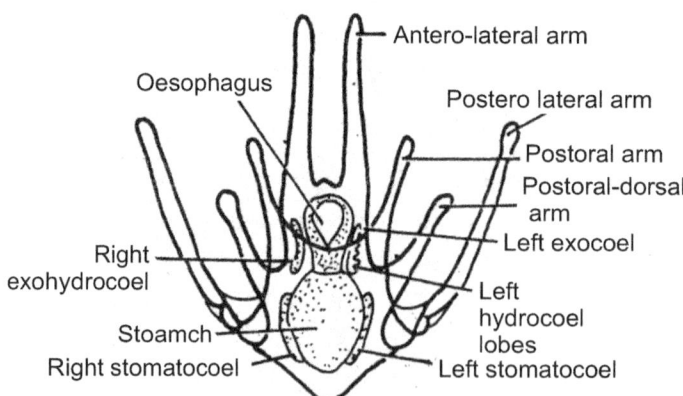

Fig. 8.6: Ophiopluteus larva

8.3.5 Auricularia

After the gastraulation and formation of coelomic sacs and gut, within three days a free swimming auricularia larva is formed. It is transparent and pelagic in nature. It measures 0.5 to 1 mm in length. It swims with the help of ciliated bands. One of these bands encircling the mouth and is called pre-oral loop. Similarly, the ciliated band around the anal opening is called the anal loop. Internally, the larva contains a curved gut. The stomach is sacciform. Hydrocoel and the right and left somatocoels are also present. Lobes appear in the hydrocoel forming the primary tentacles which are connected with the hydropore by means of a duct. Some giant auricularia of unknown adults measuring 15 mm in length, have been reported from Bermuda, Japan and Canary islands. They possess a frilly flagellated band.

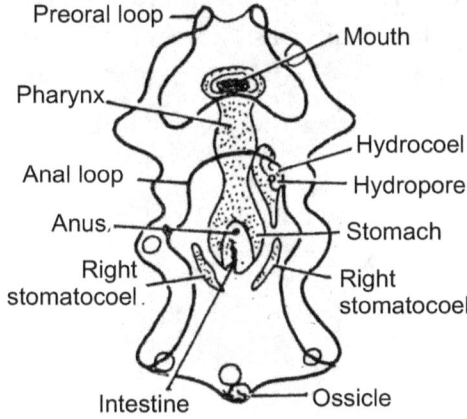

Fig. 8.7: Auricularia larva

8.3.6 Doliolaria

The auricularia larva soon changes into a barrel-shaped form, the *doliolaria larva*. In doliolaria stage, the continuous ciliated bands break to form 3-5 flagellated spheres. The mouth has shifted to the anterior pole and the anus to the posterior pole.

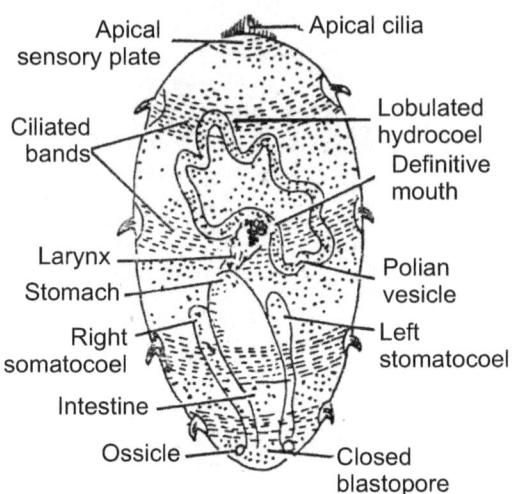

Fig. 8.8: Doliolaria larva

There are some species of holothuroids that possess a non-feeding barrel shaped vitellaria. This type of larva, which is found in crinoid and a few ophuroids, possesses ciliated bands but no arms. In Cucumeria planci, the auricular stage is ommited and the embryo directly develops into the doliolaria larva. In Holothuria the embryo directly develops into young stage from the egg.

Significance:

All the larval form of echinodermis have a bilateal symmetry. Hence, it is believed that the ancestor of echinoderms was bilaterally symmetrical animal. According to Semon (1888) the radial symmetry secondary as the primary radial symmetry is seen in coelenterates and poriferans. The adult echinoderms are more primitive than their larvae because the adults possess the characters of the lower animals like coelenterates etc. During metamorphosis the advanced larva becomes a primitted adult. Such a metamorphosis is called retrogressive metamorphosis.

Practical 9...

Aim:

(A) Identification, Classification and Study of habit, habitat and economic importance of the following: Rohu, *Catla*, *Mrigal* and *Pomphret* [D].

In this practical, selected fishes of India have been described with latest classification, diagnostic features which are used for the laboratory study.

9.1 *Rohu*

Systematic Position:

Phylum	–	Chordata
Sub-phylum	–	Vertebrata
Class	–	Pisces
Sub-class	–	Teleostomi
Order	–	Cypriniformes
Family	–	Cyprinidae
Genus	–	*Labeo*
Species	–	*rohita*

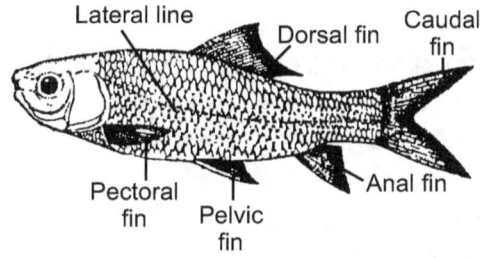

Fig. 9.1: *Labeo rohita*

Habit and Habitat:

Labeo rohita is commonly found in fresh water ponds, rivers, lakes and esturies. It is herbivorous and bottom feeder feeding on algae, aquatic plants. It frequently comes to water surface to take air into air bladder. *Labeo* is the major carp distributed in the plains of India except Southern part.

Identification Characters:

(1) *Labeo rohita* is commonly known as *rohu* in Hindi.

(2) Body is elongated, spindle shaped, with gray colour on back and silvery white on the two sides and belly.

(3) Adult ones are measures about 1 metre in length with 20 to 25 kg weight.

(4) Body is divisble into head, trunk and tail.

(5) Scales are large, orange to reddish in colour in the centre and are cycloid type.

(6) Head is prominent with blunt snout.

(7) Mouth is large transverse aperture bounded by thick and fleshy lips.

(8) Trunk is thick. Lateral line is present on either side of trunk and tail.

(9) Trunk bears single dorsal fin, pectoral fins and pelvic fins.

(10) Tail is laterally compressed and has homocercal caudal fin.

(11) Air bladder is large and divided into anterior and posterior fin.

(12) It is economically important due to its food value.

9.2 *Catla*

Systematic Position:

Phylum	–	Chordata
Sub-phylum	–	Vertebrata
Class	–	Pisces
Sub-class	–	Teleostomi
Order	–	Cypriniformes
Family	–	Cyprinidae
Genus	–	*Catla*
Species	–	*catla*

Habit and Habitat:

It is distributed throughout India, Pakistan, Bangladesh, Nepal and Thailand. It inhabits the surface layer of fresh water and found in Krishna river. *Catla* is a surface feeder feed on plankton, insects, vegetable debris, algae, crustaceans etc.

Identification Characters:

(1) *Catla catla* is largest Indian carp commonly known as *Katla* in Hindi.

(2) Body is deep, stout with broad snout. Mouth is large, provided with promient lower lip and large gill apparatus.

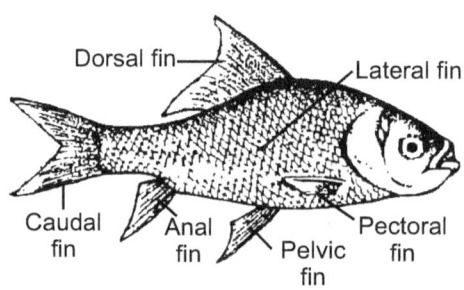

Fig. 9.2: *Catla catla*

(3) The colour is greyish on the dorsal side while silver on the ventral side.

(4) Dorsal profile is more convex in comparison to the ventral one.

(5) Scales are pink in the centre of dorsal side and whitish below.

(6) Eyes are large situated in the anterior half of the head.

(7) Dorsal fin is quite large. Caudal fin is bilobed.

(8) Air bladder is large consists of two parts.

(9) It is grown in polyculture system.

(10) It is economically important as a food-fish.

9.3 *Mrigal*

Systematic Position:

Phylum	–	Chordata
Sub-phylum	–	Vertebrata
Class	–	Pisces
Sub-class	–	Teleostomi
Order	–	Cypriniformes
Family	–	Cyprinidae
Genus	–	*Cirrhinus*
Species	–	*mrigala*

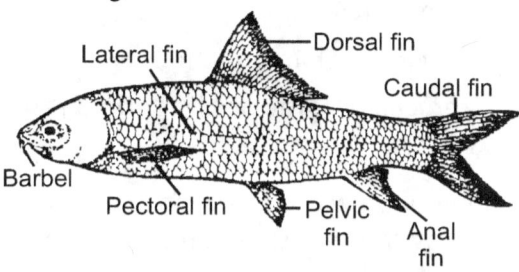

Fig. 9.3: *Cirrhinus mrigala*

Habit and Habitat:

It is found in fresh water bodies like lakes and ponds, rivers. It is bottom feeder and feeds on green algae, decayed vegetable, mud and detritus. *Mrigala* is distributed in river systems of India, Pakistan, Bangladesh and Burma.

Identification Characters:

(1) *C. mrigala* is commonly called *mrigal* and is a fresh water carp of India.

(2) The body is elongated and compressed and measure about 66 cm with 1.4 to 2.8 kg in weight.

(3) The body is silvery but dark grey along back. The body is covered by large cycloid scales but absent on head.

(4) The mouth is wide and lips are thin.

(5) Snout is rounded.

(6) 2-4 barbels are small in fold of lip.

(7) Pectoral, pelvic and anal fins are orange with black tips.

(8) Caudal fin is strongly forked.

(9) Lateral line is clear.

(10) Upper margin of the body is concave particularly in the posterior side.

(11) Economically very important as tasty and delicious fish.

9.4 Pomphret

Systematic Position:

Phylum	–	Chordata
Sub-phylum	–	Vertebrata
Series	–	Pisces
Class	–	Teleostomi
Sub-class	–	Actinopterygii
Order	–	Perciformes
Family	–	Stromateidae
Genus	–	*Stromateus*
Species	–	*Sinensis* (white pompfret) and
		argenteus (grey or silver pompfret).

Habit and Habitat:

Pompfret are mainly marine but few are estaurine and fresh water in habitat. Pompfrets are famous in east, also known as "butter fishes" on account of their soft flesh and flavour, therefore highly priced food fish.

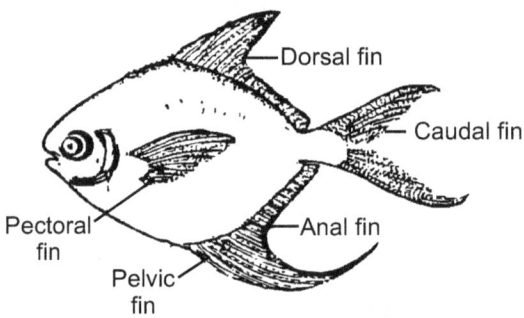

Fig. 9.4: *Pompus argenteus*

Identification Characters:

(1) Body oval and compressed from side to side and covered with thin, small scales.

(2) Head is short and compressed.

(3) Snout is blunt, overhanging the mouth.

(4) Eyes are large situated laterally in the middle region of head.

(5) Jaws equal, lips thin.

(6) Lateral line is smooth, indefinite.

(7) Two dorsal fins continuous, first dorsal fin with 5 to 6 rudimentary spines.

(8) Anal fin deeply forked with 32-42 rays.

(9) Commercially very important food fish.

Aim:

(B) Identification, Classification and Study of Habit, Habitat and Economic Importance of the following Prawn, Crab and Oyster [D].

9.5 Prawn

Systematic Position:

Phylum	–	Arthropoda
Class	–	Crustacea
Order	–	Decapoda
Family	–	Palaemonidae
Genus	–	*Palaemon* or *Macrobranchium*
Species	–	*rosenbergii*

Habit and Habitat:

P. rosenbergii is freshwater inhibitant found in streams, rivers, ponds and lakes in Central and South India. It is benthic animal and omnivorous feeding algae, organic matter, insect larvae and small insects.

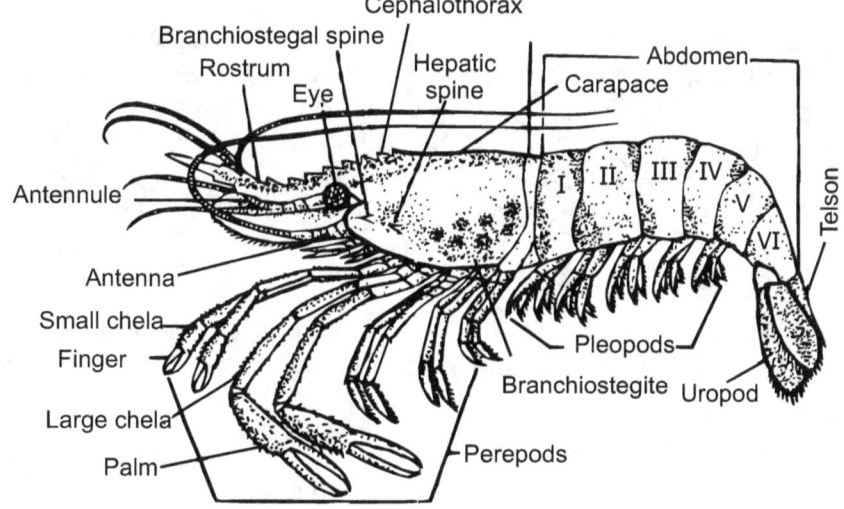

Fig. 9.5: Prawn (*Macrobrachium rosenbergii*)

Identification Characters:

(1) *Palaemon resenbergii* is commonly called as freshwater prawn.

(2) The body is elongated, spindle shaped and about 25-40 cm long.

(3) The body is bluish green with brown or orange red patches.

(4) The body is divided into distinct two parts – an anterior cephalothorax and a posterior abdomen. The cephalothorax is formed by fusion of head and thorax and abdomen is formed by six-movable segments.

(5) A pair of compound eyes present on head.

(6) Each abdominal segment bears a pair of jointed appendages called pleopods. The second pair of walking legs is much larger than others.

(7) The terminal conical piece of body is called as tail plate or *telson.*

(8) The cephalic region carries five-pairs of appendages namely antennules, antennae, mandibles, maxillulae and maxillae.

(9) Prawn and prawn products of India have much appreciation as food in international market, as it is highly nutritive, tasty and palatable.

9.6 Crab

Systematic Position:

Phylum	–	Arthropoda
Class	–	Crustacea
Order	–	Decapoda
Sub-order	–	Brachyura
Family	–	Calippidae/Portunidae/Grapsidae
Type	–	Edible crabs

Habit and Habitats:

Crabs occur in freshwater, marine, brakish water habitats. They generally shows aquatic respiration by gills. Crab is carnivorous, feeding copepod, shrimps and small fishes.

(a) *Matuta planipes* (Fabricius)   (b) *Scylla serrata* (Forskal)

Fig. 9.6: Marine Crabs

Identification Characters:

(1) Cephalothorax is large and covered by a hard chitinous partly calcified *carapace.*

(2) Cephalothorax has five pairs of head appendages and eight pairs of thoracic appendages. The last five pairs are the legs.

(3) First pair of legs is powerful called chelate, used for capturing food. They also serve as organs of offense and defence. The remaining organs are used for swimming and walking.

(4) Swimming organs are Oar-like for propulsion in water.

(5) The gills are in several series in branchial chamber covered by carapace.

(6) The abdomen is much abbreviated and kept flexed against the mid-ventral surface of the thoracic region.

(7) Abdomen of males is narrow with two pairs of uniramous appendages helpful in reproduction.

(8) The abdomen of female broad with four pairs of biramous appendages for carrying the eggs in berried ones.

(9) Life cycle have two larval stages, the *zoea* and the *megalopa*.

9.7 Oyster

Systematic Position:

Phylum	–	Mollusca
Class	–	Bivalvia
Order	–	Pseudolamellibanchiata
Family	–	Pteriidae
Genus	–	*Pinctada*
Species	–	*margaritifera*
		(Indian Pearl Oyster)

Habit and Habitat:

Common pearl oyster is distributed in Gulf of Kutch, Gulf of Mannar, the Pak Bay, and Indian Coast i.e. from Cape Comorin to Rameshwarm Island. They found on hard, rocky, sandy substratum in the bays and creek near coastal area. Oysters are ciliary feeder and feed on a variety of diatoms with detritus material.

 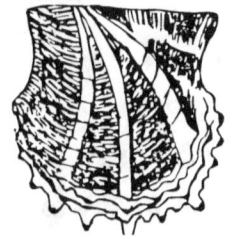 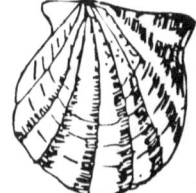

Pinctada margaritifera **Pinctada chemnitizii** **Pinctada fucata (Gould)**
(Linnaeus) **(Philippi)**

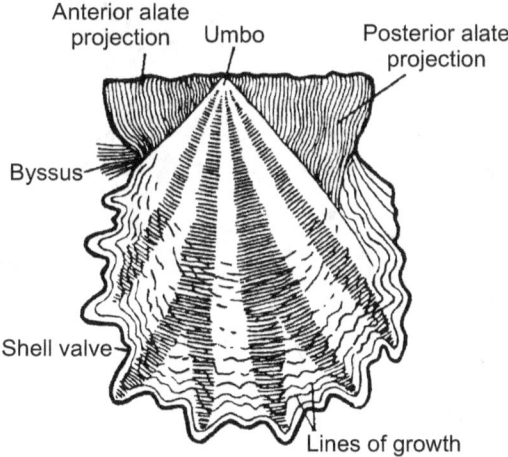

Pinctada margaritifera
Fig. 9.7: *Pearl Oysters*

Identification Characters:

(1) Shell valves may be equal or unequal and shell surface is coarse, irregular ruffled.

(2) Left shell valve is large, convex and permanently attached to rock. Right shell valve is smaller, thin and covers the viscera.

(3) Gills plated with vertical folds and ciliated.

(4) Only posterior single adductor muscle present, which is very large and strong.

(5) Body measures about 25 cm in length.

(6) Oysters are economically very important because they produce high quality pearls as gems.

9.8 Lobster

Systematic Position:

Phylum	–	Arthropoda
Class	–	Crustacea
Sub-class	–	Malacostraca
Order	–	Decapoda
Sub-order	–	Macrura
Family	–	Palinuridae
Genus	–	*Palinures*
Species	–	*polyphagues* (Herbst)

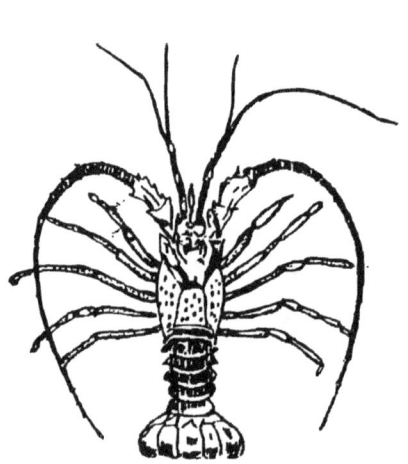
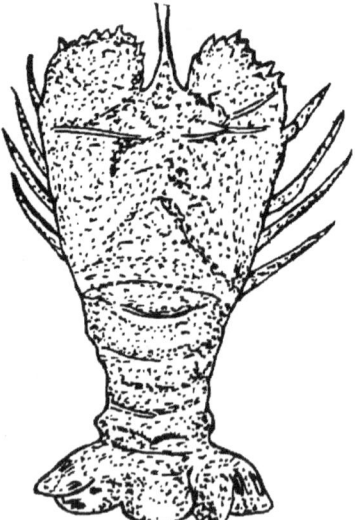

Fig. 9.8 (a): *Panulirus polyphagus* (Herbst)   **Fig. 9.8 (b): *Thenus orientails* (Lund)**

Habit and Habitat:

The common lobster found in the Pacific and the Atlantic Oceans and spiny or rocky lobster found in Indian waters under rocks, coral reefs and muddy bottom of seas. Lobster are primarily scavengers feed on carrions but also feeds on polychaetes, molluscs, crustaceans.

Identification Characters:

(1) The body is divisible in cephalothorax and abdomen. Abdomen ends into a fan-like tail fin.

(2) Telson and uropods reddish-tinged; legs brownish red with cream coloured joints.

(3) Cephalothorax and abdomen is muddy brown in colour. Carapace shows a row of six white spots on lateral side.

(4) Cephalothorax covered by chitinous carapace.

(5) Stalked eyes, a pair of *antennules,* and a pair of *antennae.*

(6) Five pairs of walking legs, prominent and strong.

(7) Abdomen bears five pairs of uniramous *pleopods* which are small and leaf-like.

(8) Carapace bears spines.

(9) The body of lobster is strong and robust.

(10) In male, the third leg is longest which help in copulation.

(11) In earlier days, Lobsters was food of poor people; but now it becomes a delicious food item in Western countries.

Practical 10...

Aim:

To study Maintenance of Fish Aquarium [E].

AQUARIUM

Small fishes are controlled and maintained in a small tank either in a personal house or in the laboratory. Its purpose may be commercial, decorative, hobby or scientific studies. The tank (rectangular), partly filled with water should be equipped with thermostat heater, a reflector and some sort of vegetations. These are basic requirements of an aquarium. For ideal aquarium following should be considered while setting aquarium.

(1) Tank: It is rectangular and have slate glass at bottom with sides of thick glass set in an angle iron/aluminium frame-work. The glass are held with special aquarium cement. The aquarium can be prepared in three different sizes i.e. 21" × 12" × 15" or 24" × 12" × 15" or 36" × 12" × 15".

Fine gravel is mixed with sand and spread over the floor of the tank. The tank should have a tank cover with 60 watt electric lamp. The aquarium may be placed on a table near a window.

(2) The Aquatic plants for the aquarium: Some sort of vegetation is essential for the aquarium, which produce and provide oxygen for fishes. Following are some important plants used for aquarium setting.

    (i) Fanwort *(Cabomba Caroliniana).*

    (ii) Tape grass *(Vallisneria americana).*

    (iii) Sagittaria *(Sagittaria gigantea).*

    (iv) Hygrophila *(Hygrophila polysperma).*

(3) Aquarium fishes: Generally, small sized fishes are selected for aquarium. Both live bearers and egg laying fishes are kept in the aquarium. For example,

    (i) *Lebistes reticulatus* (Guppy).

    (ii) *Gamburia affinis.*

    (iii) *Belta splendens.*

    (iv) *Colisa latia.*

    (v) *Pterophylum eimeki* (Angle fish).

    (vi) *Barbus ticto.*

    (vii) Gold fishes and other fishes.

(4)   Thermometer: It is required to check water temperature.

(5)   The aerator: It is electrically operated. It can pump a continuous stream of bubbles through water of the aquarium. The bubbles produce the movement of water from the bottom towards the top and thus the water gets oxygenated when it contacts with atmospheric air.

(5)   Feeding net: It is made up of plastic and floats on the water surface. It is used for feeding micro-organisms and dried foods.

(6)   Steel wool: It is used to clean and clear the glass of aquarium.

(7)   Electric heater: It is made up of an element perfectly set in glass tube and is thermostatically controlled. The heater is usually set at a temperature of 72°F. Its functions automatically.

(8)   Live food: In addition to dried, and aquatic vegetation. Live food is also give to aquarium fishes which include *daphnia, tubifex, infusoria*, mosquito larvae, earthworms, brine shrimps, microworms etc.

(9)   The pH: The pH of aquarium water should be maintained i.e. for the inland fishes it is 7 and for marine fishes pH 8 is suitable.

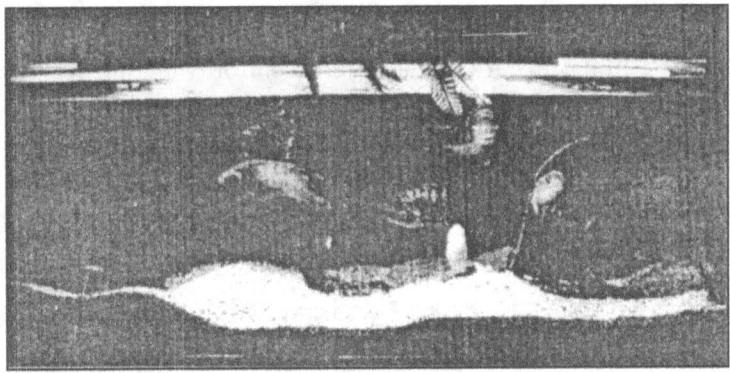

Fig. 10.1: Home Aquarium

Practical 11...

Aim:
Study of any three types of Crafts and Gears in Fishing [D].

The sea coast and riverine & estuarine water of India, have wealth of fish fauna. For this, simple, crude rafts and canoes to well-built; boats are used by man. A number of crafts and gear have been device to hunt or capture fishes. Now-a-days, motor boats and modern steam vessels are being used. These devices are divided on the basis of their form, function and mode of operation.

In fishing technology, crafts and gears are real means of production. Fishing method means the way in which fish can be captured. Gears are the instruments used for fish catching and the crafts provide platform for the fishing operations carrying the crew and fishing gear. There are several types of crafts and gears operated in sea and inland waters. There are some gears which can be operated without the help of craft. Crafts and gears used in the different parts of country are mostly indigenous, non-mechanised and locally built.

The farm fish can be captured in two ways - Drying out (i.e. emptying the ponds or farm) and Non-drying out (i.e. ponds or farm can not be completely dried out).

To minimise considerable losses to fishing, the following precautions should be taken at the time of capture.

1. Feeding should be stopped before 2 or 3 days of capturing.
2. Harvesting should be done in the cool weather preferable in the morning. It should be avoided at the time of raining and thundering.
3. Long transport may be avoided.
4. Young fishes, salmonids and delicate fishes should not be heaped up in scoop nets or any other receptacle.

Fishing crafts or boats and gears are grouped as:

(a) Marine fishing craft and gear
(b) Inland fishing craft and gear
(c) Mechanised craft.

Crafts or boats used in Indian seas are of many types such as *Catamarans, Masula boats, Dinghis, Nauka, Machwa, Tuticorin boats, Dug out canoe, Rampani, Bult-up* etc.

11.1 Important Fishing Crafts

11.1.1 Catamaran

The word 'Catamaran' is derived from the Tamil "Kattumaram" which describe the nature of craft. It is keelless craft. This is made up of numerous wooden logs tied together. The logs are arranged in such a way that in the inside center there is a shallow depression, which is used for stocking the caught fish and as manoeuvring space by the fisherman. The front end of this craft is cut slantingly to reduce water resistance during fishing. Wind sail used for streaming. Catamarans have a length of 5-12 m, width 0.7 m to 1.4 m and depth 0.3 to 0.7 m.

Generally, the catamarans consists of two main logs and two side logs. They are cut into boat shape and tied together with a rope. Catamaran is a primitive type of fishing craft. It is normally operated by 1 or 2 fisherman. The use of catamaran is restricted to the east coast from Orissa to Cape Comorin with a little extension towards north on the Kerala coast. It is a very economical and efficient craft evolved for surf beaten coasts.

There are four types of catamarans:

(a) **Orissa or Ganjam Type:** These are boat shaped catamarans made up of five logs which are pegged with wooden pieces instead of being tied together to give the shape of boat.

(b) **Andhra Type:** It is slightly larger than the Orissa type. It has 5-7 metres heavy wood. There are strong median logs used in fitting the sides.

(c) **Coromandal type:** This is the original Tamil Nadu type and commonly used around Chennai. It is made up of 3-5 logs tying together, with considerable variations in pattern. Sometimes seven logs are used for construction and then named as *Kalamaran*. This is used for catching flying fish in waters of Nagapatnam.

Fig. 11.1: Tuticorin-Type Fishing Boat (Tamil Nadu State)

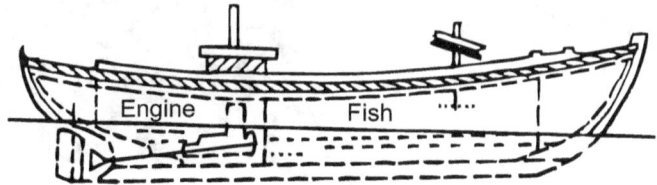

Fig. 11.2: Pablo-Type Fishing Boat of Chennai

(d) **Boat Catamaran:** It is small boat shaped vessel. It is made up of three logs, fitted into a regular boat shape. It is used on the coast around Mandapam and Mukkur regions. Wide variations of this type are found in the Tuticorin, Cape Comorin and Colachel areas.

11.1.2 Machwa Boats

This is most evolved of Indian fishing craft and is indigenous. It has broad hull, pointed bow and straight keel. There are minor modifications in the construction from place to place and locally known as *machwa* used extensively in Bassein. The *Satpati* type known as **galbat**; has a broad beam, median pointed bow, straight keel and high gunwale. **Satpati** is highly specialised as a motor engine can be fitted without change in the design of the locally assembled boat. The *Broach* type is flat bottomed and is of great use in inshore and estuarine waters.

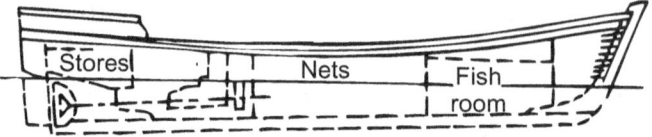

Fig. 11.3: Fishing Machwa of Saurashtra

The satpati boats are common in use on the west coasts along the Mumbai-Cambay coast and north of Ratnagiri.

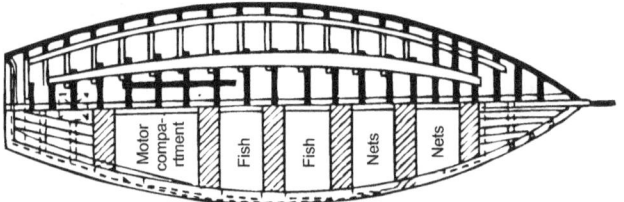

Fig. 11.4: Satpati Type Fishing Boat

11.1.3 Dinghi

Dinghi and Nauka are carvel boats commonly operated in Orissa and West Bengal respectively. These boats are highly curved boats, which are well designed and constructed upto a size of 13 m × 3 m × 2 m are quite spacious and are used for a variety of purposes including fishing operations. Naukas are larger boats as compared to dinghis.

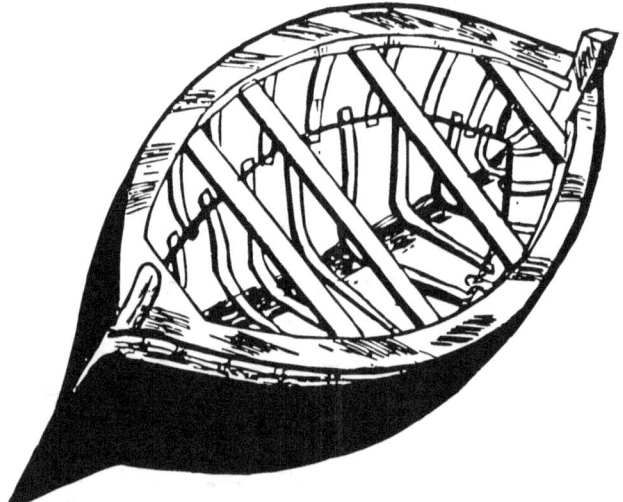

Fig. 11.5: Dinghi – A Carvel Boat of Orissa

11.1.4 Dug-out Canoes

These are made from a single logs of wood by scooping out the inner part, the keel portion being thicker than the sides. These are mainly used on the Kerala and Kanara coasts and also between Colachel and Kathiawar.

The large dug-outs known as *Vanchi* or *Odams* form the main fishing crafts of Malabar coast; operating a variety of nets. They are measuring 10-12 m long, 0.9 m wide and 0.8 m deep and of 3-5 tons displacement.

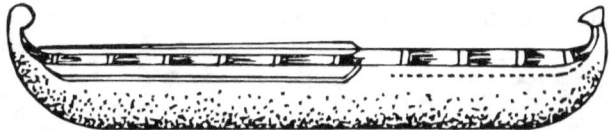

Fig. 11.6: Odam – A Dug-Out Canoe of Malabar

The smaller dug-outs known as *Thonies* are with dimension 7.3 m × 0.9 m × 0.8 m and with 2 tons capacity. Thonies are generally used for gill nets, drift net and cast net.

The dug-out canoes are operated in large numbers from the sandy beach along the south-west coast of India. Mango (*Mangifera indica*) wood is mostly used for these canoes. The dug-out canoes (thonies) of Andhra coast are made out of palm tree trunks.

11.1.5 Rampani

These are large (upto 15 m long) in size with a narrow keel and more spread out planks. Canoes with single out trigger are used on the Kanara and Konkan coasts and are called Rampani boats, as they are used for mackerel fishing with rampani net. Hence, also known as out trigger canoes. These are large with dimensions with 15 m × 3 m. Smaller out trigger canoes are also largely used in the area between Bhatkal and Majali.

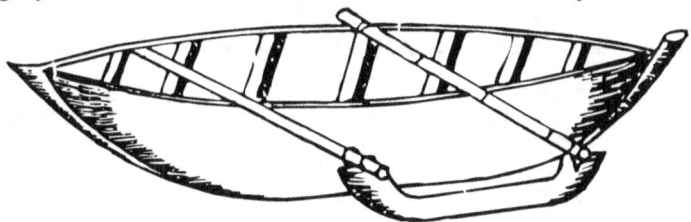

Fig. 11.7: Rampani Boat – An Outrigger Canoe of Karwar

11.1.6 Built-up Boats

These boats are operated on the west coasts of Mumbai-Cambay and North coasts of Ratnagiri. These boats have pointed bow, straight and narrow keel and low gunwale. The built-up boats can be easily mechanized (i.e. motor machines are mounted).

Following are some built-up boats:

(a) Shoe Dhonie: The shape of this craft is like a shoe. It is used in rivers and seas. It is very common in Godavari. This is made up of teak wood and is constructed with planks grooved with ribs and frames. Nails are also used while construction. It is wide and flat forward. 3-4 persons can operate this craft for fishing with gill nets.

(b) Coracle: It is like a round basin. Its frame is constructed with split bamboos, the outer surface is covered with leather. It can be operated in rivers, canals and reservoirs with a stout, short stick by 2-3 fishermen.

(c) Kakinada Nava: It is a keelless boat with about 9.5 m length; and made from teakwood and carvel built. They are constructed with frames and ribs. Nails are also used in their construction. It is open type with a little space decked. This craft is very common for inshore fishing. These built up can be used in rivers, lakes and reservoirs also.

Fig. 11.8: Kakinada Nava (Andhra State)

11.2 Principal Fishing Gears

The equipment used effectively to collect fish from water body is called fish gear or fish nets. Nets, the main gears are made of cotton yarns, hemp or other special yarns. They can be prepared by the fisherman themselves or they are products of cottage industries.

A net is basically a piece of webbing in which the twines are intersected into regular meshes, given a certain form. The fishing twines are made up of any thing natural product (cotton, silk, flax, flax-hemp) to synthetic material (nylon and kapron). At the point of intersection between twines there may be knots or simple interlacing. Mesh size represents the distance between two points of intersection, and it is very important factor in determining the selectivity in fishing. The accessories include, Ropes and Cables, Stakes, Floats, Sinkers or Weights, Anchors, Thimbles, Swivels, Shackles, Gables, Snoods and Reinforcement ropes and webbings.

Setting of net depends upon the nature of active netting or passive netting when operated in water.

Active Netting: In active netting, the net carries a float line with a number of floats and a foot rope to which a number of sinkers are tied.

Passive Netting: In this, the net is either set at the bottom with the help of anchors and skates. It is held suspended near the surface by its own float line, but the net is attached by means of ropes to larger sinkers.

In our country, though a large number of fishing methods are in use but all are not of common use throughout the country. Some common methods of fishing are described here.

11.2.1 Gill Net

Gill nets are wall-like nets with floats attached to the head rope and sinkers fixed to the foot rope with a mesh opening of varying size with type of fish to be fished. The net is set on the transverse direction of the migrating fish. The net is made up of common hemp fibres but now-a-days nets are prepared from synthetic impermeable fibres due to which it is not possible for the fishes to see the nets. So, as fishes try to swim through a net wall, the meshes form a noose round its head and they are caught because they get entangled in the fabric mesh. As the fish tries to escape, it gets stuck up behind the opercle hence these nets are called "*gill nets*". The various dyes are used to make the net invisible. These nets are generally used to catch big varieties of fish viz. *Seenghala, Pangasius, Silonia, Major carps* etc. This net is fit for fishing in fast current therefore made of strong material with large sized mesh. These nets are left over night i.e. they are stretched across the river banks and fixed by poles. The net is hauled up in the morning and the fish entangled are collected.

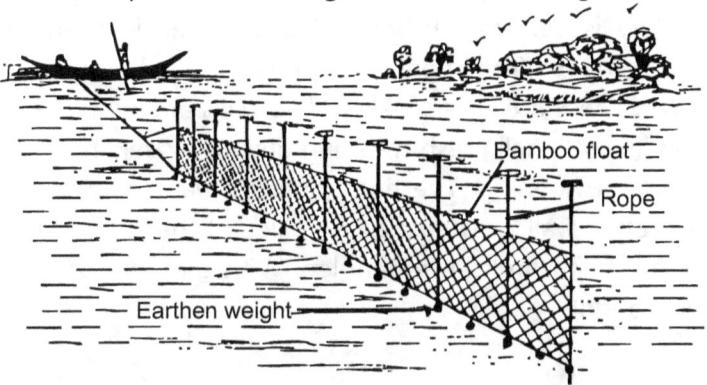

Fig. 11.9: Chandi Jal – A Drift Gill – Net of West Bengal

Depending on the manner of entangling fish, gill nets are classified into two types i.e. (i) *Simple Gill Nets* and (ii) *Trammel Nets*.

(A) Simple Gill Nets: In these case, a loose net webbing is set in the path of fish movement. When the fish tries to swim through a mesh, only its head passes through the mesh, but its large body can not pass through it. When fish tries to withdraw its head, twines slip under the gill cover and the fish is entangled. Thus, they cannot escape and the fish is caught by gill.

The gill nets are generally set in three ways namely *floating*, *anchored*, and *staked*.

(i) Floating or Drift Gill Net: The floating type (drift net) is simply a vertically suspended wall of net with a float line and a lead line.

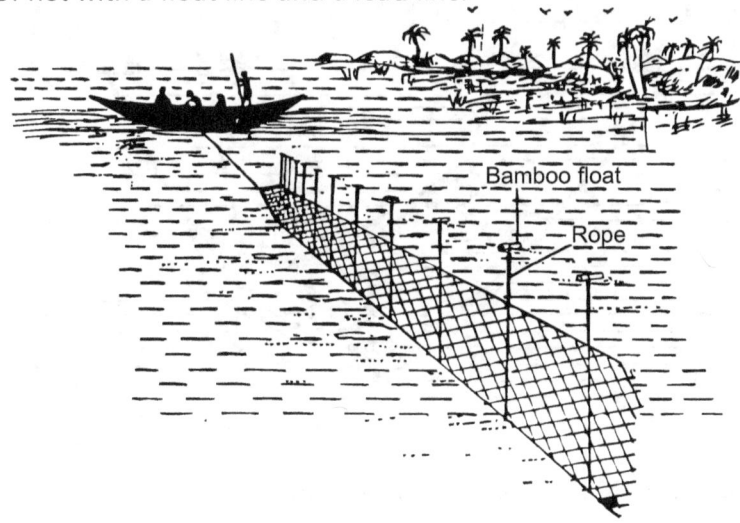

Fig. 11.10: Karal or Katla Jal - A Drift Net

(ii) Anchored Type Gill Net: It is a modification of drift net. In such cases an anchor is used which does not permit free drifting and the net is held stationary either at the surface or at any depth in the mid water. They are used in large lakes or coastal fisheries and are set as straight walls or in bow shaped pattern.

(iii) Staked Nets: In this case, the net is fixed at the bottom with the help of stakes or anchors. The gill nets are generally rigged with vertical snoods and frames. Snoods are twines attached at intervals between the float line and lead line. Snoods increase fishing efficiency and frame provide reinforcement.

(B) Trammel Net: These are 2 or 3 walled. The walls are jointed above at the float line and below at the lead line. A small mesh webbing (lint) is loosely hung between two lightly netted walls of large mesh webbing. The tightly netted wall has twines 3-4 times stronger than those of loosely netted wall. Small fishes are gilled at the lint and large size fish pushed a bag of the loosely hung lint and get entangled. With the help of these nets a wide size range of fishes can be caught.

11.2.2 Dol Net

Fixed/stationary or dol nets are conical or rectangular in shape. These are of various sizes and meshes. Panch, Kathia-kool jal, Behundi or Ghurni jal and Panch-kathiaber jal are conical nets used in West Bengal and Orissa. Jadi or intagh jal of Gujarat and Kathiawar coasts, Kalam-Katti valai (Mada Valai) of the Gulf of Manaar and some parts of the Palk Bay are some of the important examples. All these nets may be fixed in the tidal regions of inshore water during the low tide with the help of the floats, stakes or sinkers. The high tide brings the fish in the net which are subsequently trapped.

Dol net is a specialized fixed bag net, which has the characteristics of both bag net and a fixed trap. Dol net is used in Mumbai and Gujarat areas. It is fixed in the sea by stakes or buoys. These nets are used in waters, where the current is strong and high enough to keep the net in horizontal expanded position.

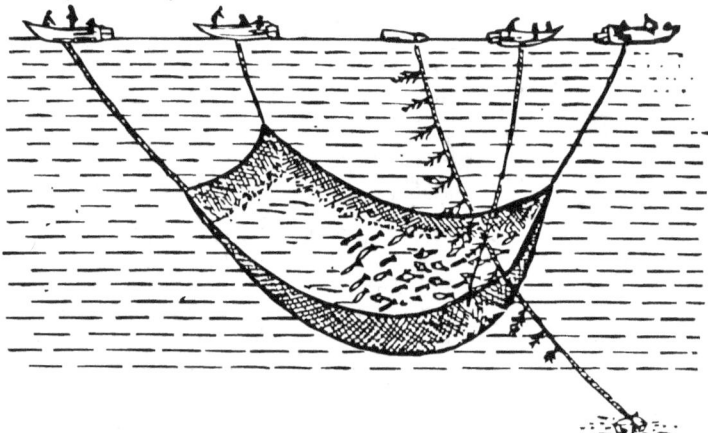

Fig. 11.11: Mada Valia – A shore-Seine of Coromandel Coast

11.2.3 Purse Net

Purse nets are generally used to capture the migrated fishes *Hilsa* in the month of October to January and large sized carps and cat fishes are fished in May to July. This is a purse shaped net and operated from the vessel (boat). In the hanging condition, the float line of the net wall remains at the surface, the lead line is at certain depth from the surface and does not touch the bottom. The fish is prevented from escaping below the lead line by the net being pursed during the hauling. For this purpose there is in addition to the lead line a purse line of strong cable. There is no 'bag', the net consists of a single wall of net with equal height throughout. The central part acts as the bunt, has the thickest twines.

During operation, one end of the net is held on a small boat and then the net is laid out by a large vessel cruising at high speed and making a circle so that it comes back to the small boat. The purse line is handed on board the vessel. The net then takes the shape of a purse. The pull on the purse line increases at the end

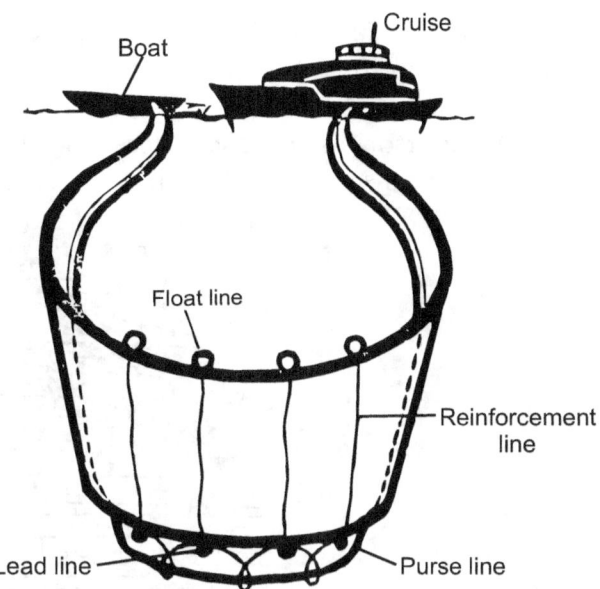

Fig. 11.12: Purse Siene (Before Pursing)

of the operation and it equals the weight of the lower half of the net. Finally, the entire net is hauled along with the catch.

In India, the common purse net used are *'Kharki Jal'* and *'Shangla Jal'* are made up of tanned cotton and have rectangular shape.

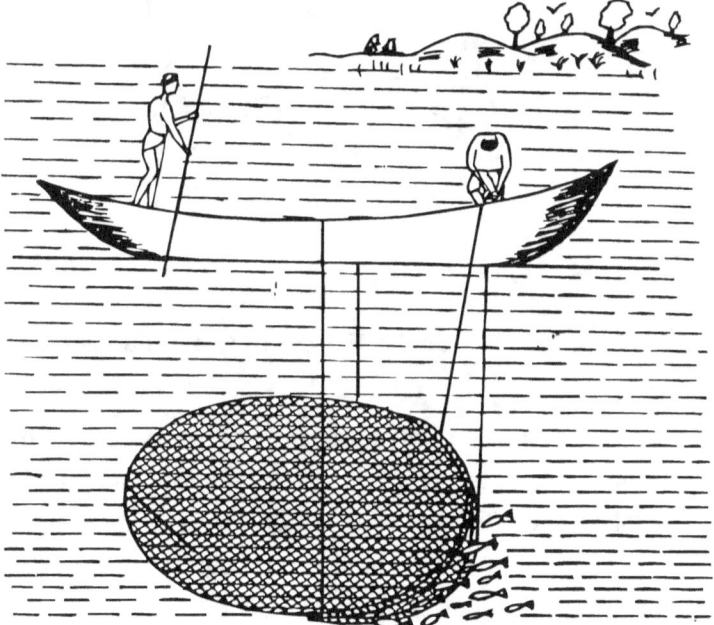

Fig. 11.13: Shanglo Jal – A Purse Net

11.2.4 Rampani Net

These are very large nets for active fishing and operated from sea-shore. The biggest shore seines used in India is Rampani of Konkan and Malbar Coasts are largely used for mackerel fishing. Each net contains a bag with wings and scare lines are used for driving the fish into the bag. The net is kept in position by wooden floats and stone sinkers held in the head and foot ropes. One end of the net remains on the shore and the other extremity carries the rest of the net and places it in the semicircular way. Finally, the two ends are slowly dragged by groups of fishermen. It is used to catch the Indian Mackerel etc.

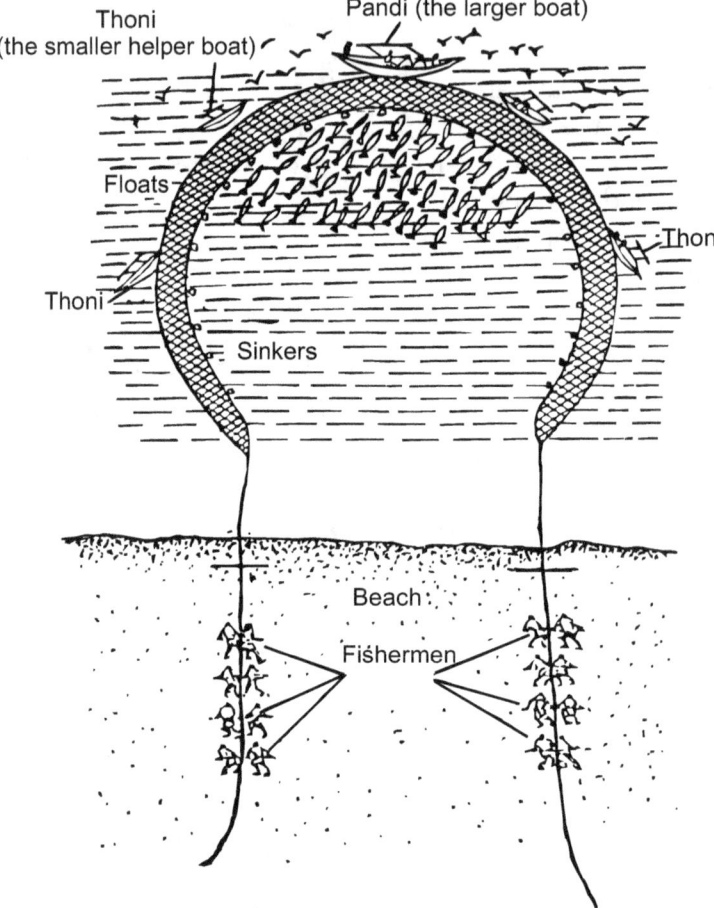

Fig. 11.14: Operation of Rampani Net for the Fishing of the Indian Mackerel in a Large Scale

11.2.5 Cast Net

This is a circular, umbrella-shaped net made up of cotton twine. This is operated from boat. It is skillfully thrown over water, but is held by a rope (hauling line) attached to its center. The net spreads like umbrella over a group of fishes. The perimeter (circular line), is weighted with sinkers, which increase the weight and facilitate (dragging) sinking the entire net towards bottom. The circumference is inwardly recurved so as to form an inner circular pocket around the perimeter; this prevents the escape of fish during hauling. When perimeter touches the bottom, hauling line is pulled to raise the net on board and thus the trapped fish is collected. The net is used to catch small fish in shore waters or in riverbanks. Cast nets are hand operated nets with string or without string.

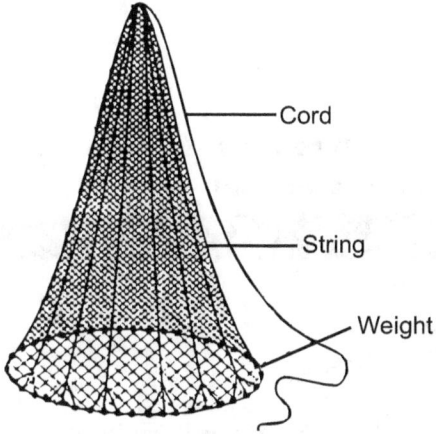

Cord

String

Weight

Fig. 11.15: Stringed Cast Net

✳✳✳

Practical 12...

Aim:

To study insect pests with respect to marks of identification, nature of damage and economic importance [D].

12.1 Jowar Stem Borer

Class	–	Insecta
Order	–	Lepidoptera
Family	–	Pyralidae
Genus	–	*Chilo*
Species	–	*zonellus = partellus* (Swinhoe)

Jowar is the most important staple food crop of the Maharashtra state. Besides being staple food crop of the people, it also supplies very good fodder for the cattle. It is cultivated in Kharif, Rabi and also in hot weather. Jowar stem borer is one of the major pests of jowar.

Distribution:

It occurs throughout India. The jowar stem borer is commonly called as *spotted stalk borer* or *pink borer*.

Identification Marks:

The adult moth is a medium sized insect with 3 cm wing span. Its forewings are straw or light brown in colour with numerous shining brown spots on the margin and hindwings are white and papery. The caterpillars (Larvae) are dirty white in colour with dark brown head with mandibulate type of mouth parts. Many dark spots are appeared on the body. Mature caterpillars are measured about 12-20 mm in length and shows four broad and patchy strips on the body.

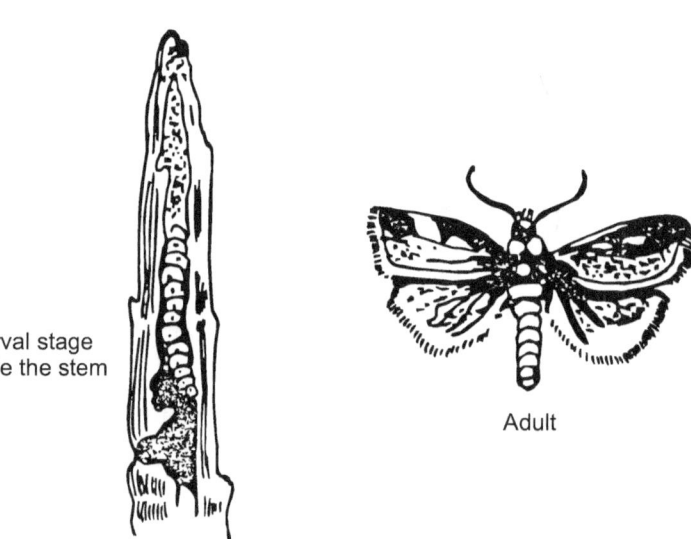

Larval stage inside the stem

Adult

Fig. 12.1: Jowar Stem Borer

Host Plants:

This is the major pest of jowar and maize but also recorded on bajra, ragi and other grasses.

Life Cycle:

A female lays about 50-300 eggs in clusters arranged in two rows on the under surface of the leaves during April-May. Eggs are creamy white in colour. They hatch into the young caterpillar in about six days of incubation period. The young caterpillar feeds on tender leaves for a day or two and bores into the central shoot. The larval stage last for about 3-4 weeks and have normally five moults. Pupation takes place inside the stem and it last for about 7-10 days. The adult lives for 2-4 days. The pest is generally active from June to November and about four generations are completed in a year. The pest hibernates in the larval stage in stubbles during unfavourable period.

Nature of Damage:

Newly hatched caterpillars initially feed on the leaves causing numerous small holes in the leaf lamina and attack all parts of jowar plant except the roots. The larvae on entering the leaf, whorl and cut the leaves, which on emergence manifest characteristic pin holes, shoot holes and longitudinal streaks. At times the growing point is cut which results in drying of the central shoot and subsequently formation of dead-heart. The larvae after entering the stem, feed on the tissues (pith) and tunnels or galleries are formed.

Control Measures:

Cultural Method:

(i)   Hand picking or light trapping of adult moths and collection of their eggs for destruction.

(ii)   Burning of stubbles and trash which harbour borers and act as source of infestation for the next crop.

(iii)   Growing resistant varieties of jowar like CHS-7, CHS-8, Indian sorghum types IS-5566, 5285 and 5613.

Chemical Method:

(i)   For the *Chilo* on jowar a spray of 0.05% lindane or 0.1% endosulfan on 15 days old plants has been found effective. This may be followed after another fortnight with a second application of 1.0% lindane or 4% endo sulfan granules. A third application with 0.2% carbaryl spray may be carried out, if found necessary.

(ii)   If the crop infestation is noticed, dusting of crop in the early stage with 10% BHC at the rate of 25 kg per hectare or spraying the crop with 350-400 ml of aldrin or dieldrin in 200 litres of water helps to control the pest.

Biological Method:

(i) The hymenopteran, *Trichogramma minutum* is employed as egg parasite.

(ii) *Apanteles flavipes* and *Bracon brevicornis* as larval parasites.

(iii) *Sexmaculata* have been recorded predating on early stages of the larvae of this pest.

12.2 Red Cotton Bug

       Class   –   Insecta

       Order   –   Hemiptera

       Family   –   Pyrrhocoridae

       Genus   –   *Dysdercus*

       Species   –   *cingulatus = koenigii* (Fab.)

The red cotton bug has wide distribution, it is a minor pest in cotton growing region of northern India particularly Punjab and Uttar Pradesh. This pest also occurs throughout the Maharashtra state but is minor importance. It is commonly known as a *"cotton stainer"*.

Host Plants:

Cotton, bhendi, ambadi, hollyhock and several other malvaceous plants.

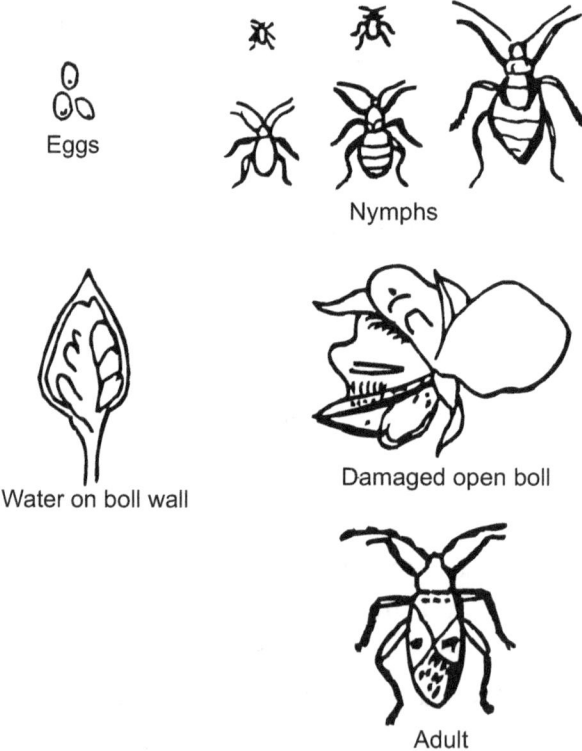

Fig. 12.2: Red Cotton Bug

Identification Marks:

The adult bug measures about 12-15 mm in length. The females are longer (15 mm) than the males (12 mm). It is blood red in colour except eyes, scutellum, and antennae which are black coloured. Besides, there is a black spot on each of the membranous forewings. A series of white transverse bands are present on the ventral side of the abdomen. Mouth parts are adapted for piercing and sucking. They form a straight beak or rostrum. The nymphs are smaller than adults and are wingless.

Life Cycle:

The mature female lays eggs during spring in clusters of 70-80 eggs each under the moist soil surface; fallen leaves and in crevices. The eggs are spherical, yellowish-white about 1.2 mm in length. After 7 days of incubation period and moist weather, eggs are hatched into active 1 mm long red coloured nymphs which are resemble the adult except size and absence of wings. The nymphs feed gregariously on the cotton bolls. The nymphs undergo 5-moults within 49-89 days to reach adult stage. In winter the life of the adult is about three months but in summer it is varied. Pest breeds on cotton from August-November; takes shelter under leaves or debris from December-middle of March and feeds on bhendi from April-July. The life cycle of bug is completed within six to eight weeks.

Nature of Damage:

Both nymphs and adults, suck the cell sap from the leaves and tender shoots and impair the vitality of the plant. If the attack is severe, bolls open badly and the lint is of poor quality. In addition they also feed on the seeds and lower their oil content and low percentage of germination; such seeds are unfit for sowing. The lint is stained by the excreta of bugs or by their body juice as they are crushed in the ginning factories.

Control Measures:

1. Cotton field should be ploughed to expose eggs to sunlight.
2. Insects should be hand picked and killed in kerosinised water.
3. The crops of bhendi should be sown as trap crop and pests collected there, should be destroyed.
4. Moistened cotton seeds should be hunged up at different places in the field where bugs congregate, they may get killed in the kerosene mix water.
5. Spraying of Malathion 0.05% is effective to control the pest.
6. Spraying of 1 litre endosulphan 35% EC, 0.25 litre phosphamidon = 100% EC or 1 litre Fenitrothion 100% EC per hectare is very effective or reduces pest population.

12.3 Castor Semilooper

Class	–	Insecta
Order	–	Lepidoptera
Family	–	Noctuidae
Genus	–	*Achaea*
Species	–	*janata* (Linn.)

The castor semi-looper is a serious pest of castor in the larval stage and is also a serious pest of citrus in the adult stage found all over Maharashtra and throughout the country.

Host Plants:

It is a polyphagous pest and having been recorded to infest castor, citrus, pomegranate, rose, cotton etc.

Identification Marks:

The moths are stout with smoky grey or brown forewings. Hindwings are dark with white band in the middle and 3-4 white spots at the anal margin. The body measures about 60-65 mm in length. The larva is semilooper, grey or black in colour with red or whitish side strips. A full grown larva measures about 60 to 70 mm in length.

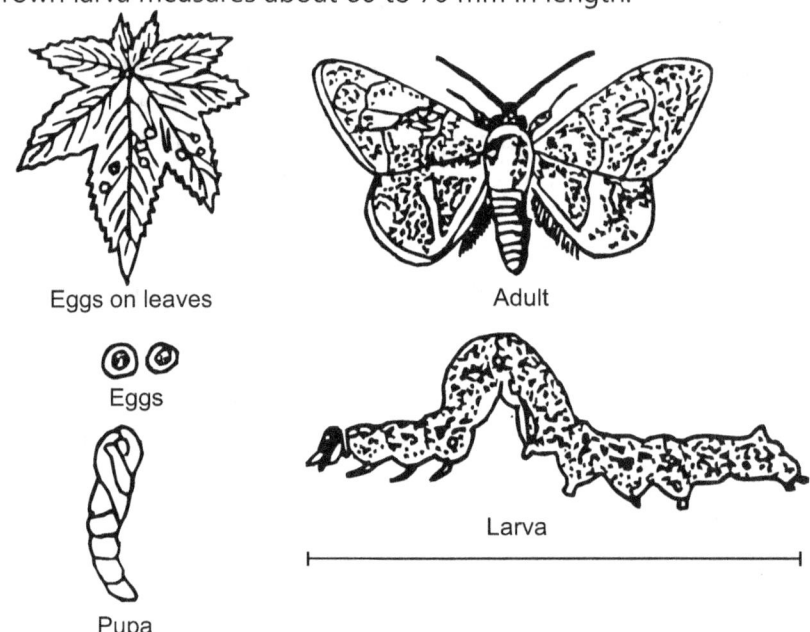

Eggs on leaves

Eggs

Pupa

Adult

Larva

Fig. 12.3: Castor Semilooper: Life Cycle

Life Cycle:

The eggs are laid singly on tender shoots and over the lower surface of leaves. The eggs are elongated and bluish-green. They hatch in 3-4 days. On hatching from eggs, the larvae start feeding on leaves and become full grown in about two weeks. The larva undergoes 4-instars, each taking 2-4 days. The full grown caterpillar is about 7 cm long and brownish black in colour with pale white stripes. It pupates in soil or in leaf folds. The pupal stage lasts about 10 days. After emergence, moths feed on citrus fruits by piercing skin and feeding on the juices. 5 to 6 generations are completed in a year.

Nature of Damage:

The caterpillar is a voracious leaf-eater of castor, starting from the margins, eating inwards and leaving behind only the mid-rib and the stalks. Maximum damage is caused by the second and third instars caterpillars; with the excessive loss of foliage, the seed yield is drastically reduced. The adult moths feed on citrus fruits juice.

Control Measures:

1.   The caterpillars should be handpicked and destroyed.

2.   The population of castor semi-looper can be considerably suppressed by spraying the plants with any of the following insecticides.

Insecticide	Concentration (%)	Quantity per litre of water
Carbaryl (Sevin) 50 w/p	0.1	2.0 g
Quinalphos (Ekalux) – 25 EC	0.1	4.0 ml
Fenitrothion 50 EC	0.1	2.0 ml
Endosulfan (Thiodan) 35 EC	0.075	2.1 ml
Methyl parathion 50 EC	0.05	1.0 ml

3.   1.5% quinalphos dust @ 20 kg/ha may be dusted on the infested crop.

4.   In biological control, the larval parasites *Apanteles sudanus* Wlk., *A. ruidus* Wlk. and *Tetrastichus ophiusae* craw and egg parasites *trichogramma* achaeae and *Telenomus* spp. are successful.

12.4 Brinjal Fruit Borer

Class   –   Insecta
Order   –   Lepidoptera
Family   –   Pyralidae / Pyraustidae
Genus   –   *Leucinodes*
Species –   *orbonalis* (Guenee)

Common Name:

Brinjal shoot and fruit borer.

Host Plants:

Brinjal (main) and other solanaceous plants and peas (alternative).

L. orbonalis is the most important and destructive pest of brinjal and has a countrywide distribution.

Identification Marks:

The moths are medium sized of about 20 mm across the spread wings. The head and thorax are blackish brown. The wings are white and provided with small hairs along the apical and anal margins. A number of black, pale and light brown spots are found on the fore and hindwings of the moth. The caterpillars are pale white and about 12 mm long when fully grown.

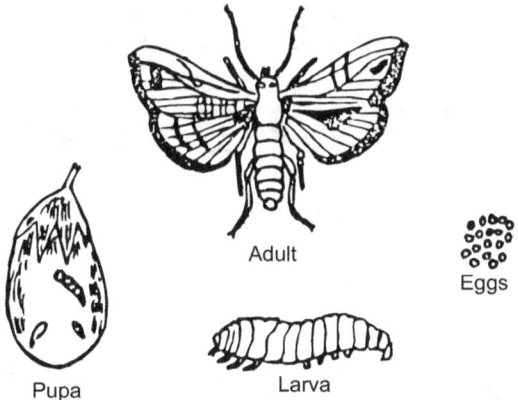

Adult

Eggs

Pupa

Larva

Fig. 12.4: Life history of *Leucinodes orbonalis*

Life Cycle:

The moth lays elongated eggs singly or in small batches, on the leaf surface, shoots and fruits. They hatch in 3-5 days. On hatching the caterpillars start boring into the shoot, leaf midrib, petiole and fruits and feeds on the internal tissues. The larva undergoes 5-moults in 10-15 days. The fifth instar larva is stout pink and measures about 1.6 cm in length. Pupation takes place in a cocoon on the plant and lasts for 6-8 days. Moth lives 2-5 days and the female lays upto 250 eggs. The larva is parasitized by *Pristomerus testaceus* Morl, *Cremastus flauoorbitalis* and Bracon species.

Nature of Damage:

The larval stage is the only destructive stage. In the early stages the larvae bore into tender shoot as a result the infested shoots droop down and ultimately dry up. The larvae also bore into flower buds and developing fruits under the calyx leaving no visible signs of infestation. The attacked fruits show holes on them plugged with excreta. In case of severe infestation in the initial stages, there may be no fruiting at all. The pinkish larvae make zig-zag tunnels in the fruits and fruits are holed; such infested fruits are rendered totally unfit for human consumption. Upto 70% loss of crop is caused by this pest.

Control Measures:

1. The affected fruits and drooping shoots, containing caterpillars inside, should be clipped off and destroyed.

2. The crop should be sprayed with suspension/emulsion of any of the following insecticides.

Insecticide	Concentration (%)	Quantity per litre of water
Carbaryl (Sevin) 50 w/p	0.2	4.0 g
Malathion 50 EC	0.1	2.0 ml
Endosulfan (Thiodan) 35 EC	0.1	3.0 ml
Phosalone (Zolone) 35 EC	0.075	2.1 ml

3. The biological agencies like, Braconid wasps (*Bracon chinensis, shirakia schoenobi*) and Inchenumonid wasps (Trathela flavoorbitais) parasitize the larvae of this pest.

12.5 Mango Stem Borer

Class   –   Insecta
Order   –   Coleoptera
Family   –   Cerambycidae
Genus   –   *Batocera*
Species   –   *rubus* (Linn)

The mango, the king of fruits in India suffers from many serious pests. Among them mango stem borer is the most important. It is very common in Maharashtra and Uttar Pradesh.

Host Plants:

This pest is found on the planted plants like mango, fig, rubber and jack.

Identification Marks:

The adult beetles are well built, large sized, measuring about 5 cm long in length and brownish yellow/grey coloured. It has orange yellow spots on thorax and has hard forewings (elytra); lateral spines on the prothorax and long antennae and legs. The grubs are large, yellowish white in colour, fleshy in appearance and measures about 100 × 18 mm with black head bearing strong mandibles.

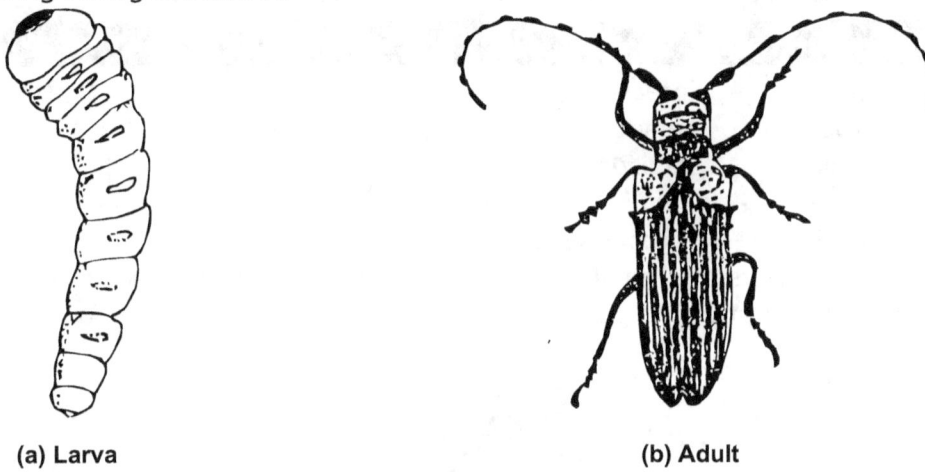

(a) Larva   (b) Adult

Fig. 12.5: Mango Stem Borer

Life Cycle:

The female beetle lays single egg under the loose bark or in a diseased part of trunk or in the crevices of stems. After the incubation period of 14 to 17 days the egg hatches out. The grubs on hatching penetrate into the stem or even the roots feeding on the woody tissue and make tunnels. The larval stage last for 3 to 6 months; then they pupate in the stem and remain in the pupal stage for 3 to 6 months over winter and the adults generally emerge during the monsoon. Duration of life cycle may extend from 1-2 years.

Nature of Damage:

The grubs make zig-zag galleries beneath the bark and tunnel into the trunks or main stems. As a result of feeding on the internal tissues, the attacked branches and stem die and wither away. Sometimes, frass and masses of refuse exude may be seen on the opening of the bored holes. In severe cases of attack, the branches may collapse and the tree may die.

Control Measures:

1. The population of grubs and pupae of stem borer can be reduced by cutting and destroying the infested branches.

2. The best way to control the grubs is to just inject borer solution (i.e. 2 parts of carbon disulphide + one part of chloroform and cresole) in the holes after which it should be closed by mud.

3. Pest population can also be effectively reduced by injecting 0.05% spray fluid of the following into the borer holes.

Insecticide	Quantity (ml)/litre of water
DDVP (Dichlorvos) 76 EC	0.7
Endosulfan (Thiodan) 35 EC	1.5
Chlorpyriphos (Durshan) 20 EC	2.5

Immediately after insecticidal treatment the holes must be sealed with mud.

12.6 Lemon Butterfly

Class   –   Insecta
Order   –   Lepidoptera
Family   –   Papilionidae
Genus   –   *Papilio*
Species –   *demoleus* (Linn.)

There are many pests of citrus trees in the state of Maharashtra. Out of which lemon butterfly is a highly destructive pest of citrus in India. The genus *Papilio* is distributed throughout the world.

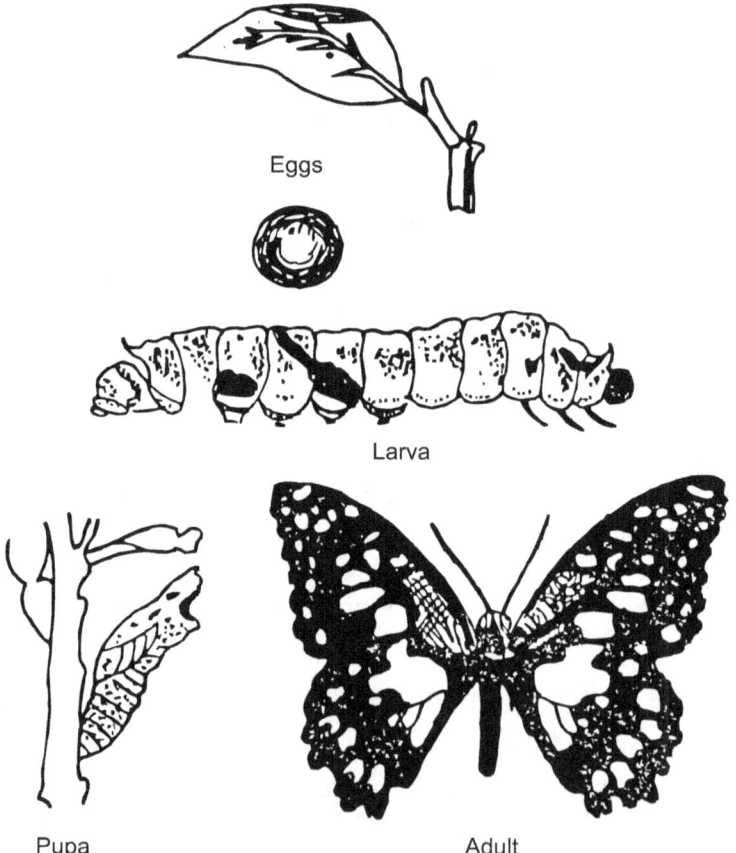

Eggs

Larva

Pupa   Adult

Fig. 12.6: Life Stages of Lemon Butterfly

Host Plant:

Citrus is the only host plant of this pest.

Identification Marks:

It is a beautiful butterfly of large size measuring about 2.8 cm in length and 9.4 cm on wing expanse. The adult is a black and yellow, swallow tail butterfly. Its hindwings have a brick red oval patch near the anal margin and a tail like extension behind on account of which it is commonly known as a swallow tail butterfly. The antennae are black and club shaped. It has black coloured head and thorax, whereas, creamy yellow coloured abdomen. The young caterpillar is darkish-brown in colour with irregular whitish stains. On maturity it turns deep green in colour and cylindrical in form and measures about 38 mm length with a hump-like appearance in front.

Life Cycle:

Eggs are laid singly or in small group of 2-3 on the under surface of leaves and shoots; upto 180 eggs are laid by each female. The eggs are minute, spherical and white turning grey on maturity. They hatch in 3-6 days. The larva has five instars; the first three are brownish black with white patches. The last two are greenish with brown and grey markings. When disturbed the caterpillar pushes out from the top of its prothorax a bifid, purple structure called the **osmenterium** which emits a distinct smell. The larva becomes full grown in 13-26 days and is stout and 4 cm long. Later they pupate on the plant itself and remain attached to it by silken girdles. The pupal period lasts about 2-3 months in winter and emerges out as adult. The peak population of the pest is in April and again from July to October.

Nature of Damage:

The caterpillars cause destruction of the citrus plants. They usually feed on the tender leaves and terminal shoots. It has been observed that they start feeding from margin and reach the mid-rib. The severe attack by full grown caterpillar causes complete defoliation of citrus plants thus rendering them unfit for fruit bearing. Seedlings and young plants suffer the most.

Control Measures:

(1) Handpicking of the caterpillar and pupae from plants in the initial stages of infestation and removing alternative host plants are mechanical control measures.

(2) In case of severe infestation, the plants may be sprayed with suspension/emulsion spray of any of the following insecticides.

Insecticide	Concentration (%)	Quantity per litre of water
Carbaryl 50 w/p	0.1	2.0 g
Quinalphos (Ekalux) 25 EC	0.1	4.0 ml
Chlorpyriphos (Dursban) 20 EC	0.05	2.5 ml
Phosalone 35 EC	0.1	3.0 ml
Methyl parathion 50 EC	0.1	2.0 ml
Thiodan 35 EC	0.1	3.0 ml

(3) The pests can also be controlled by treating the plants with a short term contact insecticide such as 0.04% monocrotophos or phosphamidon.

(4) *Trichogramma evanescens* and *Telenomus* sp. parasitize the eggs of *P. demoleus* while the larvae are parasitized by *Erycia nymphalidaephaga*, charops spp. and *Brachymeria* sp. are the biological agents to control the pest population without any harmful effects.

12.7 Sitophilus Oryzae Linn

Common name	–	Rice weevil
Class	–	Insecta
Order	–	Coleoptera
Family	–	Curculionidae
Genus	–	*Sitophilus*
Species	–	*oryzae*

This is a serious pest of stored grains as well as grains in farm storage. It is cosmopolitan in distribution.

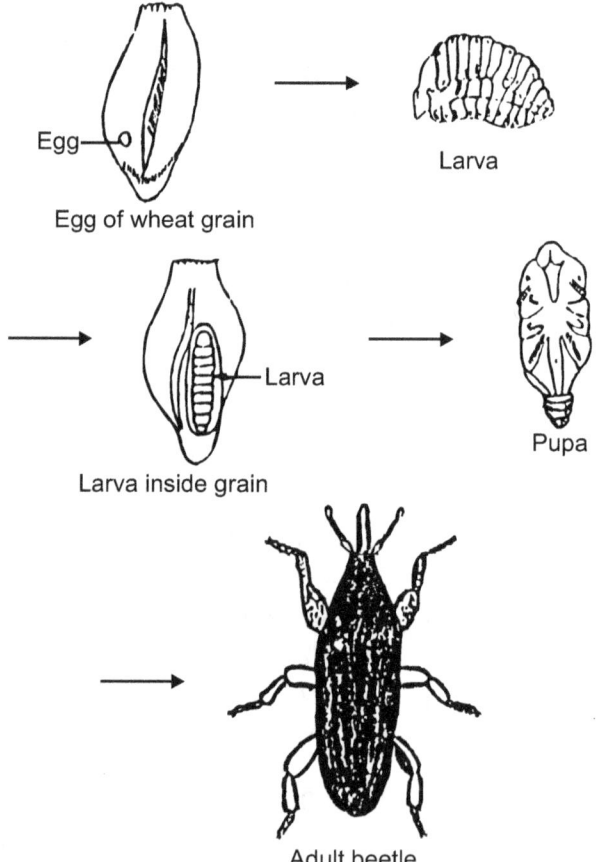

Fig. 12.7: (a) Life Stages of *Sitophilus oryzae* (Gram)

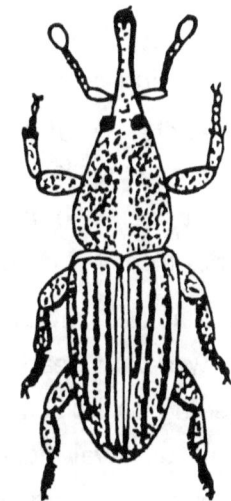

Fig. 12.7: (b) *Sitophilus oryzae* (Rice)

Identification Marks:

The adults are small weevil, about 4 mm in length with reddish brown, dark brown or almost black in colour with cylindrical body and a long curved rostrum. The head is prolonged into a slender snout with chewing mouth parts located at its tip. The functional wings hidden beneath the dark brown elytra with four light reddish or yellowish spots and the insect is able to fly. The life span of adult weevil is 4-5 months. The grubs are whitish in colour, small (i.e. 5 mm in length) and legless with yellow brown head. They are always found inside the kernels.

Host:

S. oryzae prefer rice, they can be found feeding on wheat, maize and other grains.

Nature of Damage:

Generally, infestation starts in grains only during storage. The *S. oryzae* feeds on whole grains of rice, wheat, jowar, bajri, maize, barley etc. Both adults and larvae feed voraciously on the grains so that the grain becomes unfit for consumption and seed purposes. A thin tunnel (hole) is formed by the grub from the surface towards inside of the grain. Circular exit holes and stained spots on the surface of the grain kernel is the symptom of damage. In case of heavy infestation, the grains become a mass of broken vegetable matter. The adults eat a small amount of grain, making shallow holes with rugged edges but the amount of damage thus caused is negligible as compared to the complete hollowing of grain by the larval stages results into hollowed grains leading to reducing in weight and food value.

Life Cycle:

The female starts laying eggs 5 days after the emergence. The female bores a small, round hole in the soft part of a grain by means of mouth parts and there she lays a single egg and sealing it with a mucilaginous secretion. The eggs are translucent, white, oval, minute (0.7 × 0.3 mm in size). A female lays a total of 300-400 eggs during her life-time. The incubation period varies from 4-7 days in summer to 6-9 days in winter.

The **grub** (larva) hatches out of the egg is legless (Apodous), translucent white with fleshy body and yellow-brown head. The young tiny grub bores into the grain kernel and lives within grain; feeding on its starchy content and hollows it out, leaving only the outer shell intact. There are four larval instars and the larval period lasts for 25-35 days. The full-grown grub makes a pupal cell inside the grain. The **pupa** is curved or humpy in appearance and takes 3-6 days to emerge as an adult. The emerged weevil immediately starts breeding and gives rise to new generation for destruction of grain. Several generations are possible during a normal storage season of grains. The adults live on an average for 2 to 5 months.

Control Measures:

To control the stored grain pest. Both the control methods are adopted i.e. the preventive and curative.

1.　Preventive Method:

This control measure is employed to protect fresh stocks from the attack of pests.

(i)　　After harvesting, dry the grains in sunlight sufficiently so that the moisture content is reduced to less than 8% moisture because most of the stored grain pests cannot multiply in grain at such percentage of moisture.

(ii)　　After drying in sunlight, the grains store in new gunny bags so that grains will be free from infection.

(iii)　　Use of neem leaves, mercury, mixing of ash, powder of sweet flag rhizome (*Acorus Calamus* Linn), etc. in grains or smearing the grains with plant oils are the indigenous practices used by rural peoples for protecting the stored grains from the attack of different pests.

If the old bags are to be used, they should be fumigated with EDBR (Ethylene di-bromide) at 3 kg/100 cu.m for 5 to 7 days which helps to check the cross infestation. It also achieved by applying 5% BHC or 0.06% pyrethrum dust at 25 gm/sq.m or sprays of BHC, pyrethrum or malathion. The bags should then be stored in an insect free godown.

(iv) To make the insect free godown one or more of the following methods may be used.

(a) All dirt, refuse material should be removed and destroyed and all the cracks, crevices, holes in walls, floors or ceiling of the godown should be filled in with cement.

(b) The rat holes should be closed by filling them with cement or sand mixed with glass pieces.

(c) Fumigate the godown with EDBR.

(d) Spray with insecticides like Pyrethrum, Malathion or BHC to avoid the chance of contamination.

2. Curative Measures:

This measure becomes essential when the grains get infested with the stored grain pests.

(i) Sieving and cleaning removes all the stages of pests.

(ii) After above method the grains must be followed by sunning and fumigation with suitable fumigants.

(iii) The larvae and adults are killed by exposing them for 48 hours to the vapours of ethylene dichloride - carbon tetrachloride mixture under gas proof covers. Fumigation of infested grain with methyl bromide is also effective and kills all stages of the pest including eggs.

12.8 Pulse Beetle

Class   –   Insecta

Order   –   Coleoptera

Family   –   Bruchidae

Genus   –   *Callosobruchus* (= *Pachymerus*) or *Bruchus*

Species   –   *chinensis* Linn.

Common Name:

Gram dhora / mung dhora.

Distribution:

All over India and many other countries though not world wide. This is very important pest of various pulse crops in India, both in field crops and in stores.

Host Plants (main):

Gram, peas, cowpeas, lentile, arhar (C. cajan).

Alternative:

Chick pea, maize, soyabean, other pulses.

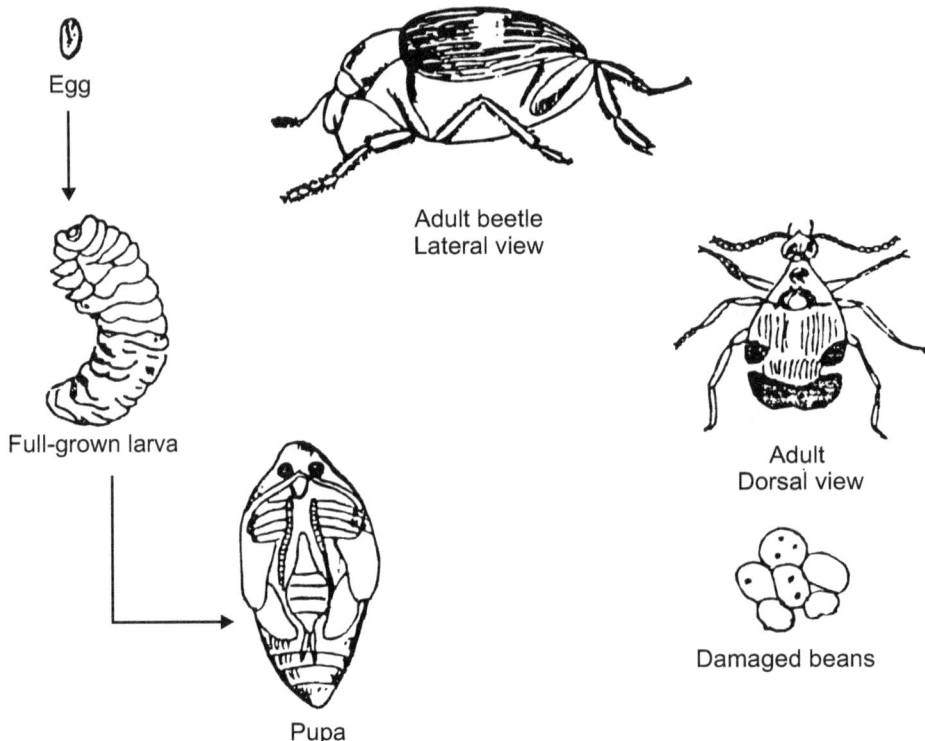

Fig. 12.8: Life Stages of *Callosobruchus chinensis*

Identification Marks:

The adults are small, roundish chocolate or brown beetles, 4 mm long. There are dark markings on the elytra and a white, raised spot on the middle of the body; when observed from above, the beetle presents a heart-shaped appearance, with two ivory coloured spots in the middle of the dorsal side of its body. The beetles has a conspicuously swollen abdomen. The grub is white, cylindrical fleshy and wrinkled, found always inside the grain and it has brown head.

Life Cycle:

The mature female lays upto 90 eggs. Singly on the seeds or on the pods in the field. The incubation period is 4-6 days. The young larvae burrow into the grain and feed inside for 2-3 weeks, undergoing 4-5 moults. The full grown larva is about 1 cm long, white and curved in appearance. Pupation occurs within the grain or grain dust and takes about 7 days to complete. The adult emerges from the grain after cutting a small, round hole. 6 to 7 generations in a year of the pest are common in India.

Nature of Damage:

The pest attacks leguminous pods in the field from where they are carried to storage godowns. The mung, gram, tur, lang, bean, masur (lentil) and udid are generally infested when the grain is whole. The larvae bore into the pulses and grains and feed and develop inside. The infestation in case of grains in early stages cannot be detected since the hole through which the larva enters is very minute. The damaged grains are hollow inside, bearing small holes and are unfit for human consumption.

Control Measures:

(i)   Cultural control can be achieved by growing susceptible crops atleast a kilometre away fin storage godowns which are the main source of infestation.

(ii)   Fumigation with methyl bromide in the stores is very effective but proper precautions must be taken because of the high toxicity of this compound.

(iii) Remaining measures are same as rice weevil.

Practical 13...

Aim:

Study of plant protection appliance (sprayers and dusters) (D).

The usefulness of any pesticides depends upon its proper application by judicious selection of the plant protection appliances. Insecticides may be applied in liquid, solid or gaseous forms. It is important to determine the form, formulation, application, timings etc. of insecticides.

There are three methods of application of insecticides.

(a) **Spray**, in which a carrier like water or oil is used for the preparation of formulations of pesticides.

(b) **Dust** in which a fine dry powder is the carrier and

(c) **Fumigants** are applied as a gas.

Ideal equipment for using the different types of insecticides should possess the following qualities:

(i)   It should be simple and easy to operate.

(ii)   It should be cheap.

(iii) Spare parts should be readily available.

(iv)   It should be handy and cost of operation should be low.

(v)   Its performance should be of a high degree.

Spraying:

It is done with liquid insecticide formulated as suspension, emulsion or solution. The spray droplets of the liquid insecticide vary widely in size from 30-150 microns. The size depends on the type of sprayer used. The droplets combine to form a film on the surface of which after sometime a deposite of insecticide is left after the water or oil or any other solvent is evaporated.

Stomach poisons kill the insect when they feed on the sprayed surface. Contact poisons are sprayed either on the insects or on the surface on which the insects crawl. The flying insects are brought in contact with the insecticide by spraying directly on them.

When water is a carrier, the usual method of application of the spray is by passage under pressure through special nozzles which distribute the chemical in a fine spray over the crops. Due to the increased effectiveness of new organic insecticide, spraying is the most common means of application. Knapsack sprayer is successfully used throughout the world for spraying pesticides over small areas.

(a) Knapsack Sprayer:

It consists basically of a spray container which mounts comfortably on the back of the operator and supported by straps over the shoulder. A double action pump is built either inside or outside the spray container and is operated by working a lever which projects alongside of the operators body. In some models, the pump lever also operates on agitation paddle in the spray tank. The spray liquid is applied through a lance held in the operators free hand.

The lance is connected to the spray tank by a long flexible hose. The tank capacity is usually about 5 gallons. The sprayer being portable and handy; it can be used for spraying in inaccessible areas. About half hectare of crop field can be sprayed per day.

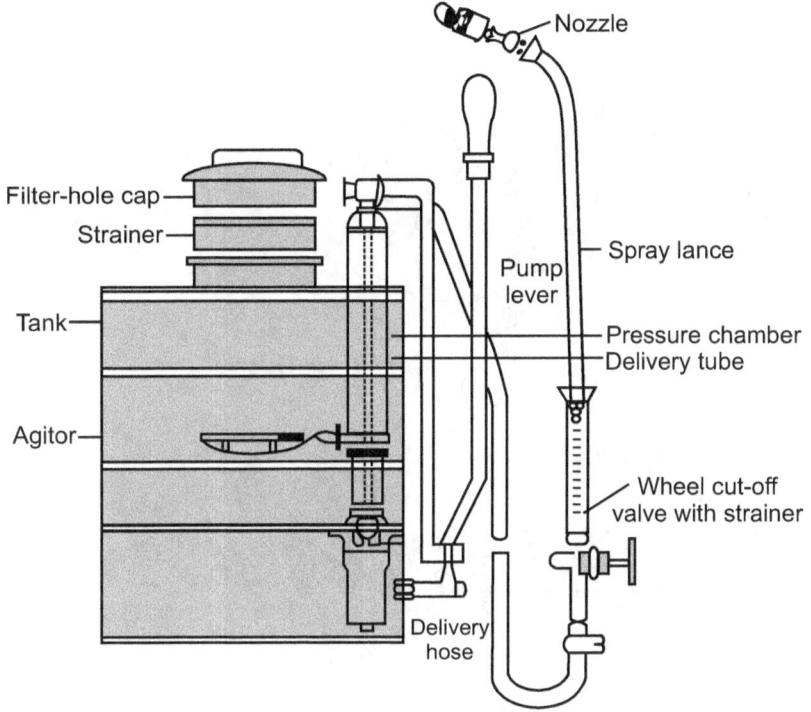

Fig. 13.1: Knapsack Sprayer

(b) Dusters:

Duster is an equipment used for application of dry powdered poison to plant body or insect. Dusting in general is best done easily in the morning when there is no wind or late in the evening after the dew has fallen. Dusting is commonly used in the regions of limited water supply. It is very effective against the pests which infect crops nearing harvest.

Shoulder Type Rotary Duster:

It consists of a container (hopper) for the dust, a system of agitation to disturb the dust and a feed mechanism to pass the dust into a current of air which is carried through an outlet as an turbulent cloud. This is a manually operated rotary type of duster.

In this type of duster, a fan is driven off and hand crank through a reduction gear produce an air stream. The air stream passes through a exhaust pipe on which a hopper is mounted just away from the tip of the exhaust pipe mouth. The powder is released into a mixing chamber by simple agitator. The air mixed with dust then travels through a pipe and comes out as finely dispersed dust particles in air through the terminal opening. The duster is provided with shoulder straps for fastening to the shoulder of the operator. The operation of the machine is less tedious than other hand dusters and dusting is smooth and uniform. The capacity of the hopper ranges from 4-5 kg and is useful for dusting row crops as well as bushy trees. This type of duster can dust half to one hectare of field crops per day.

Fig. 13.2: Shoulder Type Duster

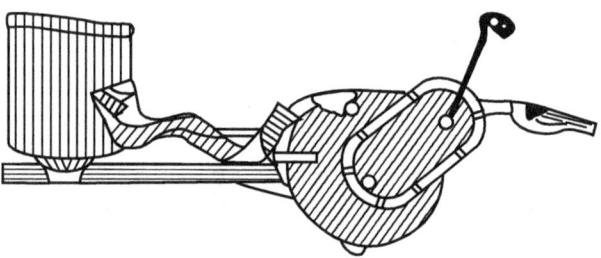

Fig. 13.3: Shoulder Type Rotary Duster

Advantages of Dusting Over Spraying:

1. Prepared in less time.
2. Economical where water is scarcity.
3. Easier to apply.
4. Machinery for application is light and less complicated.

Practical **14**...

Aim:

To study the classification with reasons of the following:

Class: Cyclostomata - *Petromyzon and Myxine.*

Class: Reptilia - Cobra, Garden, Lizard, Turtle, Rat snake and Draco [D].

14.1 *Petromyzon*

Classification:

Phylum – Chordata	–	Dorsal tubular nerve cord, paired gill slits.
Group – Craniata	–	Definite head, cranium with brain present and notochord present.
Subphylum – Vertebrata	–	Notochord is replaced by vertebral column.
Superclass – Agnatha	–	Jaws and appendage are absent.
Class – Cyclostomata	–	Mouth circular, suctorial, without jaws.
Order – Petromyzontia	–	Mouth with funnel, without tentacles, Gills 7-pairs, well developed branchial basket.
Genus	–	*Petromyzon*
Species	–	*marine*

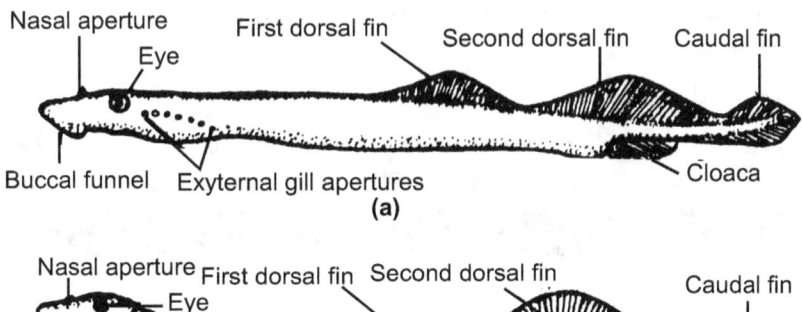

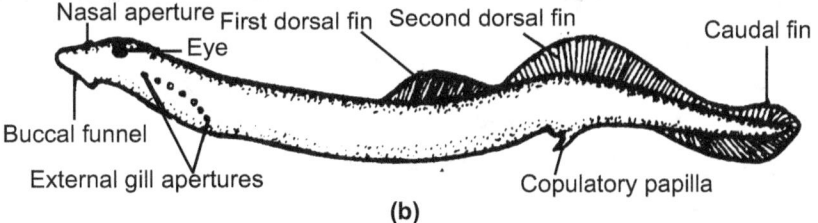

Fig. 14.1 : *Petromyzon.* (a) - Female; (b) - Male

Characters :

(1) It is commonly called as lamprey and found in fresh and salt waters.

(2) Body is eel-like measuring about 90 cm and differentiated into head, trunk and tail with two dorsal and one caudal fin.

(3) Skin is without scales, slimy, green brown with strong metallic lusture.

(4) Mouth has no jaws. It is circular, suctorial and armed with numerous horney teeth. The tongue is toothed and piston like.

(5) The paired eyes are relatively large and functional. Pineal body is present behind nasal opening. Two small median eyes, namely pineal and parietal are also present.

(6) Nasal opening is single and dorsal.

(7) Seven pairs of gill slits are present and branchial basket is well developed.

(8) Sexes are separate in adults and there is only single large gonad. Female with large anal fin. Male with copulatory papilla.

(9) Fertilization is internal.

(10) Development includes ammocoete larva which is very important phyllogenitically as it is regarded as connecting link between amphioxus and cyclostomes.

(11) It leads an ectoparasitic life on fishes. They injure and destroy fishes by sucking blood and causing secondary infection.

(12) Larval lampreys are used as bait for sport fishing and commercial fishing.

Habit and Habitat:

Petromyzon is found in fresh and salt waters. They lead an ectoparasitic life on other fishes by attacking on host by buccal funnel and secreting anticoagulant for continuous flow of blood. They show anadromous migration i.e. ascending river for spawing. They are carnivorous and predator.

Geographical Distribution:

Petromyzon has world wide distribution in sea waters, coastal regions, streams and lakes of North America, Europe, West Africa, Japan, Chili, New Zealand and Tasmania.

14.2 *Myxine*

Classification:

Phylum – Chordata	–	Dorsal tubular nerve cord, gill-slits and notochord present.
Group – Craniata	–	Definite head, cranium with brain present.
Sub-phylum – Vertebrata	–	Vertebral column is present.
Superclass – Agnatha	–	Jaws and appendages are absent.
Class – Cyclostomata	–	Mouth circular, suctorial, without jaws.

Order – Myxinoidea   –   Mouth without funnel, with 8 tentacles, gills 10-14 pairs. Branchial basket feebly developed.

Genus   –   *Myxine*

Species   –   *glutinosa*

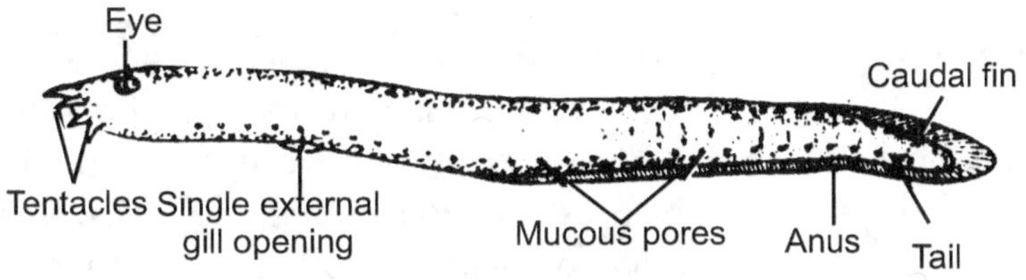

Fig. 14.2: *Myxine glutinosa*

Characters:

(1) It is commonly known as hagfish. It is found burried in the sea bottom.

(2) Body is soft, without scales, worm-like, measuring about 60 cm in length and differentiated into head, trunk and tail.

(3) Mouth is terminal and supported by soft lips.

(4) Mouth has a no buccal funnel and jaws. Branchial basket is also reduced.

(5) Mouth is surrounded by four tentacles supported by skeletal rods.

(6) There is a single nostril present close to the mouth.

(7) Single pineal eye is visible on the top of the head.

(8) There is a single dorsal fin which extends upto caudal fin.

(9) Paired eyes are vestigial or degenerated due to bottom dwelling habit.

(10) It secretes large amount of mucous through mucous pores.

(11) 10-14 pairs of gills open into a branchial chamber, which opens to the exterior by a single branchial opening.

(12) It is hermaphrodite and protandrous. The eggs are enclosed in horny shell, with hooks which are useful for attachment to the weeds.

Habit and Habitat:

They are nocturnal feeders. During the day time they live burried in the sea bottom mud at the depths of over 630 metres. They are also parasitic or quasiparasitic and generally found attached to the body of fishes, especially around gill area. They enter the body of host and eat entire visceral organs and muscles.

Geographical Distribution:

Myxine is widely distributed along sea coasts of both Atlantic and Pacific Oceans in North Europe, North Atlantic, America, Chili and Japan.

14.3 Indian Cobra (Nag)

Phylum	–	Chordata
Group	–	Craniata
Sub-phylum	–	Vertebrata
Division	–	Gnathostomata

Characters same as rabbit

Class – Reptilia   –   Cold blooded, terrestrial, single occipital condyle, 12 pairs nerves, vertebrae gastrocentrous

Order – Squamata   –   Body covered with horny epidermal scales, teeth are pleurodant, cloacal opening transverse, male possesses a pair of eversible copulatory organs

Family	–	Elapidae
Genus	–	*Naja*
Species	–	*naja*

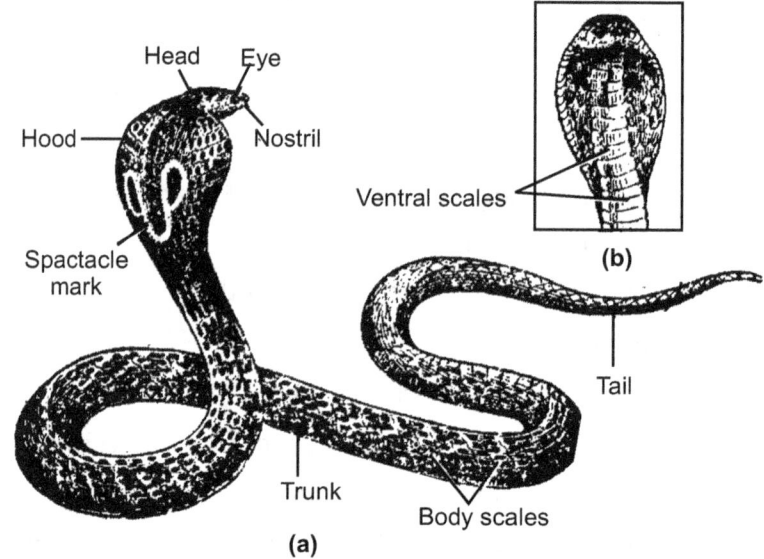

Fig. 14.3.: *Naja naja.* (a) - Hood expanded; (b) - Ventral view of hood

Naja is found from Transcapsia to China and Malay Islands and India.

Characters:

(1) *Naja naja* is commonly called Indian cobra or nag.

(2) Body is elongated, measuring upto 2 meters in length. Body colour is brown or blackish.

(3) Body is covered with smooth oblique scales without pits and are arranged in 15-25 rows. Sub-caudal scales are arranged in two rows.

(4) Head is not differentiated from neck. Neck is dilatable and the cervical ribs are elongated. The expansion of the neck and cervical ribs form the **hood**.

(5) Hood bears a binocoellate mark to which people call a mark of spectacle or the figure of ten.

(6) Eyes are very small with round pupils.

(7) Each nostril lies between two nasals and the inter-nasal.

(8) Loreal is absent. Frontal shield is truncated. Three post-occular scales are present.

(9) Third supra-labial is large and touches the eyes and the nasal.

(10) Poison fangs are followed by 1-3 small teeth.

(11) Tail is cylindrical and tapering posteriorily.

(12) Oviparous and carnivorous.

(13) Cobra is deadly poisonous and venom is neurotoxic and fatal. When it bites there is light pain, swelling and irritation. Death due to respiratory failure.

14.4 *Calotes* (Garden-lizard)

Phylum	–	Chordata
Group	–	Craniata
Subphylum	–	Vertebrata
Division	–	Gnathostomata

Characters same as rabbit

Class – Reptilia	–	Cold blooded, terrestrial, single-occipital condyle, vertebrae gastrocentrous, respiration by lungs, heart with two auricles and incompletely divided ventricle, embryo with amnion and allantois.
Order – *Squamata*	–	Body covered with horny scales, single supra-temporal vacuity, teeth pleurodont, vertebrae are procoelous, cloacal aperture is transverse, male have a pair of eversible copulatory organ
Genus	–	*Calotes*
Species	–	*versicolor*

Calotes is found in India, Malaya Islands, Afghanistan and Southern China.

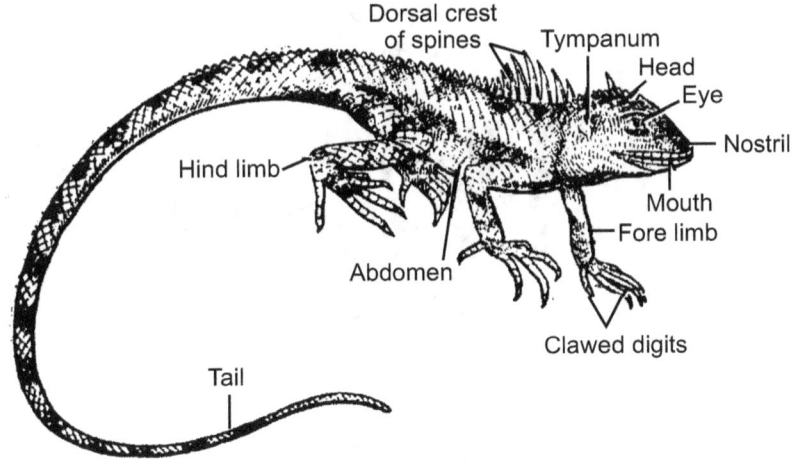

Fig. 14.4: *Calotes versicolor*

Characters:

(1) *Calotes versicolor* is commonly called garden-lizard or girgit. Found in open fields and hedges.

(2) Length is upto 35 cm and body is divisible into head, trunk and tail and is covered with epidermal horny scales.

(3) Mouth is placed anteriorily on the head, Gular sac is absent.

(4) Cloacal opening is transverse at the root of tail on ventral surface.

(5) Tail is long and cylindrical.

(6) Oviparous.

(7) Insectivorous.

(8) It changes colour but normal colour is olive-green; but in courtship body becomes yellow and neck slides head becomes red.

14.5 *Chelone*

Phylum – Chordata – Dorsal tubular nerve chord, notochord, and gill-slits are present.

Group – Craniata – Definite head, cranium with brain present.

Sub-phylum – Vertebrata – Verterbra column is present.

Superclass – Gnathostomata – Jaws and paired appendages are present.

Class – Reptilia – Scaly vertebrates, single occipital condyle, pulmonary respiration, heart with two auricles and one incompletely divided ventricle, 12 pairs of cranial nerves. Embyro with amnion and allantois.

Sub-class – Anapsida – Primitive reptiles, skull with solid roof. Body enclosed in carapace and plastron.

Order – Chelonia – Tail short, teeth absent, thoracic vertebrae and usually fused with the carapace.

Genus – *Chelone*

Species – *mydas*

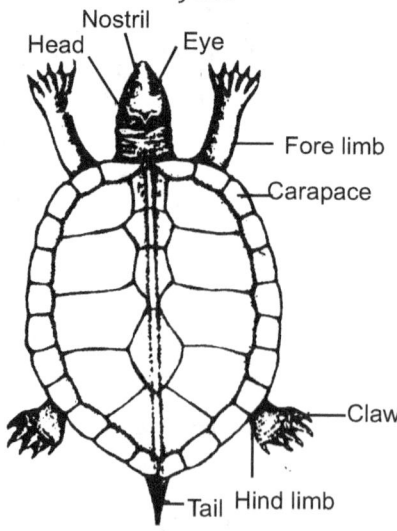

Fig. 14.5: *Chelone mydas*

Characters:

(1) *Chelone* is marine animal commonly called as green turtle. They come at shore only to lay eggs which are incubated under sand.

(2) It measures 85 to 110 cm in length.

(3) Body is enclosed in rigid case. Carapace is flat, heart shaped and covered with smooth bony shield.

(4) Dorsal shields are juxtaposed fitting closely into each other. There are four pairs of coastal shields.

(5) Head is covered by single pair of prefrontal shields, others are small. Head is partially retactile into shell.

(6) Eyes are well developed with nictitating membrane.

(7) Fore and hind limbs are adpated for swimming and they are paddle like. In case of forelimbs only first digit is clawed while hindlimbs are clawed.

(8) Tail is short.

(9) The head, tail and limbs are retractile inside the carapace.

(10) Jaws are not hooked.

(11) It is herbivorous, feeding mostly on marine algae.

Geographical Distribution:

It is found in Atlantic India, Pacific Oceans and Coasts of United States.

14.6 *Zamenis* (Rat Snake)

Phylum	–	Chordata
Group	–	Craniata
Subphylum	–	Vertebrata
Division	–	Gnathostomata
Class	–	Reptilia
Order	–	Squamata
Family	–	Colubridae
Genus	–	*Zamenis* (Ptyas)
Species	–	*mucosus*

Characters same as cobra

Zameins is found in France, Italy, North-West Africa, America and India.

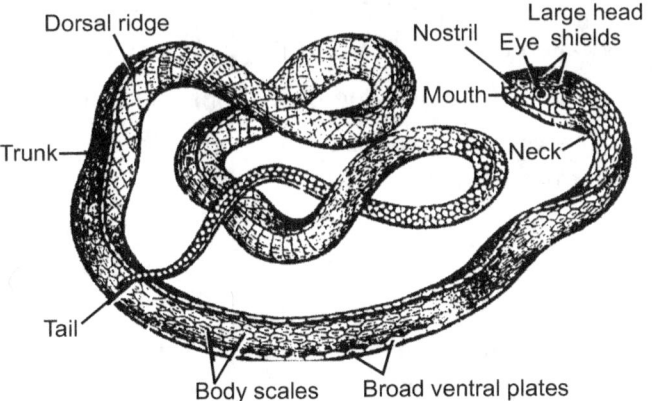

Fig. 14.6: *Zamenis mucosus* (Dhamen)

Characters:

(1) *Zamenis* is commonly called as *Dhaman* or rat-snake.

(2) It is more than two meters long. It is brown above and yellowish ventrally.

(3) Presence of a prominent dorsal ridge of the backbone along the mid-dorsal line.

(4) Head is distinct from the neck. Eyes are large with round pupil.

(5) 4th and 5th supra-labials are touching the eye.

(6) Teeth are present but fangs are absent.

(7) Tail is long and prehensile.

(8) It can climb a tree and feeding on frogs, toads, lizards and mammals.

(9) Oviparous.

(10) Non-poisonous.

14.7 Draco (Flying Lizard)

Classification:

Phylum – Chordata	–	Dorsal tubular nerve cord, notochord and gill slits are present.
Group – Craniata	–	Definite head, cranium with brain present.
Superclass – Gnathostomata	–	Jaws and paired with right and left aortic arches. Single condyle. Respiration by lungs. Embryo with amnion and allantois.
Order – Squamata	–	Lizards and snakes with horny epidermal scales and shileds. Anal opening transverse, procelous vertebrae.
Genus	–	*Draco*
Species	–	*volans*

Characters:

(1) It is commonly called as flying lizard or flying dragon.

(2) Body is dorsoventrally flattened and divided into head, neck, trunk and tail.

(3) The head is more or less triangular with pair of eyes, typanum behind eyes and nostril. Eyes are small with eye-lids.

(4) There are three pointed hooks on sides of neck.

(5) Gular pouches are sac like structures present below the neck. These structures are larger in males than females and are useful in copulation.

(6) On the sides of body, between fore and hind limbs membraneous wing like structure called patagia is present useful for flying mode of life. This membrane is supported by 5 to 6 elongated ribs.

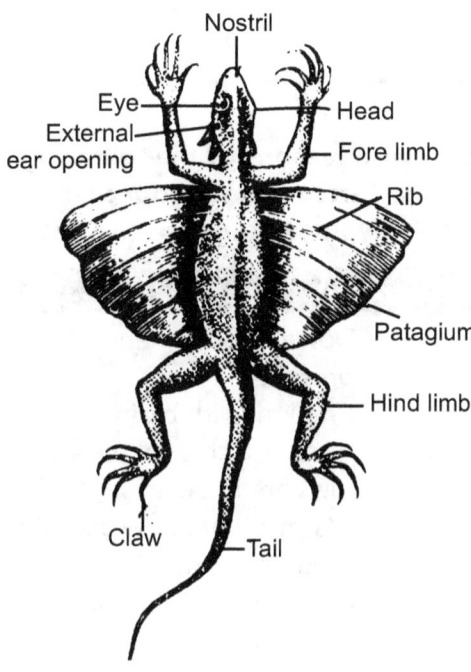

Fig. 14.7: *Draco volans*

(7) Tail is long and slender.

(8) Male has small nuchal crest.

(9) Teeth are acrodont.

(10) Vertebrae are procoelous.

(11) They use the patagia like parachutes.

Habit and Habitat:

Draco is flying and arboreal animal adapted for climbing and gliding from higher to lower branches of trees. It has brilliant colours hence look very beautiful like flowers of trees in which it lives and thus it shows camouflage (mimicry). It is insectivorous.

Geographical Distribution:

Draco is commonly distributed in Burma, India, Malaysia, Europe, Asia and Australia, Sumatra, Java, Borneo.

Practical 15...

Aim:

To study the classification with reasons of the following:
Class - Aves: Sparrow, Crow, Parrot and Woodpecker
Class - Mammals: Rabbit, Platypus, Mungoose and Bat [D].

15.1 Passer (House Sparrow)

Phylum – *Chordata*	–	Dorsal tubular nerve chord, notochord and gill-slits are present
Group – *Craniata*	–	Cranium with brain
Subphylum – *Vertebrata*	–	Vertebral column present
Division – *Gnathostomata*	–	Jaws are present
Class - *Aves*	–	Warm blooded, exoskeleton of feathers, forelimbs are modified into wings, horny beak, heart four chambered, oviparous, embryo with amnion, allantois and yolk sac.
Order – *Passeriformes*	–	Toes three infront and one behind; adapted for perching; beak are adapted for cutting.
Genus – *Passer*		
Species - *domesticus*		

Passer domesticus is distributed world wide except the Andaman and Nicobar.

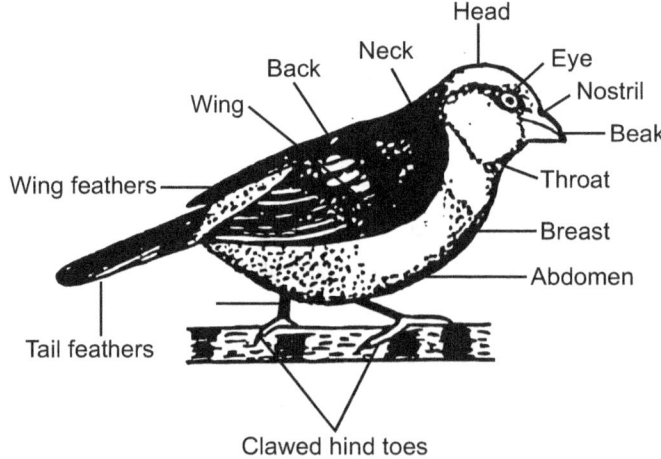

Fig. 15.1: *Passer domesticus* (House sparrow)

Characters:

(1) *Passer domesticus* is commonly called as house sparrow.

(2) It is a small bird growing upto 10-12 cm in length. The upper surface is earthy-brown and underparts are whitish.

(3) The male has a black area on the throat and breast.

(4) Three clawed toes directed forward and one backwords.
(5) Nest made of straw and rubbish stuffed into a wall.
(6) *Passer* is a commensal on man.
(7) It feeds chiefly on seeds and grain etc.

15.2 Corvus (Crow)

Phylum	–	Chordata
Group	–	Craniata
Subphylum	–	Vertebrata
Division	–	Gnathostomata
Class	–	Aves
Order	–	Passeriformes
Genus	–	*Corvus*
Species	–	*splendens*

Characters same as sparrow

Corvus is found in India, Pakistan, Srilanka and Burma.

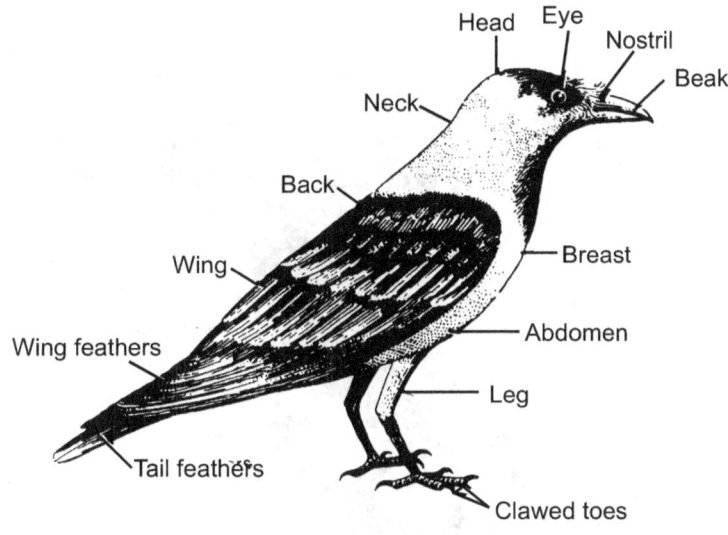

Fig. 15.2: *Corvus* (Crow)

Characters:

(1) *Corvus* is commonly known as crow and in Hindi it is called *Kowwa*.
(2) It is most familiar bird of Indian towns and villages.
(3) The length is upto 42 cm.
(4) Body is divisible into head, neck and trunk. Neck is grey in colour.
(5) Each leg have four clawed toes out of which three directed forewards and one backwards.
(6) Nest is constructed on twigs.
(7) Omnivorous. It eats anything dead rat, kitchen refuse, fish, insects, grains, fruits etc.
(8) It is useful scavenger and commensal of man.

15.3 *Psittacula* (Parrot)

Phylum	–	Chordata
Group	–	Craniata
Subphylum	–	Vertebrata
Division	–	Gnathostomata
Class	–	Aves

Characters same as sparrow

Order – Psittaciformes – Feathers are green, yellow or red; beak stout, sharp-edged and hooked on the tip; feet zygodactylus (i.e. two toes infront and two toes directed backwardly

Genus – *Psittacula*

Species – *krameri*

Psittacula is distributed throughout India, Pakistan, Srilanka and Burma.

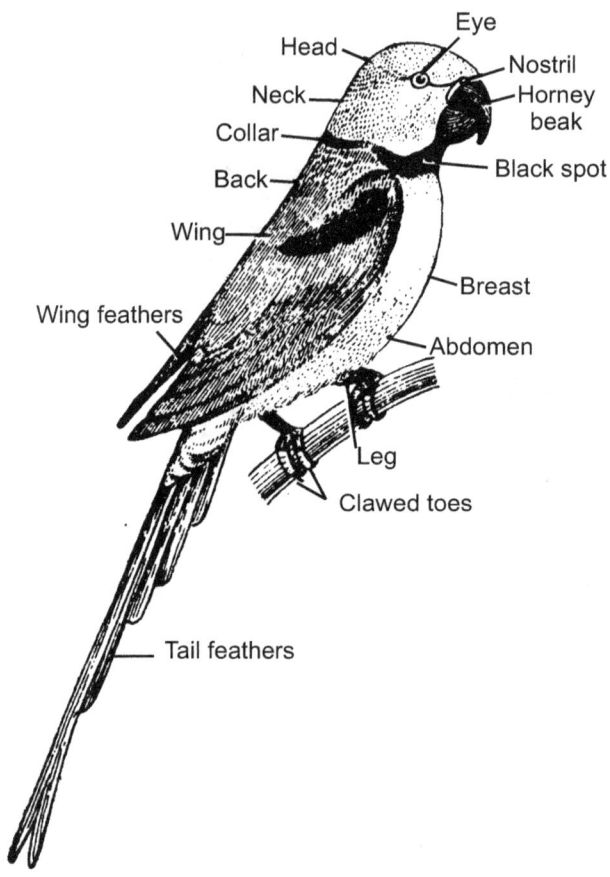

Fig. 15.3: *Psittacula* (Parrot)

Characters:

(1) *Psittacula* is commonly called Rose-ringed-Parakect and in Hindi, Tota.

(2) Body is grass green in colour. It is slender with a long pointed tail and measures 25 cm in length.

(3) Beak is red, short, stout and deeply hooked.

(4) Black and rose-pink collar is present in the male and it is absent in female.

(5) Feet are adapted for grasping.

(6) Food chiefly includes the fruits and ripening grains.

(7) Parrots are always found in large flocks and it is destructive to crops and orchard fruits.

(8) It is a popular cage bird and can be taught to repeat few words and sentences.

15.4 *Dinopium* (Woodpecker)

Phylum	–	Chordata
Group	–	Craniata
Subphylum	–	Vertebrata
Division	–	Gnathostomata
Class	–	Aves

Characters same as sparrow

Order – Piciformes   –   Tail feathers stiff with pointed tips; beak stout, tongue is protrusible; two toes in front and two toes behind

Genus   –   *Dinopium*

Species   –   *benghalense*

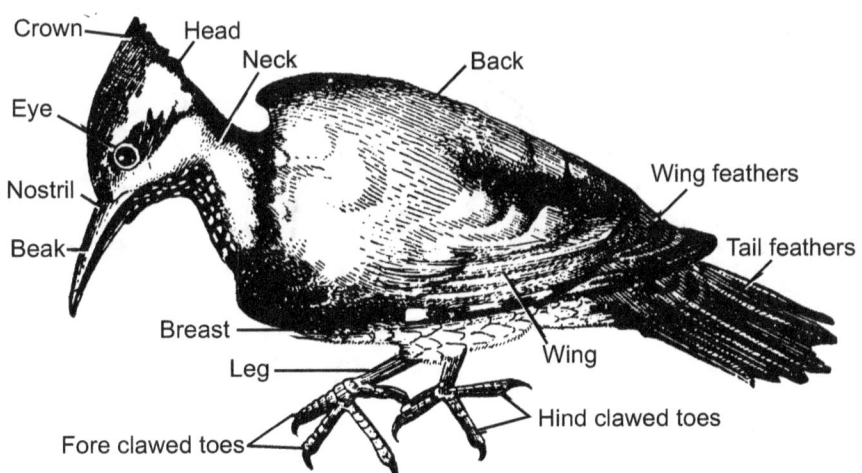

Fig. 15.4: *Dinopium*

Dinopium is found in India, Pakistan and Sri Lanka.

Characters:

(1)   *Dinopium* is commonly known as golden-backed woodpecker.

(2)   Bird is small in size and measure about 22 cm in length.

(3)   Upper plumage is golden-yellow and black while lower is buffy-white in colour.

(4)   The male have crimson crown in colour.

(5)   Bill is long, stout and pointed.

(6)   Tongue is protrusible and barb-tipped.

(7)   Topes are four, two directed forward and two backward.

(8)   The tail is stiff and wedge-shaped.

(9)   Food comprises wood-boring bettles, grubs, ants and other insects pests of trees.

15.5 *Oryctolagus* (Rabbit)

Phylum – *Chordata*	–	Dorsal tubular nerve cord, notochord and gill-slits present.
Group – *Craniata*	–	Cranium (brain box) with brain.
Subphylum – *Vertebrata*	–	Vertebral column present
Division : *Gnathostomata*	–	Jaws and paired appendages are present
Class : *Mammalia*	–	Females have mammary glands and body covered with hair
Order – *Lagomorpha*	–	Upper incisors two pairs
Genus – *Oryctolagus*		
Species – *Cuniculus*		

Fig. 15.5: Rabbit

Habit and Habitat:

Cosmopolitan, inhabiting in the fields, grasslands and woodlands. Gregarious, crepuscular (i.e. coming out of burrows for feeding in twilight), coprophagous (eating their soft stool for nourishment) and polygamous.

Characters:

(1) Body divisible into head, neck, trunk and tail and cat like appearance.

(2) Head possess external nares, short eyes and mouth. External ears drooping and snout bears long tactile vibrissae or whiskers.

(3) Forelimbs usually used for digging and hindlimbs for leaping.

(4) Males have muscular skin and covered penis.

(5) Females have clitoris.

(6) Rabbit is fast runner, it covers 30-40 km per hour.

Economic importance:

Rabbit is used as important experimental animal for classroom and research. The fur of rabbit is used to make purses, caps and gloves and also used as food.

15.6 Platypus (*Ornithorhynchus*)

Classification:

Phylum – Chordata — Dorsal tubular nerve cord, gill-slits, and notochord present.

Group – Craniata — Definite head, cranium with brain present.

Sub-phylum – Vertebrata — Body column present.

Class – Mammalia — Body covered with hairs.

Sub-class – Prototheria — Females with mammary glands.

Order – Monotremata — Cloaca present.

Genus — *Ornithorhynchus*

Species — *anatinus*

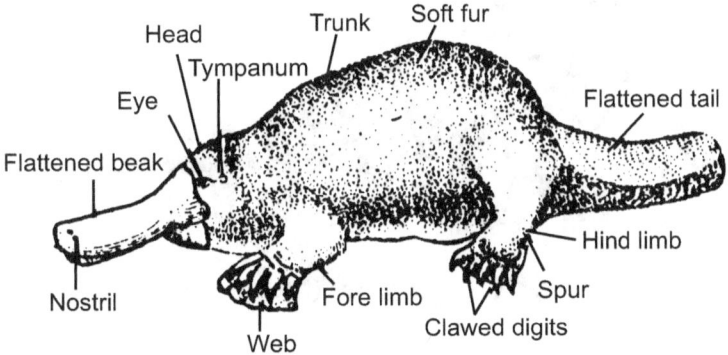

Fig. 15.6: Duck-billed Platypus (*Ornithorhynchus*)

Characters:

(1) It is commonly called duck billed platypus.

(2) Body covered with fur.

(3) Body shows head, trunk and tail.

(4) Head is distinct. The bill or beak is broad and flat and covered with soft, sensitive naked skin having tactile sensory organs.

(5)   External pinnae absent.

(6)   Teeth are absent in the adult but broad horny plates are present inside the bill.

(7)   Limbs are five clawed and webbed digits.

(8)   Tail is flat and adapted for swimming.

(9)   The male has a spur on the heal.

(10)   It is carnivorous and food consists of molluscan shells, crustaceans and worms.

(11)   It is aquatic in habitat and lives in burrows on the bank of rivers and streams.

(12)   Eyes are small with nictitating membrane.

(13)   Mammary glands without nipples.

(14)   Cloaca present. Testes are abdominal.

Habit and Habitat:

It lives in rivers, pools and streams. It makes tunnel or burrow about 40 feet long in river banks. It is carnivorous and feeds on aquatic invertebrates carried in check pouches.

Geographical Distribution:

It is found in Eastern and Southern parts of Australia and Tasmania.

15.7 *Herpestes* (Mongoose)

Phylum – *Chordata*   –   Dorsal tubular nerve chord, notochord and gill-slits are present

Group – *Craniata*   –   Cranium with brain

Subphylum – *Vertebrata*   –   Vertebral column present

Division – *Gnathostomata*   –   Jaws are present

Class – *Mammalia*   –   Females have mammary glands and body covered with hairs

Order – *Carnivora*

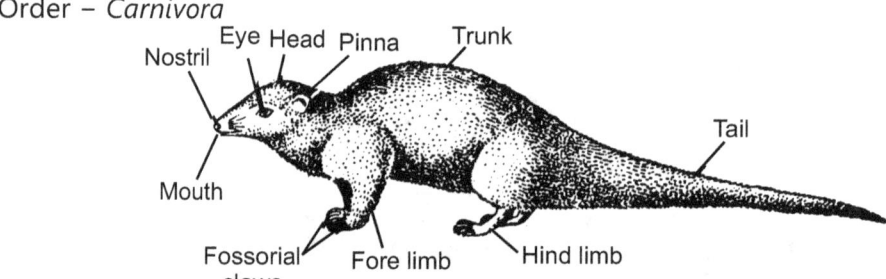

Fig. 15.7: *Herpestes* (Mongoose)

Habit and Habitat:

Found in Asian and African countries. It is nocturnal and eats small mammals, birds, reptiles and eggs. It is having burrowing habit.

Characters:

(1)   The snout is pointed, eyes and pinna are small and rounded.

(2)   Tail is elongated and bushy.

(3)   Forelimbs and hindlimbs have five digits with fussorial claws.

(4)   Body is covered with greyish fur.

(5)   Skull is long with small brain.

(6)   Legs are short.

(7)   Teeth thecodont and heterodont with well developed canines.

(8)   The fight between mongoose and snake is famous. The mongoose wins the fight and kills the snake hence it is herpestes.

15.8 *Cynopterus* (Bat)

Phylum – *Chordata*   :   Dorsal tubular nerve chord, notochord and gill-slits presents

Group – *Craniata*   :   Definite head, cranium with brain present

Subphylum – *Vertebrata*   :   Vertebral column present

Division – Gnathostomata   :   Jaws are present

Class – Mammalia   :   Female having mammary glands and body is covered with hairs

Order – Chiroptera

Genus – *Cynopterus* (Indian fruit bat)

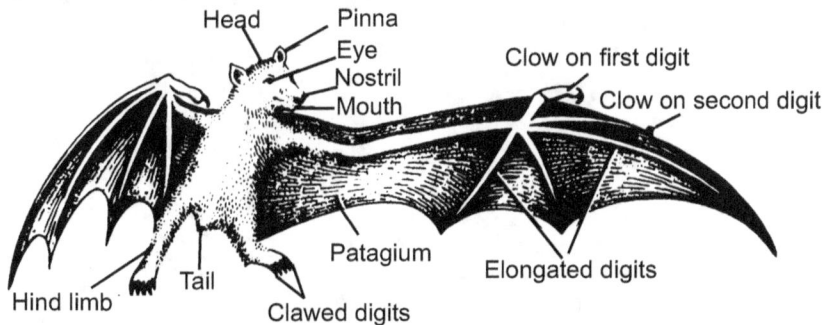

Fig. 15.8: *Cynopterus* (Bat)

Cyopterus is distributed in South-Eastern Asia, especially in India.

Habit and Habitat:

Bat have arboreal and aerial mode of life. Live in groups and feed on fruits (Fruigivorous).

Characters:

(1)   Body is dark-brown in colour and shoulders are golden yellow in colour.

(2)   Forelimbs are modified into wings. Each wing are formed by a fold of skin (patagium) which are supported by elongated forelimb and 2nd to 5th fingers. Only 1st and 2nd fingers bears claws.

(3) Hindlimbs and tail are also included in patagium. Hindfeet small with sharp and curved claws.

(4) Tail is small and stumpy.

(5) Head small with external ears, large eyes, snouth and small teeth.

(6) During sleep, head hangs downwards with wings folded around body.

(7) *Cynopterus* is commonly called fruit bat.

(8) Bat shows the following important features:

   (i) They have phylogenetic significance and insectivores

   (ii) They are the only flying mammals.

   (iii) Faeces of bats are used as fertilizer.

   (iv) Bat have highly developed sonar or echo-apparatus (i.e. a kind of radar). During flight they send out ultrasonic sound waves which strike on objects or wire and reflected back to bat.

   (v) Bats are used as experimental animals.

Practical **16**...

Aim:

Identification of Poisonous and Non-poisonous Snakes with the help of identification key with two examples of each [D].

16.1 Introduction

The snakes are elongated and limbless reptiles with body covered by scales. A majority of the snakes are non-poisonous and they are beneficial to man since they destroy harmful insects and destructive rodents. There are very few snakes which are deadly poisonous and cause death from snake bite. According to the estimate of World Health Organisation (W.H.O.) every year 1000 to 1200 people die in our country due to snake bite. Majority of people die because of sheer fright about snakes and some due to ignorance and unscientific methods of treatment. Therefore, it is necessary to have the knowledge about snakes, their importance and identification of poisonous snakes from non-poisonous snakes, which can reduce high mortality from snake bite.

Some of the common poisonous snakes of India are Cobra, King Cobra, Krait, Pit viper, Indian Viper, Rattle snakes, Russell's Viper, Coral snakes and Sea snakes. The common non-poisonous snakes are Python, Rat snake, Trinket; Earth snake (Sand boa), Blind snakes. There are also semi-poisonous snakes like Golden Tree snake or flying snake, Green Tree snake, Dog faced water snake.

Poisonous snakes can be identified from non-poisonous snakes by using the following key :

(1) If the snake is a marine with laterally compressed tail, it is poisonous e.g. **sea-snake**.

(2) The terrestrial snake show rounded or cylindrical and not laterally compressed tail. Examine its ventral scales.

    (i) If all the ventral scales are small or somewhat broad, then it is non-poisonous snake.

    (ii) If the ventral scales are large transverse platos extending fully across the ventral side or belly, the snake may be poisonous or non-poisonous. Then examine the dorsal surface of the head.

(a) If all the dorsal scales of the head are small and uniform it is poisonous and it may be a **viper**.

(b) If there is a **loreal** pit between the nostril and the eye, then it is a **pit viper**.

(c) If the subcaudals are double and there is a loreal pit, then it is **Russel's viper**.

(d) If dorsal side of the head has both small scales and large shields, the snake may or may not be poisonous, then examine the lateral side of the head.

(3) If the third supra-labial shield touches the nostril and eye, then it is a poisonous snake, may be **Cobra**, **King cobra** or **Caral snake**.

(4) If the dorsal side of the head has both small scales and large shields but there is no loreal pit, and the third supra-labial shield does not touch the eye, examine the back of the snake and ventral side of the lower jaw.

   (i) The middle row of scales on the back called vertebrals may be larger than other.

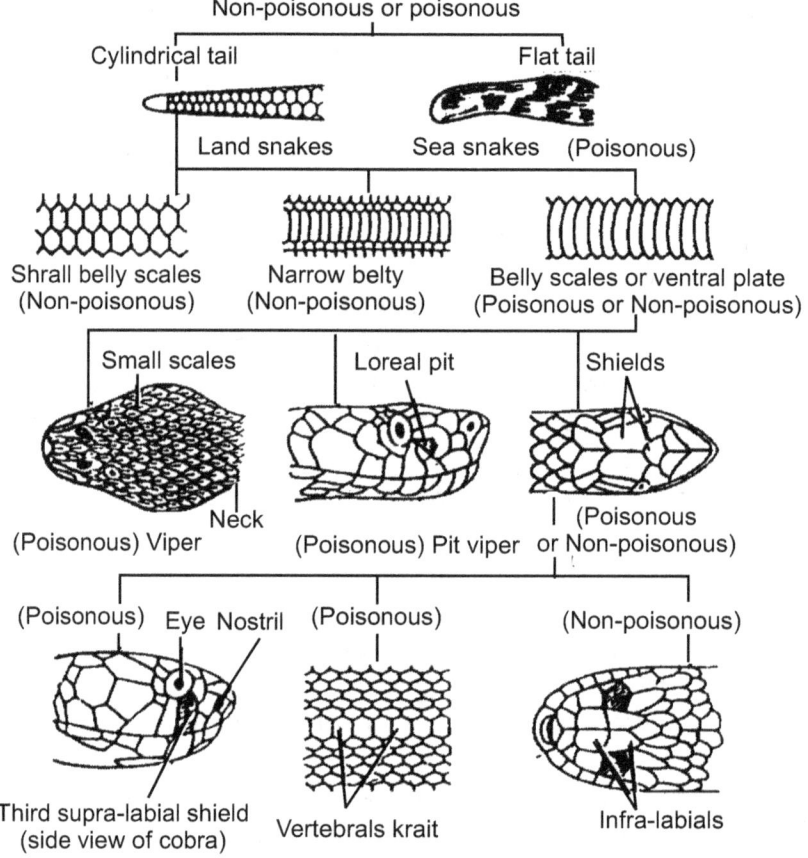

Fig. 16.1 : Key to identification of poisonous and non-poisonous snakes

   (ii) On the ventral side of the lower jaw has fourth infra-labial shield larger than the others. If both characters are exhibited by snake, then it is krait.

(5) If the head of snake shows small scales and large shields then it is non-poisonous snake.

Key to Identification of Poisonous and Non-Poisonous Snakes

Key to Identification of Poisonous and Non-poisonous Snakes

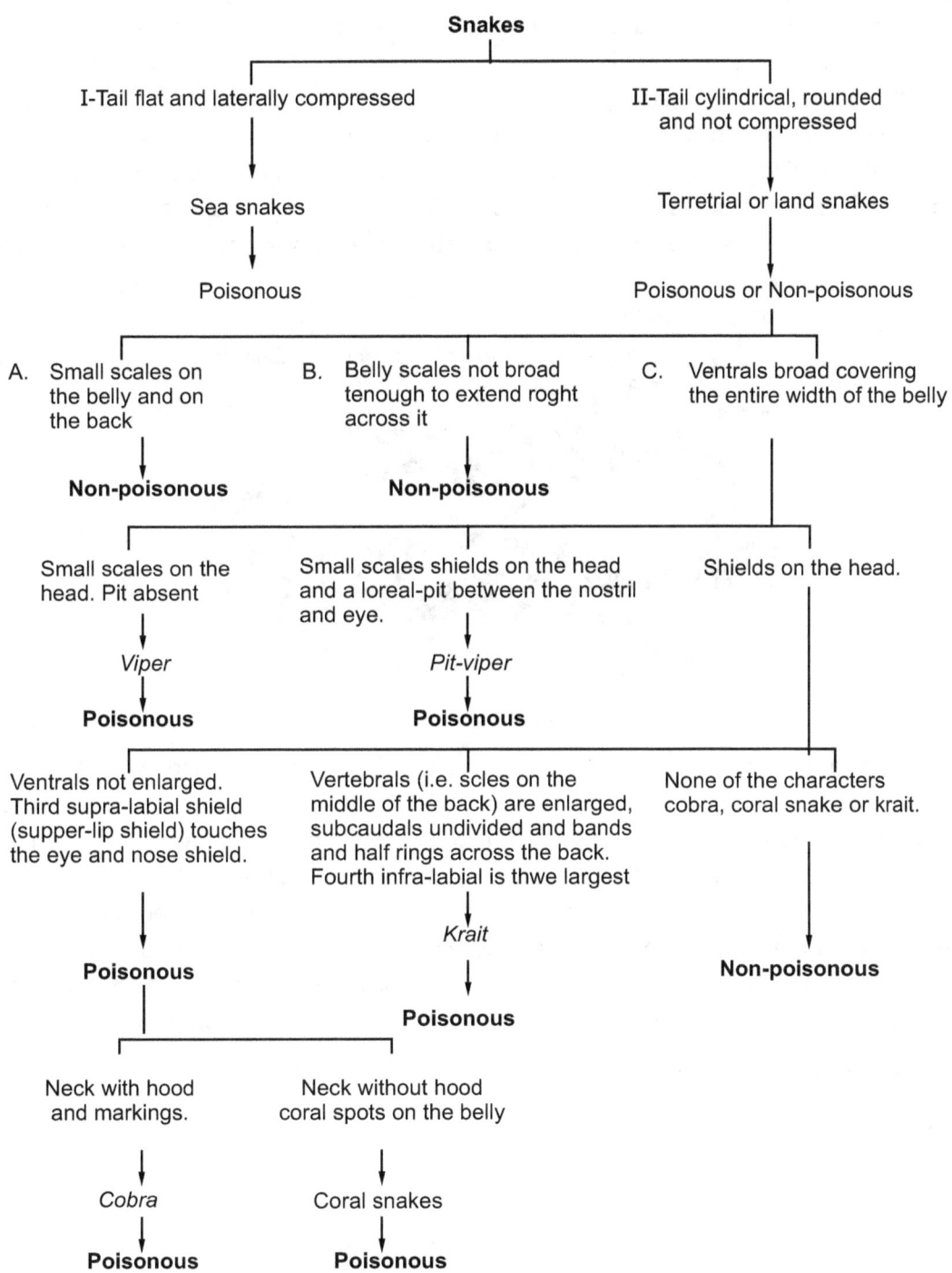

16.2 Poisonous Snakes

(1) Krait : *Bungarus* is commonly called *krait* which has many species found in India and Malaya. Krait shows elongated cylindrical body, measuring one metre in length. The body colour is steel blue and dark blue, with white cross bars. The scales are on the body are smooth, the backbone is ridged having a central row of hexagonal enlarged scales. Ventral surface is white. Krait is oviparous snake and female incubates the eggs showing parental care. It feeds on mice, rat, toads and smaller snakes. It is a deadly poisonous snake and its venom being more poisonous than that of cobra. Its venom is *neurotoxic* affecting brain. The person with krait bite feels sleepy and if immediate antivenom is not given, the patient may die.

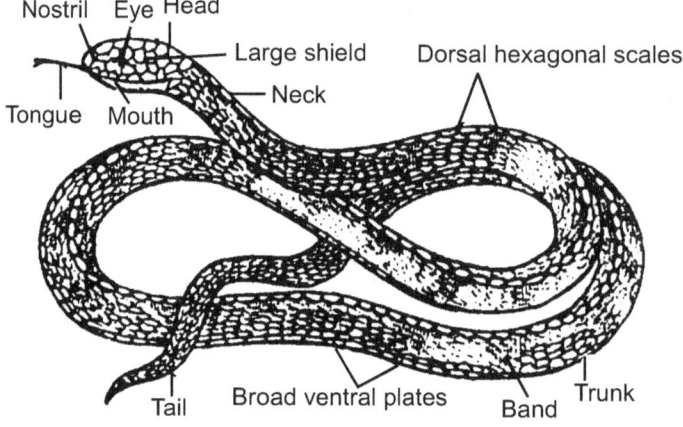

Fig. 16.2: Krait

(2) Cobra : *Naja naja* is commonly called *Indian Cobra* or nag. Which has wide distribution found in India, Afria, China, Australia, New Guinea and Egypt. It is deadly poisonous snake growing upto 2 metres. It has of brown or blackish colour. It is diurnal, shy, living in holes and understones, mud walls and in thick vegetation, but it also comes into human dwellings. It feeds on lizards, frogs, rats and other snakes. It hibernates, scales are smooth, dorsal surface of the head has small scales and large shields. Third supralabial shield touch eye. The head is small, the cervical ribs when raised form a hood on the sides of the neck. Fangs are small and non-movable. There are three varieties of Cobra found in India.

(i) *Binocellate* form having spectacle like mark connected by U found in Maharashtra.

(ii) *Monocellate* with single oval mark surrounded by ellipses found in Bengal.

(iii) *Non-cellate* without mark found in Rajasthan, Gujrat and M.P.

Cobra is deadly poisonous snake, when annoyed it raises the front part of the body about one foot, spreads to its hood and hood sways back and forth and striking the object. During this period it produces hissing sound. Fangs are small and relatively non-movable. On each side a large poison gland enclosed in a fibrous capsule and it's duct runs into a canal in the fang. The Venom is *neurotoxic* and fatal. King cobra is another species which grows upto 18 feet. It is the world's largest poisonous snake which injects large quantity of the venom and causes quick death due to respiratory paralysis. Cobra is viviparous snake and feeds on other non-poisonous snakes. There are many blind faiths regading cobra in our country. Such as presence of juwel on the head, it protects wealth, it can drink milk and hence worshipped on Nagpanchami day, snake bite cured some times in villeges by snake charmers by mantras. These are all misconcepts regarding snakes.

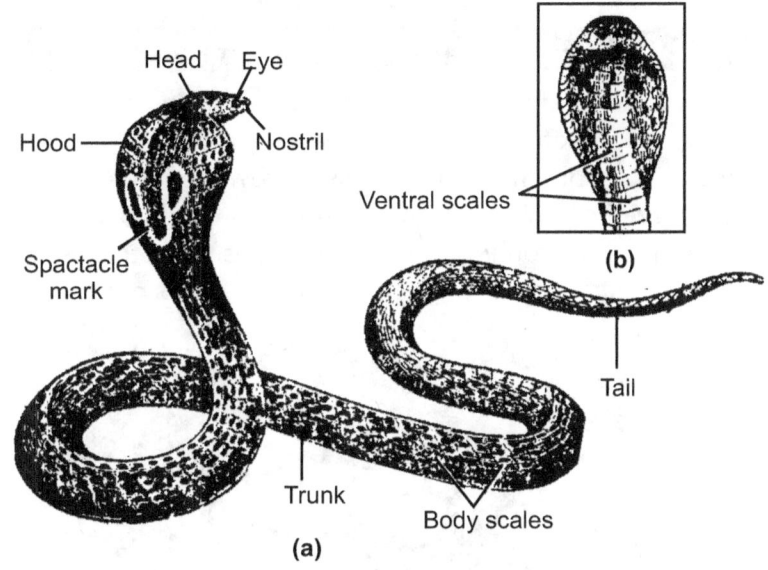

Fig. 16.3: (a) Corbra (*Naja naja*) having hood expanded.
(b) Ventral view of head

(3) Viper: Viper is poisonous snake found in India, Burma, Sri Lanka, Europe and Africa. It is found in rocky and bushy regions and feed on mice, rats, lizards and birds. There are two types of vipers called pitless viper e.g. *Vipera russeli* or Russel's viper is Indian viper. The another type called Himalayan pit viper or *Ancistrodon* or *Himalayan*.

The body of viper is thick and grows upto 5 feet long. The head is large, flat and covered with uniform small scales which is the identification mark of this poisonous snake. It shows lateral nostrils, eyes are far forwards and there is sensory pit between eye and the nostril in pit viper. This organ is also useful for detection of prey. The scales on the body are keeled. Tail is short and tapers abruptly. The Indian Russel's viper has large nostrils, its colour is pale brown above with three longitudinal series of black rings and ventrally it is yellowish. The snake bears long, movable fangs with canals. At the time of biting the fangs are erected and folded back against the roof of the mouth when not in use. The snake remains coiled with the head in the centre of the coil, when disturbed; tongue is protruded, body rhythmically swells and hissing sound is produced. Vipers are nocturnal, in biting it opens its mouth very wide and strikes like lightning, thrusting its long fang and its bite is fatal to man. Vipers are viviparous snakes.

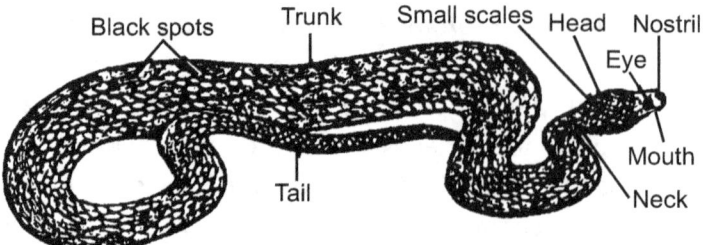

Fig. 16.4: *Vipera russelli*

16.3 Non-Poisonous Snakes

(4) Rat snake: It is common non-poisonous found in India, Pakistan, Sri Lanka and Afganistan. It grows up to 3 metres. The rat snake or dhaman *Ptyas mucosus* is common species found in India. It is greenish or greenish brown on the back and pale yellow ventrally. Head is elongated, distinct from the neck and covered with large, symmetrical shields. Eyes are large and with rounded pupil. Trunk has smooth scales, which present a distinctive pattern of cross bars. Tail is long and carries two rows of scales ventrally.

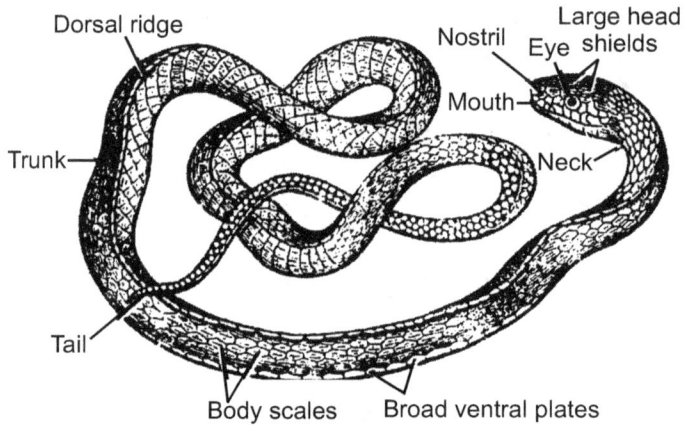

Fig. 16.5: *Rat snake (Ptyas)*

Rat snake is an altive, ill-tempered, aggressive, untamable snake. It is very active snake and often attacks on the face with loud hiss. Since, it is non-poisonous snake, and feeds on rats, therefore it is considered to be friend of the farmers. It runs and swims very fast. Rat snake is viviparous. It shows sharp ridge along the backbone. It can climb on trees and it attacks forcibly like a whip and hence it is also called as rope snake. Rat snake bites viciously and coils around the victim firmly by its prehensile tail. It emits foul odour and secretes black secretion from the anal glands.

(5) Python (Ajgar):

1. Phython is commonly called Indian Ajgar.

2. It is a large, massive and non-poisonous snake.

3. It may reach the maximum length of 10 metres and is the biggest and thickest snake of India.

4. It weighs to a maximum of 125 kg.
5. The colour is brown above with rhomboid dark-grey edged spots on the body and ventral side is greyish with yellow-brown spots.
6. The scales are in 60 to 75 smooth rows, the ventrals are distinctly smaller.
7. Head is distinct from the neck and is covered with symmetrical shields or small scales.
8. Presence of a lancet-shaped brown mark on the head.
9. The eyes are without eyelids and the pupil is vertical.
10. The tail is short and prehensile.
11. Supra-labials are 11-13. The first two are full of pits and the sixth and seventh touching the eye.
12. Infra-labials are 16-18. Anterior ones are long and narrow and posterior ones have pits.
13. Parietal, loreal and temporal regions are covered with irregular scales.
14. The rostral scale on the head bears a deep pit on either side, which is probably thermoreceptive in function.
15. Rudiments of appendages in the form of two claw spurs are present near the cloaca.
16. Carnivorous, feeding on reptiles, birds and mammals.
17. Oviparous.

Geographical distribution: *Python molurus* is distributed in India and also in Indo-China.

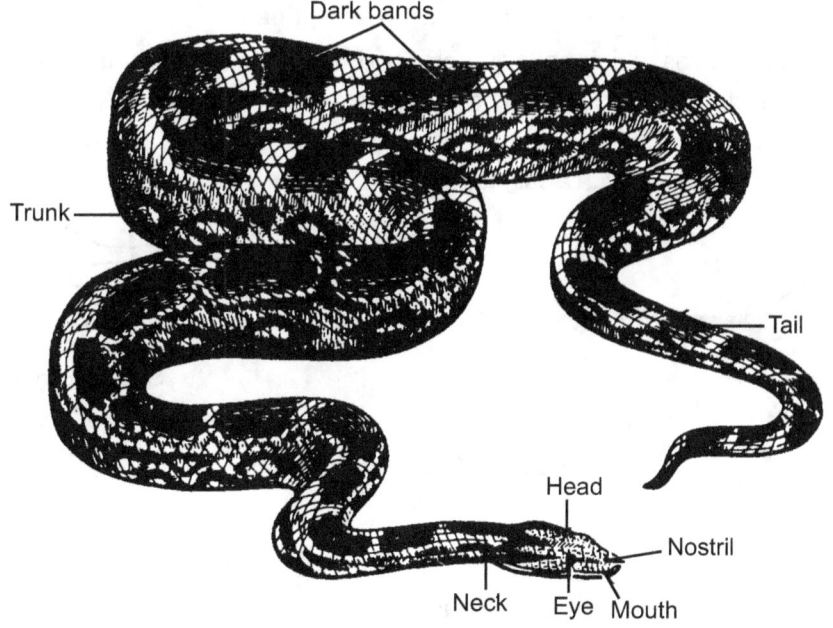

Fig. 16.6: *Python molurus*

✳✳✳

Practical 17...

Aim:

Study of Modifications of Beaks and Feet in Birds (Museum Specimen) (D).

17.1 Beaks

1. **Water and Mud Probing:**

The aquatic birds like **herons**, **king-fishers** have long, powerful and sharply pointed beaks to capture fish, frogs, toads and aquatic animals. In case of cormorants. The beak is long and narrow with the edges armed with sharp backwardly directed teeth like processes for fish capturing whereas in Indian darter or snake bird these saw-like teeth form fine needle like points.

(a) Beak of Cormorant   (b) Beak of King-fisher

Fig. 17.1: Water Probing Beaks

There are several birds which collect their food from the mud. Their beaks are extremely long and slender and slightly curved. These beaks are used as probes for thrusting in the mud for searching the food like aquatic worms, insects and larvae. Mud probing type beaks are found in **stilts**, **sandpipers**, **jacanas**, **lapwings**.

(a) Beak of stilt   (b) Beak of Yellow Leg

Fig. 17.2: Mud probing beak

2. **Tearing and Piercing:**

The carnivorous birds which feed on carrion and flesh. Therefore, they have short, pointed, sharp edged, powerful hooked beaks for tearing flesh. This type of beak is operated by well developed mandibular muscles. Eagle, vulture, owls, kites, hawks are the examples of this type of beaks.

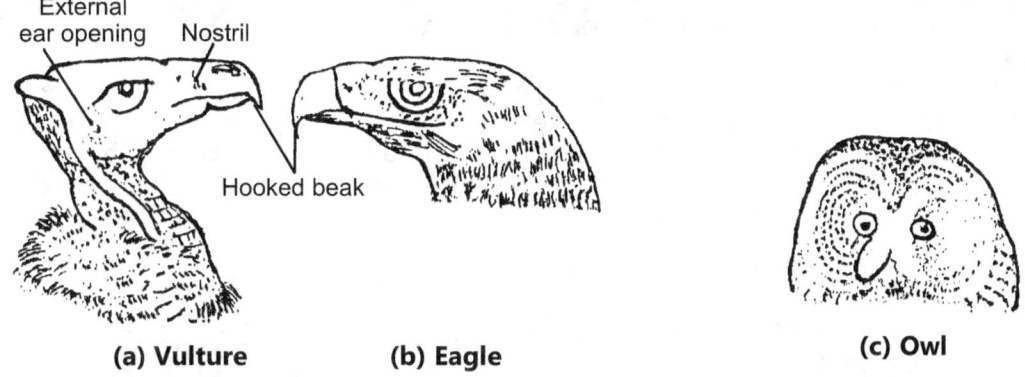

(a) Vulture   (b) Eagle   (c) Owl

Fig. 17.3: Tearing and piercing type beaks

3.   Fruit Eating Beak:

Many birds feed on fruits hence their beaks are sharp, powerful and hooked. This type of beak can break hard fruits, nuts and hard seeds. In case of **Parrot**, beak is very sharp, massive and deeply hooked and extremely strong. It is useful for gnawing or breaking open hard seeds and nuts. The beak of the hornbill is very large, enormous, heavy and cumbersome. But it is very lights, its interior structure is cellular and these cells act as resonators which enable the bird to produce exceptionally loud cry.

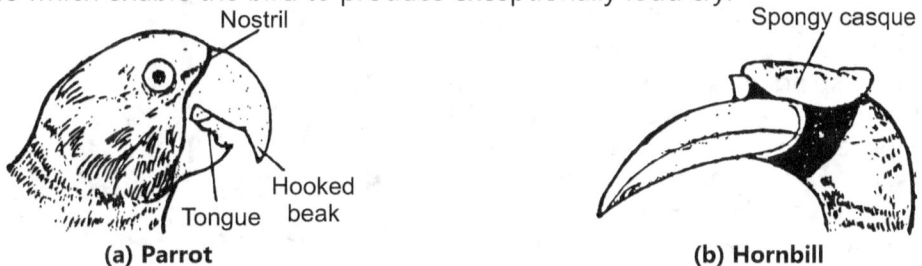

(a) Parrot   **(b) Hornbill**

Fig. 17.4: Fruit eating beak

4.   Mud and Water Straining Beak:

This type of beak is common in birds like **Duck**, **Geese**, **Flemingo**. This type of beak is broad and flat. The edges of the jaws are modified into horny serrations or transverse lamellae. These lamellae acts as sieves or strainer. Through these sieves water and mud can easily pass out and food remains in the mouth.

(a) Flemingo   **(b) Duck**

Fig. 17.5: Mud and Water Straining Beak

Flemingo is another best example of this kind of beak. The beak is curved downwards at free end and furnished with transverse lamellae. In these birds, the two halves of the lower jaw are considerably enlarged so that the comparatively narrow upper jaw closes upon a wide cavity.

17.2 Feet

1.   **Perching Feet:**

Majority of the birds show perching type of feet. In this type, three toes are directed forward and they are slender. While one toe or hallux is posterior which is strongly opposable so that they can securely fasten the foot to a branch or a berch. The feet possess long and powerful ankle bones, digits and sharp, oval and curved claws i.e. crow and sparrow.

(a) Jungle Crow   **(b) Sparrow**

Fig. 17.6: Perching Type of Feet

2.   **Raptorial Feet:**

These feet are the peculiarity of the carnivorous, predatory birds like **kite**, **eagle**, **owls** etc. These birds bear such type of feet for striking and grasping their prey. The toes are armed with strong, sharp and curved claws. All the four toes are present and the hallux is strongly developed. The underside of toes show presence of large and fleshy bulbs called tylari. They are found in **sparrow** and **hawks**. In **osprey** instead of tylari, horny spines are present. These spines are useful in gripping slippery preys such as fish and frog. This type of feet is modified for grasping and holding the prey.

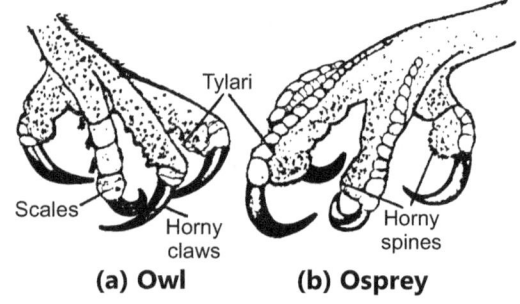

(a) Owl   **(b) Osprey**

Fig. 17.7: Raptorial Feet

3.   **Cursorial or Running Feet:**

These feet are found in birds adapted for running. **Ostrich** is the best example of cursorial feet. In this bird, the legs are very strong and powerful and number of toes are reduced. The hind toe is elevated, reduced or absent. In case of **Bustard**, **Emu**, **Rhea** and **Cassowary** only three toes are present and they are directed forward. Ostrich has only two toes of which the outer one is smaller and without a nail.

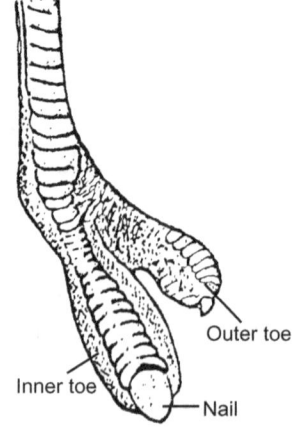

Fig. 17.8: Cursorial Feet: Ostrich

4. Swimming Feet:

In swimming birds, toes are webbed partially or completely. The feet are modified as propellers or steering organs. In case of diving birds (e.g. **coots** and **crebes**) the web is lobate and toes are free. In swimming and paddling birds (e.g. **ducks** and **teals**) only anterior, three toes are united by web whereas in Pelican and Cormorant all the four toes are united by web.

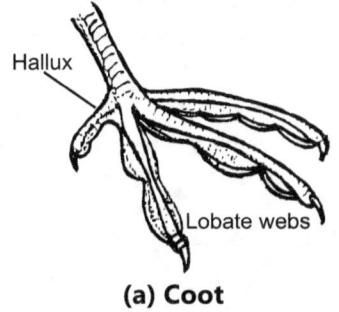 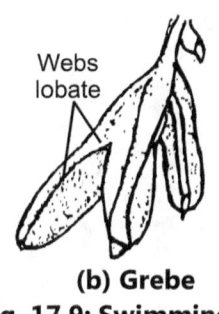 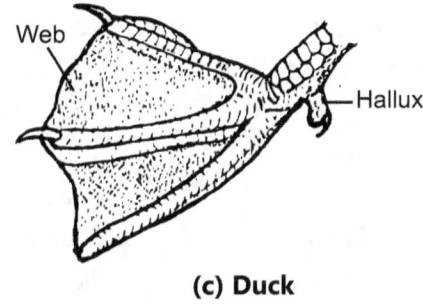

(a) Coot   (b) Grebe   (c) Duck

Fig. 17.9: Swimming Feet

✱✱✱

Practical **18**...

Aim:

Study of External characters and digestive system of Scoliodon [E].

Sharks are of great biological interest because they show the basic vertebrate plan and some of their anatomical features are seen in the early embryos of higher vertebrates.

Systematic Position:

Phylum	–	Chordata
Sub-phylum	–	Vertebrata or Craniata
Section	–	Gnathostomata
Class	–	Chondrichthyes
Order	–	Pleurotremata
Family	–	Carcharinidae scyllidae
Genus	–	*Scoliodon*
Species	–	*Sorrakowah*

18.1 Habit and Habitat

Scoliodon is a shark of the Indian seas. It has a wide distribution in the Indian Ocean, Bay of Bengal, Eastern Pacific Oceans and in the Atlantic Ocean along the coast of South America. It is carnivorous and voracious feeder. *Scoliodon* is a fast swimmer and aquatic breather. It is a viviparous.

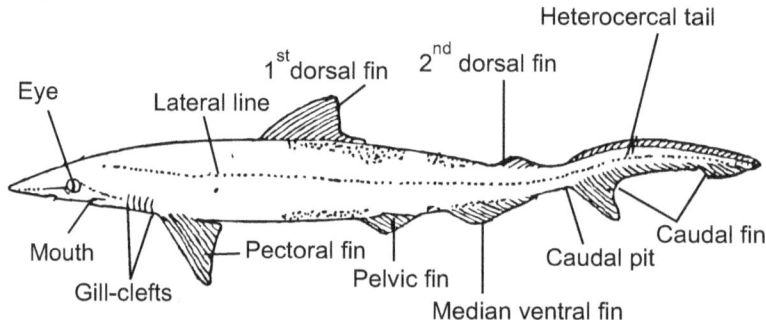

Fig. 18.1: Dog fish (*Scoliodon Sorrakowah*)

18.2 External Characters

- Take a fresh or preserved *Scoliodon*, wash it with tap water.
- Lay down the fish in dissecting tray.
- Examine and note the external features.
- Draw the lateral view of the fish, label it in your practical book.
1. **Shape:** The body of *Scoliodon* is laterally compressed and spindle shaped. Tapering at the both ends.

2. **Size:** The full grown specimen is measures about 60 cm in length.

3. **Colour:** The colour of the body is dark gray above and pale white beneath.

4. **Texture:** The skin of the shark is very rough due to the presence of placoid scales.

5. **Division of the body:** The body is divisble into head, trunk and tail; though there are no distinct boundaries between these three regions.

(I) Head: It is dorso-ventrally compressed and prolonged infront into thin, blunt snout. It possess the following structures.

Mouth: It is a wide cresentic opening situated on the ventral side of the head. It has upper and lower jaws; bearing one or two rows of backwardly directed teeth.

Eyes: These are large and situated at the sides of head. Eyes are provided with movable nictitating membrane.

External nostrils: These are present on the ventral surface of snout and olfactory in function.

Gill slits: Five vertical slits on each side of the head behind the eyes.

(II) Trunk: It is the largest region of body extends from last gill cleft to the cloacal aperture. Trunk bears two types of fins, the median or unpaired fins and lateral or paired fins.

(i) **Median unpaired fins** are:

(a) First dorsal fin, (b) Second dorsal fin and (c) Ventral fin or anal fin,

(ii) **Lateral fins** are:

(a) A pair of **pectoral fins** and

(b) A pair of **pelvic fins**.

(III) Tail: It begins from the cloacal aperture tapers posteriorly and forms about half of the body. It is laterally compressed and bend upwards. Tail is **heterocercal** and bears a caudal fin.

Caudal fin: It extends along dorsal and ventral surfaces of the tail in the median line and forms a dorsal and ventral lobe.

6. **Lateral line:** A faint longitudinal line on either side of the body which extends from the head to the posterior end of tail.

7. **Claspers:** The male Scoliodon bears a pair of claspers connected on the inner edge of the pelvic fins.

18.3 Digestive System of Scoliodon Dissection Technique

- Take a freshly killed/preserved fish wash with tap water.

- Lay down the fish in a dissecting tray facing ventro-laterally (i.e. ventral surface upwards) towards you.

- Pin the pectoral fins.

- Make the incision in the body wall from the clocal aperture to the pectoral girdle mid-longitudinally and also cut transversely along the line pectoral and pelvic fins and fix the flaps with pins and observe the digestive organs.

Digestive System of *Scoliodon*:

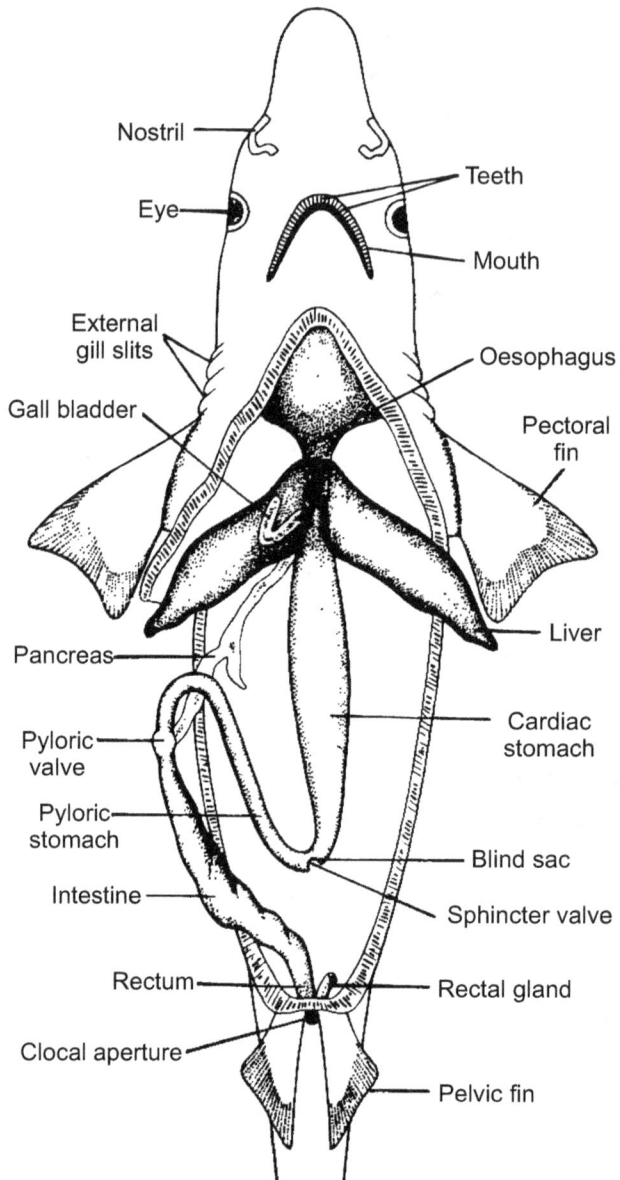

Fig. 18.2: *Scoliodon Sp.* Alimentary system

It consists of the mouth, buccal cavity, pharynx, oesophagus, stomach, intestine and the rectum.

Mouth: It is a ventral cresentic opening guarded by upper and lower jaws. It leads into buccal cavity.

Buccal cavity: It is large, dorso-ventrally flattened and lined with thick mucous membrane which forms a thick fold known as tongue. The tongue is non-muscular, non-glandular and non-protrusible. It helps in swallowing. The mucous membrane of the buccal cavity bears backwardly directed denticles.

Pharynx: Large, on each side it has five internal branchial apertures of gill clefts.

Oesophagus: It is short, muscular, and internally lined with mucous membrane which is raised into longitudinal folds called *rugae*.

Stomach: Oesophagus leads to stomach which is 'J' shaped tubular organ. It is sub-divided into the long proximal limb called *cardiac stomach* and a short, narrow distal limb termed *pyloric stomach*. At the junction of cardiac and pyloric limbs present a small out growth called *blind sac.*

Intestine: Pyloric stomach opens into a straight and wide intestine. It runs straight into the abdominal cavity. Internally, the mucous membrane folded into the scroll valve which increase the absorptive area.

Rectum: The intestine joins a short, narrow rectum which is opening externally by a cloacal aperture. The rectum receives a tubular rectal or caecal gland dorsally.

Liver: It is an elongated, bilobed yellowish gland lies below the cardiac stomach.

Pancreas: It is a compact, bilobed gland lie in the limbs of stomach. Pancreatic duct opens into intestine.

Spleen: It is a large, brownish red body situated in the coils of the pyloric stomach.

Practical 19...

Aim:

Study of Brain of Scoliodon [E].

Dissection Technique:

- Take a formaline preserved fish, wash it with tap water. Remove the skin from dorsal surface of head.
- Expose the cranium, clear it.
- Break open the cranium and expose the brain, take it out in petri dish and examine the different parts of brain.

Brain:

The brain is enclosed in a brain-case called cranium. The brain consists of three main divisions viz.,

(i)   Forebrain or *Prosencephalon*.

(ii)   Midbrain or *Mesencephalon*.

(iii)   Hindbrain or *Rhombencephalon*.

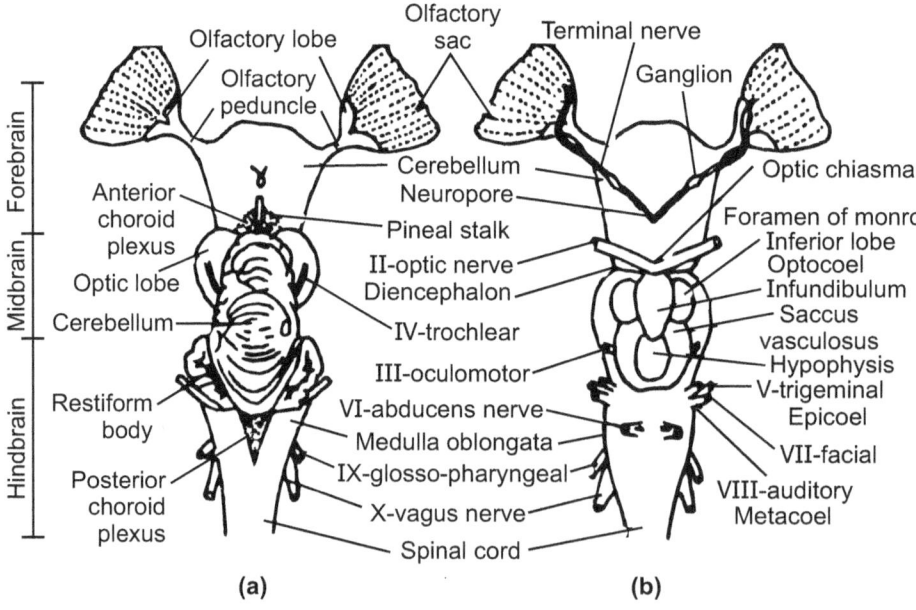

Fig. 19.1: *Scoliodon Brain. (a) - Dorsal view; (b) - Ventral view*

(A) Forebrain:

It is anterior region of brain. It consists of three parts namely *olfactory lobes, cerebrum* and *diencephalon.*

1. **Olfactory lobes:** These are bulb-like paired structure attached to the olfactory sac. The olfactory lobe is connected to the brain by olfactory peduncle. The cavity of olfactory lobe is called *rhinocoel.*

2. **Cerebrum:** It is formed of two cerebral hemispheres. Each cerebral hemisphere encloses a cavity called *lateral ventricle*. These cavities communicate with the *rhinocoels* anteriorly. Posteriorly, they open into the III ventricle by a Y-shaped opening called *foramen of Monro.*

3. **Diencephalon:** It is the posterior short part of the forebrain. It encloses a cavity called III ventricle or *diacoel*. This communicate with the IV ventricle through *iter.*

The lateral walls of the III ventricle are thickened and are called *thalami*. The roof of the diencephalon is thin, membranous and contains numerous blood vesels forming the *anterior choroid plexus*. Behind the anterior choroid plexus, the roof of III ventricle bears *pineal stalk*; which ends in a *pineal body*. The floor of the III ventricle is called *hypothalamus*. The floor of diencephalon has a cross formed by the crossing of the two optic nerves. This cross is called *optic-chiasma*. Infront of optic-chiasma has a *infundibulum*. On the sides of *infundibulum*, there are two lobes called *lobi-inferiores*. Posteriorly, the infundibulum is attached to a oval body called *hypophysis*. The infundibulum and hypophysis together form an endocrine gland called *pituitary gland.*

(B) Midbrain:

This is the middle region of brain. It consists of two main parts: *optic lobes and crura cerebri.*

1. **Optic lobes:** A pair of large rounded swelling on the dorsal side of mid-brain. Each lobe encloses a cavity called *optic ventricle* or *mesocoel.*

2. **Crura cerebri:** The ventral side of the midbrain has thick bands of nerve fibres which connects the forebrain with the hindbrain. This thick band of nerve fibres are called *crura-cerebri*. Midbrain encloses a narrow canal called *iter* or *aqueduct* of *sylvius.*

(C) Hindbrain:

It is the posterior region of brain. It consists of two parts namely *cerebellum* and *medulla oblongata.*

1. **Cerebellum:** It is a large, elongated and rhomboidal structure. Anteriorly, it covers the optic lobes and posteriorly, it covers the medulla oblongata. Its dorsal surface is thrown into numerous irregular folds.

2. **Medulla oblongata:** It is the posterior part of brain. Anteriorly, it is broad and posteriorly, it tapers into the spinal cord. The antero-dorsal end of medulla oblongata bears a pair of hollow outgrowth called *restiform bodies* or *auricular lobes.*

The medulla oblongata encloses a wide cavity called *myelocoel* or IV ventricle.

Spinal cord: It extends from medulla oblongata almost to the end of the tail. It has shallow *dorsal fissure* and well marked *ventral fissure.* Spinal cord has its centre a narrow cavity called *central canal.*

(D) Functions of Brain:

- Olfactory *lobes* and *cerebrum* are useful for sense of smell.
- Cerebellum is the seat of regulation of balance and muscular control.
- *Hypothalamus* concerned with gustatory and olfactory impulses and control of visceral function.
- The *lobi* inferiores and *sacci-vasculosi* are centres for smell and taste.
- *Optic lobes* has optic, olfactory, gustatory and acoustico-lateral sensory centres.
- The *medulla oblongata* contains the respiratory centres besides the centres of number of involuntary activities.

Practical **20**...

(A) Aim:

Temporary perparation of placoid scales from *Scoliodon* [E].

20.1 Placoid Scales

(i) **Location:** These are embeded in the dermis of the skin in oblique rows and form the exoskeleton, covering entire body surface.

Method: Cut a small piece of skin from the dorsal surface of fish. Boil it in 5%-10% KOH solution in a test tube till skin dissolves. Cool and allow the scales to settle at bottom of the test tube. Decant KOH solution slowly. Wash the scales in water. Stain in borax carmine or picroindigo carmine and mount in glycerine temporarily.

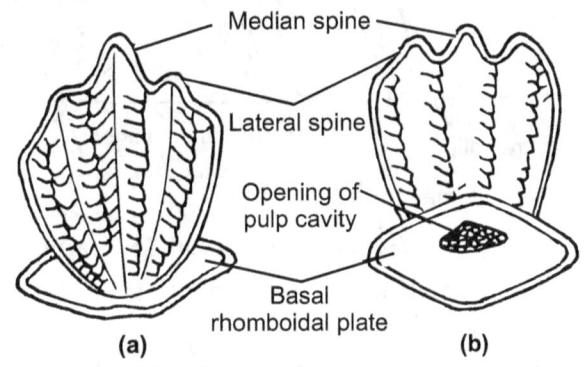

Fig. 20.1: A placoid scale. (a) - Dorsal view; (b) - Ventral view

Structure : The scales are embedded in dermis obliquely and forms exoskeleton. Each placoid scale has a *basal plate* and a *spine*. The spine is a trident, externally coated with *enamel*. It encloses a pulp cavity which is filled with *pulp* containing *odontoblasts*; blood vessels and nerves. The basal plate is diamond shaped with a central opening leads to pulp cavity.

***

(B) Aim:

Study of cranial nerves, eye ball muscles and their innervations and membraneous labyrinth of Scoliodon (D).

20.2 Brain and Cranial Nerves

The nerves arising from the brain are called cranial nerves. There are 10 pairs of cranial nerves numbered I to X, besides these, there is zero or pair of anterior terminal nerves, which originates from the cerebrum through the neuropore and innervate the nasal septum and external nostrils.

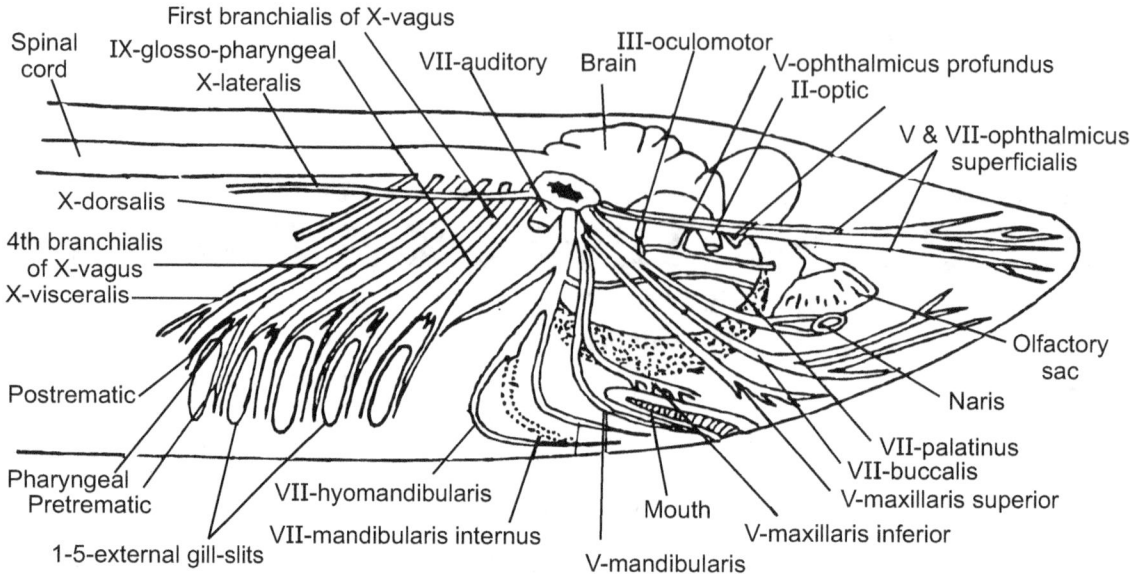

Fig. 20.2: *Scoliodon Sp.* Brain and cranial nerves. Lateral view

1. **I or olfactory nerve** arises from the olfactory lobe and distributed to the olfactory sac of its own side.

2. **II or optic nerve** arises from the optic thalamus. The nerve of each side crosses the other to form optic chiasma and passing over to the opposite side, enters the orbit and distributed to the retina of the eye.

3. **III or occulomotor nerve** arising from ventral surface of mid-brain. It divides into branches which innervates the anterior, superior and inferior recti muscles and inferior oblqiue recti muscles of eye-ball.

4. **IV or pathetic or trochlear nerve** arising from the dorso-lateral surface of the mid-brain and innervates the superior oblique muscles of the eye-ball.

5. **V or trigeminal nerve** arises from medulla oblongata. It has three branches.
   (a) *Ophthalmic nerve* along with ophthalmic branch of the VII nerve passes through the orbit and goes to the skin of snout.
   (b) *Mandibular* and
   (c) *Maxillary* arise from common stem and then separate. The mandibular innervate the muscles of the lower jaw and maxillary forms two branches going to the skin of the upper jaw and uper lip.

6. **VI or abducens *nerve*** arises from the lower surface of the medulla, enters the orbit and goes to the posterior rectus muscle of the eye-ball.

7. **VII or facial nerve** comes out from the sides of medulla oblongata in two bundles. The first bundle is called *ophthalmic superficialis*, goes to the lateral line receptors and ampullae or Lorenzini. Other bundle divides into three branches called *buccalramus, hyomandibularramus* and *palatineramus*.

8. **VIII or auditory nerve** divides into two branches, a *vestibular* going to the membraneous labyrinth and the *saccular* or *cochlear* branch going to the lagena.

9. **IX or glassopharyngeal nerve** arises from the ventro-lateral surface of medulla. It then passes backward and downward to the region of first gill-cleft where it divides into three branches.

   (a) ***Pre-trematic* branch** running along the anterior border of the gill-cleft.

   (b) A large ***post-trematic branch*** running along its posterior border.

   (c) ***Pharyngeal branch*** which supplies receptors present in the mucous membrane of the pharynx.

10. **X or vagus nerve** is large and emerges from the sides of medulla oblongata and has wide distribution. It gives three main branches.

   (a) ***Branchialis*** are four main nerves each dividing into **pre-trematic** and **post trematics** branches going to the last four gill-clefts.

   (b) ***Visceral*** is large, it turns backward into the body cavity and sends branches to the alimentary canal, liver, lungs and heart.

   (c) ***Lateralis*** it runs deep in the lateral body wall and innervates the lateral line sense organs.

The cranial nerves are of motor, sensory or mixed type.

20.3 Eye-ball Muscles and their Innvervations

Observe the following eye-ball muscles.

1. **Superior rectus muscles:** These are inserted on the dorsal surface of the eye-ball.

2. **Inferior rectus muscles:** These are inserted on the ventral surface of the eye-ball.

3. **Anterior rectus muscles:** These are inserted on the anterior surface of the eye-ball.

4. **Posterior rectus muscles:** They are enter on the posterior surface of the eye-ball.

5. **Superior oblique muscles:** These are inserted on the dorsal surface of eye-ball.

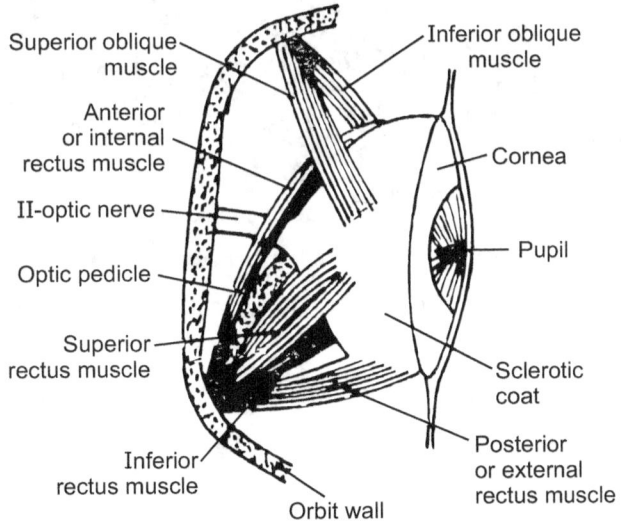

Fig. 20.3: *Scoliodon Sp.* Eye muscles

6. **Inferior oblique muscles:** These are inserted on the ventral surface of eye-ball.

   Nerves (innervations of nerves to eyeball).

   (i)   Anterior ciliary nerve.

   (ii)   Posterior ciliary nerve.

   (iii)   V, VII, VIII, IX and X cranial nerves.

✱✱✱

(C) Aim:

Study of Membranous labyrinth of *Scoliodon*.

Membraneous labyrinth is enclosed in a cartilaginous *labyrinth*.

The membraneous labyrinth made up of two chambers. viz. a dorsal *utriculus* and a ventral *sacculus*. The sacculus gives out a small projection from its ventral side called *lagena*. A small canal arises from the dorsal side of the sacculus called *endolymphatic* duct. It opens to the outside on the dorsal side but before opening to the outside, it dilates to form a sac called *endolymphatic sac.*

The utriculus has three *semi-circular* canals. Both ends of the canal open into the utriculus. One end of each tube becomes dilated to form a sac called *ampulla.* One duct is horizontal and the other two are vertical in position.

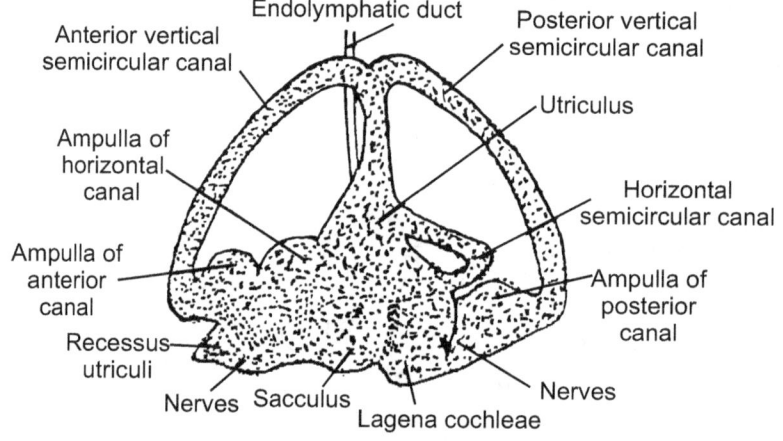

Fig. 20.4: *Scoliodon* : Membranous labyrinth

The membranous labyrinth contains a fluid called *endolymph* and one or more calcarious bodies termed as *otoliths*.

Membranous labyrinth (A pair of internal ears) serves the function of *equilibrium and hearing* in shark.

✱✱✱

Practical **21** ...

(A) Aim:

Study of Life Cycle of Honey Bee.

The honey bee shows complete metamorphosis and thus termed as holometabolous insect. The queen is functional female. The life-cycle consists of egg, larva, pupa and adult.

Nuptial flight:

A virgin queen takes her first aerial flight followed by a swarm of drones on warm, sunny days and mates with queen during which she receives spermatophores from the drone and stored in spermatheca to fertilize her eggs as long as she lives. The queen after mating returns to the hive. The Drone is always killed in the act of copulation, since he can eject the sperm by generating great pressure in his abdomen with the help of muscles and fluid pressure of blood.

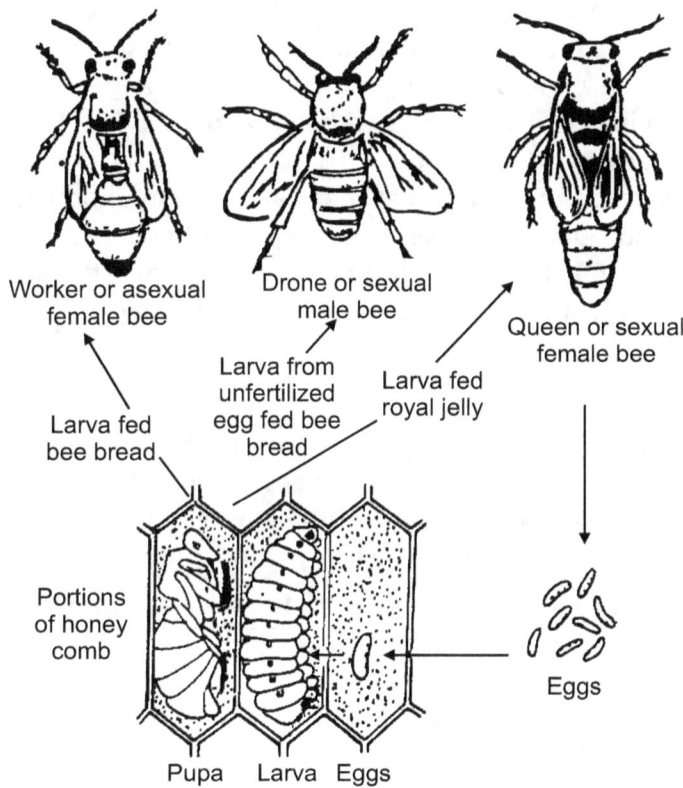

Fig. 21.1 : *Apis.* Life Cycle

Egg:

Egg laying starts after 3 days of copulation. The eggs are pinkish, elongated, cylindrical and generally attached at the bottom of the cell at the junctions of any two walls. The eggs are of two types – fertilized eggs develop into queen and workers and undertilized egg develop into drones. The fertilized eggs are laid into either queen or worker cells and unfertilized eggs into drone cells. Queen lays about 1500 egg per day. The egg hatch in three days into white, legless grubs from the fertilized as well as unfertilized eggs.

Grub:

The larvae are minute, white, apodous (legless) and with no eyes. For the first 3 days all larvae are fed on *'royal jelly'* which is produced by pharyngeal glands of young workers. After 3 days, worker and drone bees larvae are fed on a mixture of honey and pollen called *'bee bread'* but the larvae of queen are continuously fed on royal jelly. Type of food supply determine the caste. The grub grow and moult several times, then cells are sealed with a wax cap.

Pupa:

Grub transformed into a pupa in the sealed chamber. The wax lid is porous and allows exchange of air for respiration. The pupa spins a thin silken cocoon around itself and pupates completely. Pupa undergoes metamorphosis i.e. change of legless, wingless and eyeless worm like form into a winged insect with legs and eyes. The pupa is exarate type (i.e. the legs are free not adhered to the body). The worker, drone and queen pupae can be distinguished by examining the distance between eyes. In case of drone, eyes meet over the head and in worker and queen the eyes are far apart. After the pupal period is over the sealed pupae becomes tan and finally light brown in colour and the lid of cell is cut-off by the young bee, with jaws. After few hours later the pupal cuticle breaks and the adult be emerges out.

Adult:

The emerged adult chew away the cell cap and crawls out to join the other bees as a member of the hive. The morphological features are described in tabular form (Table 21.1). Emergence of the young ones takes place after three weeks and they get busy in the indoor duties for about 2-3 weeks. Later on they are sent for the outdoor duties.

Table 21.1 : Morphological feature of three caste of a honey bee

	Drone	Worker	Queen
1.	Eyes meet over head.	Eyes far apart.	Eyes far apart.
2.	Abdomen black, rectangular, blunt and without sting.	Abdomen stripped, triangular with barbed sting.	Golden (*A. florea*) or black (*A. indica*) triangular but more elongated.

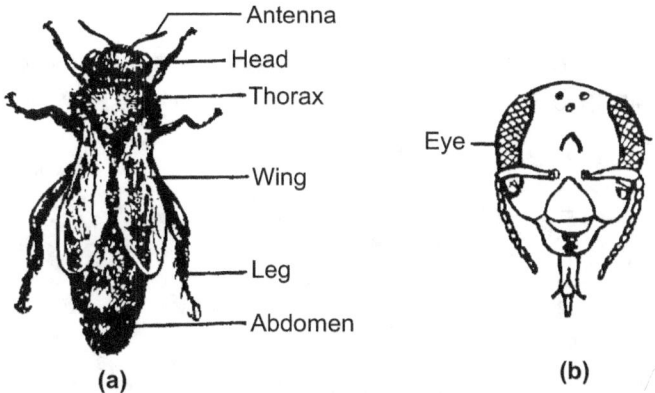

Fig. 21.2 : (a) The Queen; (b) Front view of head of the queen

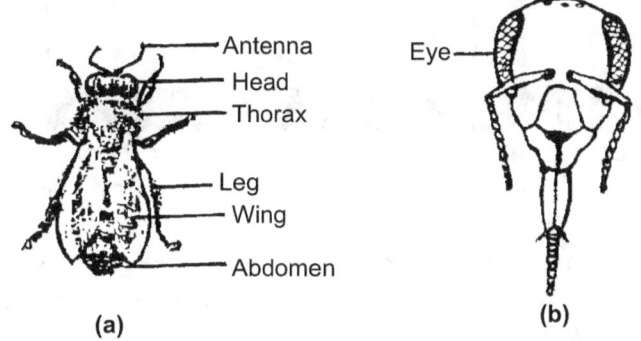

Fig. 21.3 : (a) The worker; (b) The front view of head of worker

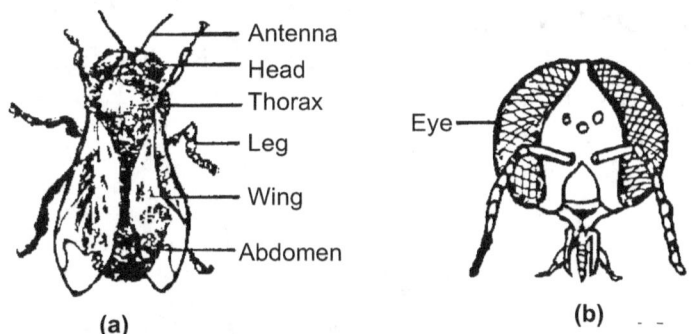

Fig. 21.4 : (a) The Drone; (b) Front view of head of drone

Table 21.2 : Periods of development of different castes of honey bees

Duration in days				
Caste	Egg	Larva	Pupa	Total
Queen	3	5	7-8	15-16
Worker	3	4-5	11-12	18-20
Drone	3	5-7	13-14	21-24

***

(B) Aim:

Study of worker bee morphology, mouth parts, appendages, pollen basket, wings, sting apparatus of honey bee.

Systematic Position:

Kingdom	–	Animalia
Group	–	Invertebrata
Phylum	–	Arthropoda
Class	–	Insecta/Hexapoda
Sub-class	–	Pterygota
Division	–	Endopterygota
Order	–	Hymenoptera
Family	–	Apidae
Genus	–	*Apis*
Species	–	(i) *mellifera*, (ii) *indica*, (iii) *florae*, (iv) *dorsata*

21.1 Habit and Habitat

Honey bees are social insect living in colonies, built by themselves. A colony may have about 50,000 individuals. They are active throughout the year. They exhibit colony organization (i.e. polymorphism) and good division of labour.

The family Apidae is main honey producing family; have five well known species in the world namely, *Apis mellifera* (European bee), *A. indica (Indian bee), A. florea* (Little bee), *A. dorsata* (rock bee) and *Apis adamsoni* (African bee).

There are three types of caste in a colony viz. workers, queen and drones.

External Morphology of Worker bee:

The worker bee is smallest member of the colony. It is black brown in colour and entire body is densely covered with hairs. The body of worker bee is divided into three regions, *Head, Thorax and Abdomen.*

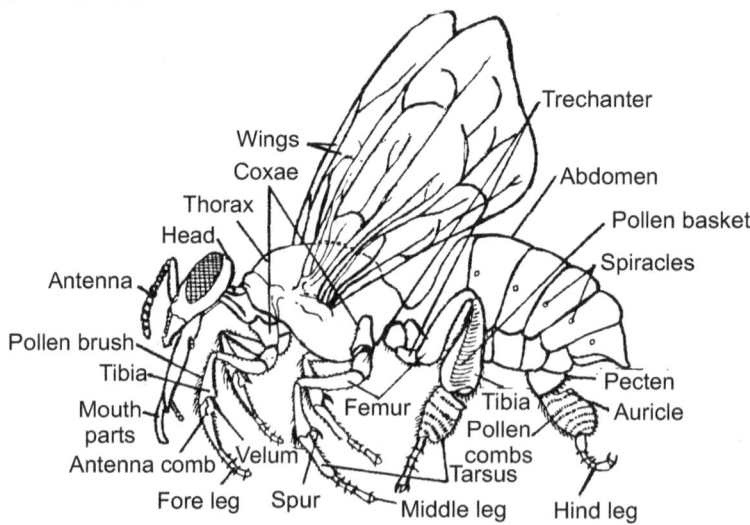

Fig. 21.5: *Apis sp.* External morphology lateral view

Head:

The head is triangular, flattened, broader on dorsal side and narrow ventrally. The head bears dorsoventrally large compound eyes and three ocelli in the middle of face. A pair of freely movable antennae are arise in the middle of the head. Each antenna is jointed, having three segments, scape, pedicel and flagellum with olfacory pits for sense of smell. Below the bases of antennae there is large plate called clypeus to this labrum is attached to lower margin. Behind the labrum are two mandibles, below this two maxillae and medium labium is seen. On the back side of head shows a central opening called occipital foramen.

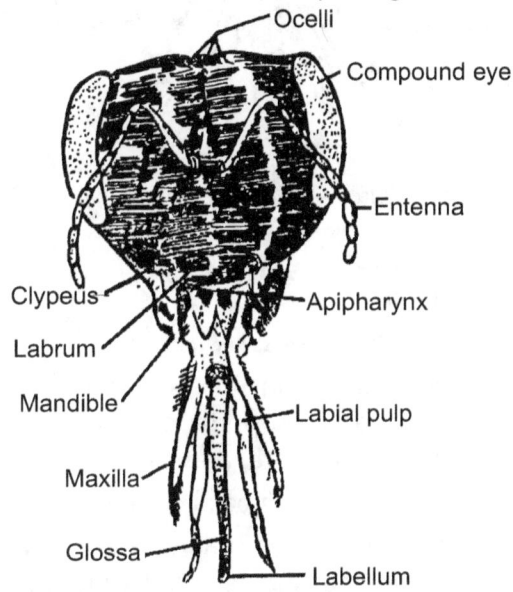

Fig. 21.6: *Apis*. Head

Mouth Parts:

These are attached to the lower part of head. The mouth parts are *biting* and *sucking* type. It consists of labrum, epipharynx, mandibles, maxillae and labium.

Labrum: Large plate like attached to lower margin of clypeus.

Epipharynx: It lies below the labrum. Fleshy in appearance. Epipharynx is a organ of taste.

Mandibles: These are two in number and lies on the sides of labrum. The mandibles of worker are spoon shaped, thick at the base and narrowed through the middle. At the base of mandibles, mandibular glands open. Mandibles are equipped with abductor and adductor muscles which work sidewise. Mandibles are useful to gather pollen and mould the wax.

Maxillae: It lies beneath mandibles. The lacinia is absent in maxillae while the maxillary palps are vestigial and the galea is elongated and blade-like.

Labium: The labium shows strongly reduced paraglosae but the glossae are very much elongated. They are united, hairy and form a honey-spoon called *labellum* at the terminal part. The labial palps are well developed and help to make the ligula up. The apparatus is well surrounded by the galeae of maxillae.

At the time of nectar feeding, the labium and maxillae come together to form sucking tube.

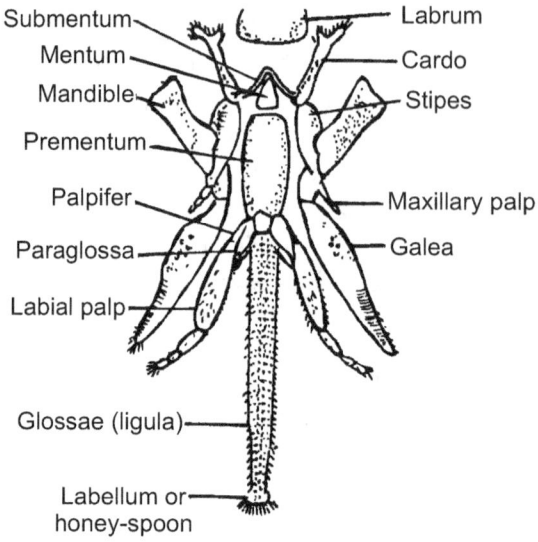

Submentum — — Labrum
Mentum — — Cardo
Mandible — — Stipes
Prementum —
Palpifer — — Maxillary palp
Paraglossa — — Galea
Labial palp —
Glossae (ligula) —
Labellum or — honey-spoon

Fig. 21.7: *Apis*. Mouth parts

Thorax: The thorax is large and strong. It is composed of four segments, namely: prothorax, mesothorax, metathorax and propodeum. Each segment has three sclerities i.e. turgum (dorsal plate), sternum (ventral plate) and pleuron (side plates).

Thorax bears two pairs of wings and three pairs of legs.

Wings: The wings are small, narrow, membraneous and transparent. They lie flat over the back at rest. Wings shows modified and reduced wing veination. The fore and hind wings are interlocked by hooks (*hamuli*) so as to work together during flight.

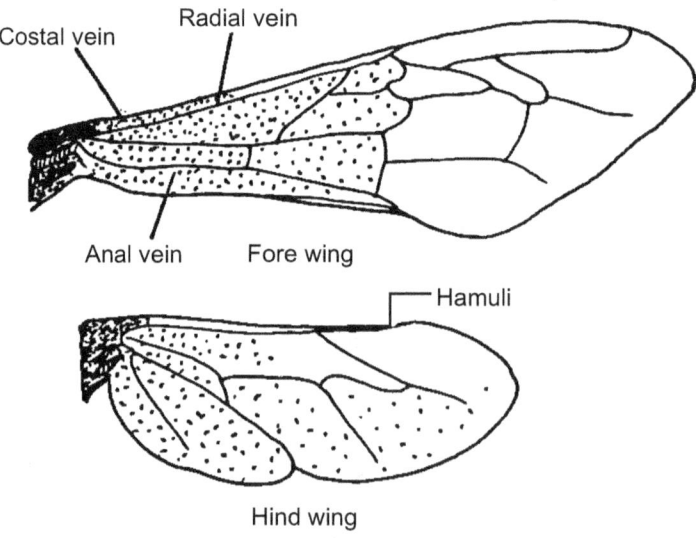

Costal vein   Radial vein
Anal vein   Fore wing
Hamuli
Hind wing

Fig. 21.8: Wings of worker bee

Legs: There are three pairs of legs, i.e. prothoracic, mesothoracic and metathoracic shows progressive increase in length from 1st to 3rd pair. Legs are densely covered with hairs. Each leg consists of five parts viz. *coxa, trochanter, femur, tibia* and *tarsus*. The tarsus is five joined and ends into the *claws* and pulvillus.

Each pair of legs are structurally modified to suit various activities/functions.

(a) Prothoracic leg: Number of stiff bristles are present on the anterior face of tibia distally, which forms *pollen brush*. On the posterior face of tibia have movable plate-like process called *velum*, which fits over a circular notch in the upper part of the first tarsal segment. The velum and antena-comb together serve as antenna cleaners.

Eye brush is present on the anterior surface of first tarsal segment which is used for removing pollen and other particles from the surface of compound eyes.

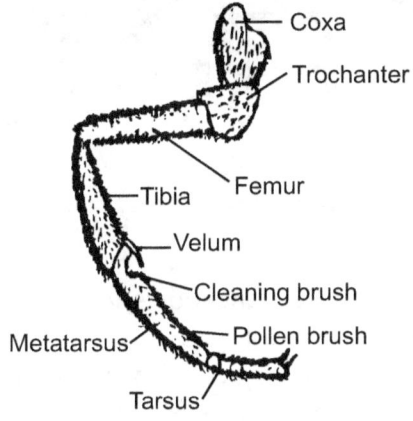

Fig. 21.9: Prothoracic leg

(b) Mesothoracic leg: The mid leg shows usual segments. The tibial segment bears a brush on its inner surface and a spine-like *pollen-spur* on its distal end. The spurs are used to remove pollen from the pollen baskets of hind-legs and to dislodge wax from wax pockets on the ventral surface of the abdomen.

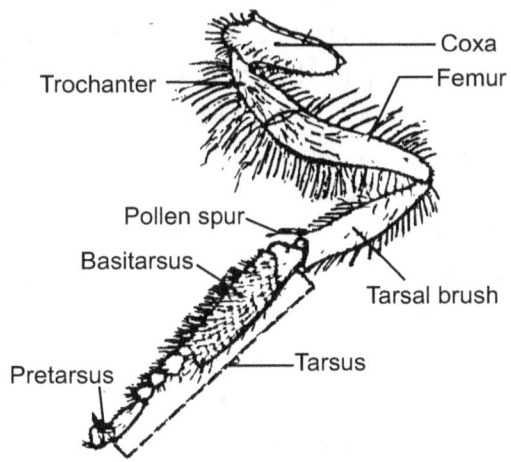

Fig. 21.10: The mesothoracic leg

(c) Metathoracic leg: Each metathoracic leg has a large tibia with a cavity with bristles forming a *pollen basket* i.e. a depression on the outer surface of tibia, used for storing pollens during collection. At the distal end the tibia has a row of stiff bristles called *pectins* below which has a flat plate, known as *auricle*. The pectines and auricle form a *pollen packet* to convey packed pollens into the pollen basket.

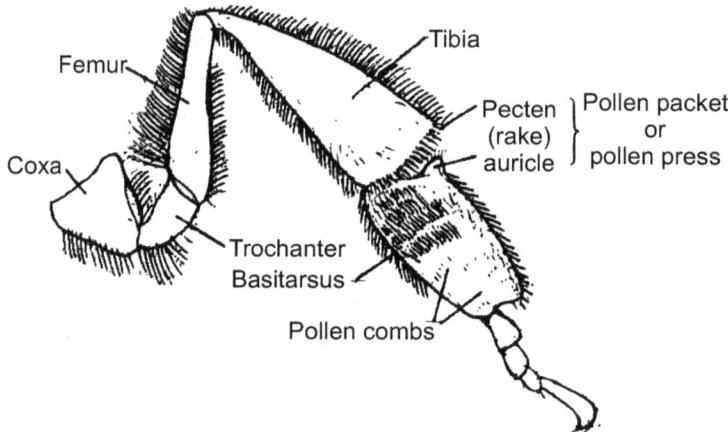

Fig. 21.11: The metathoracic leg showing pollen basket

Abdomen:

The abdomen of worker bee is oval and posterior most region of the body. It has six visible segments i.e. II to VII because the first segment (propodeum) transferred to thorax and remaining are reduced. Each visible segment has large dorsal tergum, and smaller ventral sternum. The successive terga and sterna are connected by intersegmental membrane. The posterior part of abdomen is modified into sting apparatus and wax gland on vental surface of abdomen.

(a) Wax glands: These lie on the ventral surface of the last four visible segments. Wax glands secrete wax through minute pores in the form of flat scales. Wax is used for building the cells of the honey comb.

(b) Sting aparatus: In the worker bee, the ovipositor changes so as to take the function of sting i.e. for injecting poison. The sting apparatus or poison apparatus has three components, namely, the *sting*, the plates and poison gland.

The sting: The sting is a hollow organ formed by three pieces bounding a central canal (poison canal). The dorsal part is the *stylet sheath*, and the two ventral pieces are *stylets* or *lancets*. The apices of the stylets and their sheath bear forwardly directed *barbs*. The stylet sheath expands at its base to form the *bulb* of the sting and latter a pair of diverging arms.

The plates: Three pairs of plates associated with the sting act as a lever. The innermost pair of *oblong plates* posterior in position and representing the divided 9th sternum. Two *triangular* or *fulcral* plates representing reduced 8th sternum and attached to corresponding stylets. The large *quadrate* plates lie dorsally to the triangular plates and at the posterior angle.

There are two glands which are associated with sting. Attached to the stylets porximally is a median *poison sac* into which open two acid glands and one alkaline gland.

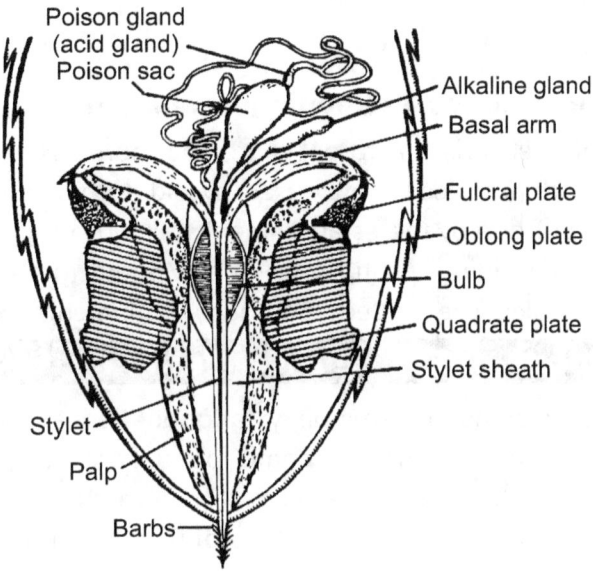

Fig. 21.12: *Apis sp.* Poison apparatus

Acid glands: It is elongated, slender gland open into the upper end of the poison sac. It discharges an acidic secretion into the sac.

Alkaline gland: It is thick, tubular gland which opens externally below the base of the bulb.

✳✳✳

Practical **22...**

Aim:

(a) To study the various Beekeeping Equipments (D).

The ultimate aim of beekeeping is to get more and more honey and bees wax in pure form. In India, old methods were commonly used by old apiculturist was very crude, cruel and of unplanned type. But due to the establishment training programmes and research of Central Bee Research and Training Institute at Pune, Modern methods of beekeeping are well acquiented to the peoples. The modern methods / equipments are described here.

22.1 Modern Methods or Frame Hive Method

For commercial beekeeping, in an apiary; a good beekeeper requires number of equipments viz. bee box, hive stand, frames, comb foundation sheet, bee escapes, smokers, queen excluder, hive tools, D.B. feeder, honey extractor, uncapping knife, bee brush, bee veil, queen cell protector etc. Now-a-days a typical type of movable hive is constructed which is capable of expansion according to the requirements of the place, season and climatic condition.

An artificial movable frame hive is rectangular wooden box based on bee space theory.

The hives are fitted with movable frames on which the bees are compelled to build their combs. Each hive is composed of several small boxes, one on top of the other, in which are suspended hive frames. The lower boxes one or two are used for keeping brood and the upper boxes are used to store honey, pollen, propolis. At present, both single walled (box) hives and double walled hives are used all over the world. Currently, there are five types of hives are in use, viz. *Smith, British Commerical, Langstroth, Newton and Modified Dadant* types. *Langstroth* in 1851 used a Wooden box, as a single brood-box-hive is good for a queen.

Bee Box:

The *Langstroth* (10-frame hive) and *Newton* frame hives are used in India, for keeping bee colonies in apiary. It is composed of the following parts: stand, floor board, brood box, hive-frames, queen excluder, supers and covers.

The details of construction are as follows:

1.   Stand: It is any, four legged structure (stand), 6-9 inches high, with dimensions to support the floor-board; on which the whole hive is constructed. The stands are adjusted to make slope for the hive, which drain off rain water. The main purpose of stand is to support the box and to prevent entry of ants and other insects.

2. **Bottom Board:** It is situated above the stand and forms the proper base for the hive having two gates in the front position. One gate is used as an entrance while the other as exit for bees. It can be constructed either by taking a piece of wood 22" long, 16'/4" broad and 7/8" thick or by joining two wooden boards together, nailing them in position with "wooden rods". Along each end of the longer side is nailed a 'wooden rod' 22" long, 7/8" broad and 7/8" thick and another "wooden rod" $14\frac{1"}{2} \times 7/8"$ is nailed at the back and this has an entrance 3" long and 3/8" deep in its middle.

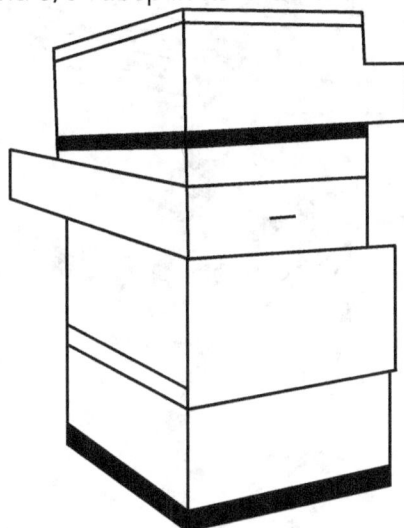

Fig. 22.1: A double walled Langstroth hive with supers

3. **Brood Chamber:** The bottom board carries the brood chamber which is the most important part of the bee hive. Brood chamber is a rectangular box without top and bottom. It is prepared of thick wood of 7/8" thick. Brood chamber is 20" from outside and $18\frac{1"}{4}$ from inside in length. Its breadth is $16\frac{1"}{2}$ on the outside and $14\frac{1"}{2}$ on the inside and its height is x $9\frac{1"}{2}$. A rabbet (scooped shelf) 5/8" deep and 1/2" wide is cut along the entire of the box to receive the ends of the top bar of the hive frames. The number of brood boxes could be increased to 2 - when the colony becomes strong. It is provided with 10 - frames.

4. **Standard Langstroth Frame:** Each wooden frame composed of a top bar, two side bars and a bottom bar. There are two types of frames: (i) Hoffman type (ii) Staple type.

(a) **Hoffman type** (Self-spacing frame):

(i) **The top bar** is 19" long, 1" wide and 7/8" thick. The ends of top bar extend beyond to rest on the rabbet scooped on the long sides of the brood box and under surface is grooved for fixing the edge of the comb foundation sheet.

(ii) **Side bar:** It is 9 – 1/8" long and made from 3/8" thick wood. Each is cut out from the middle portion at either end to accommodate the top and the bottom bars respectively. There are four holes in each side bar for wiring the frame.

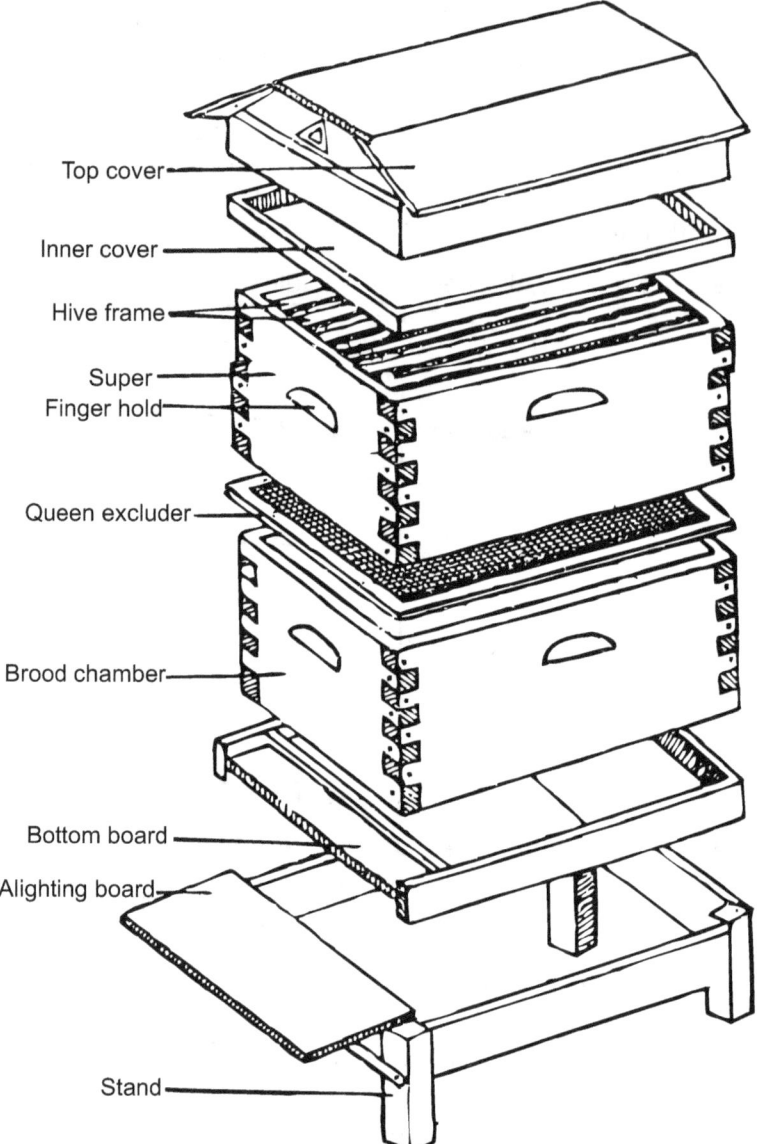

Top cover

Inner cover

Hive frame

Super
Finger hold

Queen excluder

Brood chamber

Bottom board

Alighting board

Stand

Fig. 22.2: Diagram showing different parts of a Langstroth frame hive (see text for descriptions)

(iii) **Bottom bar:** Each is 17 – 5/8" long, 3/4" wide and 3/8" thick.

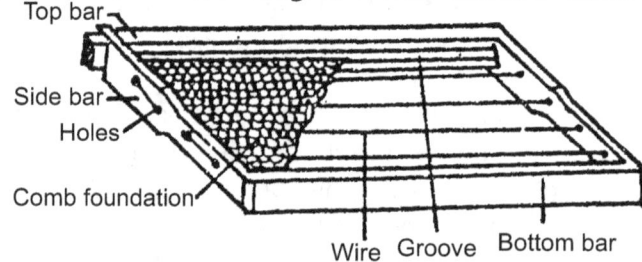

Top bar

Side bar
Holes

Comb foundation

Wire   Groove   Bottom bar

Fig. 22.3: (a) Hoffman self-spacing type

(b) Staple Spacing Frame:

(i)   **Top bar:** Top bar is 19" long, 1" wide and 7/8" thick. It has a groove as like Hoffman top bar. It is covered with metal spacing devices on each end of its opposite faces.

(ii)   **Side bar:** Each is made of 3/8" thick wood. It is 3 – 3/4" long and 1" wide. There are 4-holes in each side bar for wiring the frame.

(iii)   **Bottom bar:** It is 16 - 7/8" long, 1" wide and 3/8" thick.

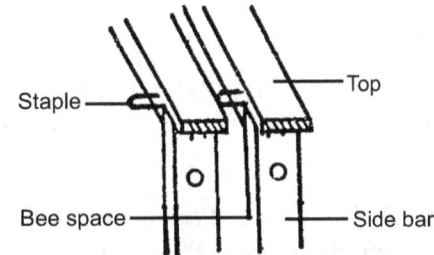

Both the type of frames are spaced apart to leave the bee-space (0.96 cm or 3/8 inch) by the width of the upper third of the side bars (Hoffman type) or by nailing two staples on ends of the tops bar on opposite sides of the frames (staple spaced frames).

Fig. 22.3: (b) Staple-spaced type

5.   **Super:** The supers are like brood box without cover and the base. Super is provided with many frames containing comb foundation to provide additional space for the expansion of the hive. It is placed over the queen excluder.

6.   **Inner Cover:** This is a wooden board to cover the brood chamber or the super. It is 20" long, $16\frac{1"}{4}$ broad and 3/8" thick wood. It has many holes for proper ventilation.

7.   **Top Cover:** It is meant for protecting the colony from rains. It is fitted with zinc sheet. There are two types of top cover: (i) Sloping and (ii) Flat top cover.

Sloping top cover is wooden, broad, 20" × $16\frac{1"}{4}$ in measurement from outside and 26" long slanting boards are nailed on top for the rain water to shed off the sides.

Flat top cover: It is made up of 3/8" thick wooden board, nailed to a rectangular frame 2" high, all covered with zinc sheet so as to make it impervious to rain water.

8.   **Queen Excluder:** It is necessary to separate the brood chamber from the supers where honey is stored. This is made with the help of a zinc or wire gauze frame with 2.3 – 3.5 mm perforations to enable the workers to pass through but not the queen whose thoracic width, is 4.3 – 4.5 mm is more in size than perforations. The queen stay within the brood box and spare the super of the eggs and brood.

9. Comb Foundation Sheet:

In nature, worker bees build new combs from bees wax secreted by wax gland and make parallel combs which are attached to the ceiling of the cavity or box.

The Central Bee Research Institute, Pune manufactures, a comb-foundation sheets artificially. In each frame a wax sheet bearing hexagonal cell impressions is held up by a couple of wires in a vertical position. Along with the margin of every hexagonal mark, the bees start making wall and ultimately the cells. This each sheet with impression of hexagonal mark is known as comb foundation sheet, which attracts the bees and provides the base for the comb preparation on both the sides. Which are kept in brood chamber.

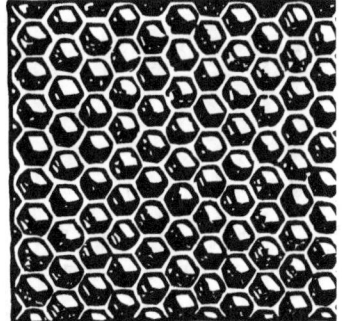

Fig. 22.4: A piece of comb foundation sheet

10. Honey Extractor:

It is a machine with which honey is separated in its purest form from the honey comb. It is made from the metal or tin material. Honey extractors are available in variety of sizes with the frames arranged tangentially or radially and is operated manually or with electric power and functions on principle of centrifugal force. When combs are centrifuged by this device the pure honey is thrown out without any damage to the comb.

Fig. 22.5: Honey extractor

11. Uncapping Knife:

When all the combs are filled with honey, they are sealed by capping with the wax. So, before such capped combs are placed in the honey extractor, the wax sealing has to be removed with the help of an uncapping knife heated by steam before use.

Fig. 22.6: Uncapping knife

22.2 Other Equipments Needed for Beekeeping

Bees have stings which they use as weapons of defence. They do not tolerate any outside interference in their home. The beekeeper has to examine the colony to find out the condition; so we required the following equipments.

(i) Smoker: It is used to give smoke gently (and not blast; it infuriates them) to the bees for easy handling. It consists of a tin can provided with a spout for directing the smoke from the smouldering material inside it with the help of a bellows.

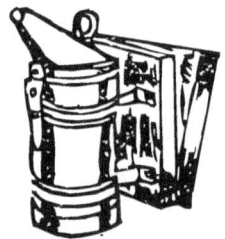

Fig. 22.7: Smoker

(ii) Hive tool: It is a flat piece of steel sharpened at one end for inserting between hive boxes to separate them and the other end bent to separate the frames. It is also used to scrape off the bee glue and pieces of comb from various parts of the hive.

Fig. 22.8: Hive tool

(iii) **Overall:** It is a protective garment worn over the clothes so that the bees cannot get under them to sting. Strong, cheap white drill could be used to make it.

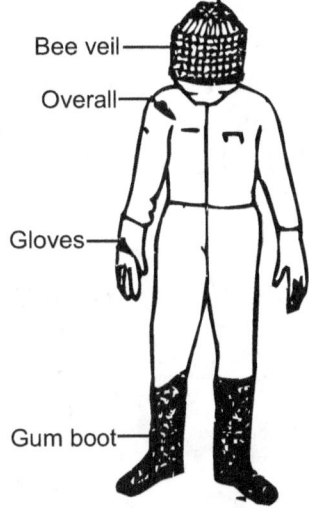

Fig. 22.9: Overall

(iv) **Bee veil:** It is made of frames covered on the four sides with small mesh wire gauge, black light material, silk, cotton and top and bottom with thick cloth. The bottom cloth is provided with rim (circular ring) with an elastic to make it stick to the neck. Bee veil is worn over the face of the person handling bees, for the protection against stings.

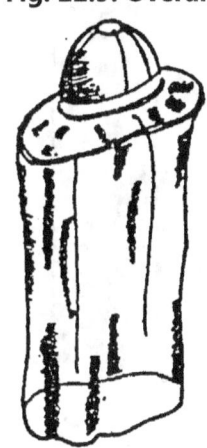

Fig. 22.10: Bee Veil

(v) **Bee gloves:** The gloves are made of thick canvass or leather with an elastic in the wrist will protect the hands from bee stings. These are most useful for beginners to develop confidence. (Please see Fig. 22.9).

(vi) **High boots:** It is made up of good plastic or rubber. Bees attack the ankles and so a pair of high (gum) boots will not only protect the ankles but will also prevent bees from climbing up under the trousers. (Please see Fig. 22.9).

(vii) **Bee brush:** A bee brush is employed to brush off the bees from a honey comb, before it is taken away for extraction.

Fig. 22.11: A bristle bee brush

(viii) D. B. (division board) feeder: The division board feeder is a wooden trough of the regular Langstroth frame dimension with its shoulders to hang in the hive boxes just like any other frame. It is used for feeding sugar syrup bees. Feeding becomes necessary if the honey store runs short before honey flow starts in the flowers, or if the bees are to abscond due to heat, shortage of water and honey. Extra feeding is also mostly used in dearth period.

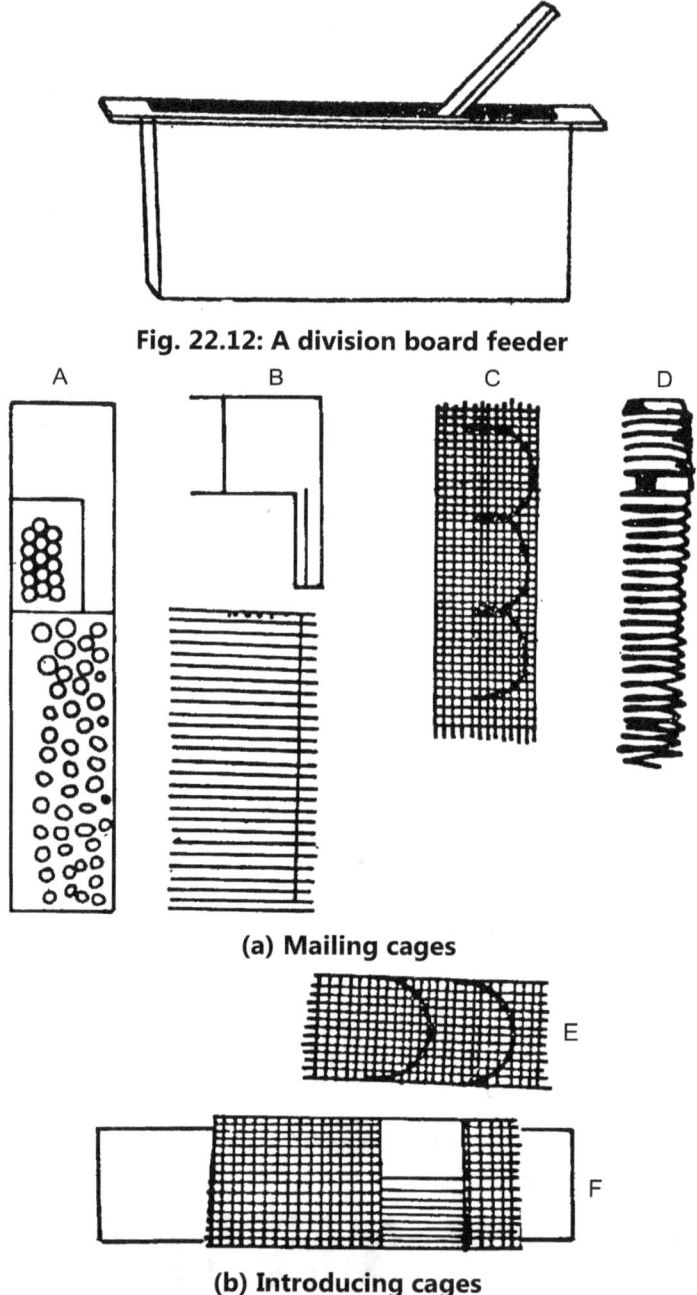

Fig. 22.12: A division board feeder

(a) Mailing cages

(b) Introducing cages

Fig. 22.13: Different types of queen cages (Eckert)

(a) **Queen Cages:** Now-a-days different types of cages are in use by beekeepers. viz. the Miller queen introducing cage, the Smith introducing cage, the queen mailing cage and the wire gauge cage. These cages are useful for introducing queen to the queenless colony. So that the bees become acquainted with the fact that she is indeed a queen. (See Fig. 22.13).

(b) **Queen cell protector:** It is made up of a piece of large-mesh wire gauge rolled into a rectangle or a cylinder. This is useful for introducing queen cell from a queen right colony to a queenless colony and often protected in a queen cell protectors until its acceptance by the workers.

Fig. 22.14: Queen cell protector

(c) **Division board (Dummy):** Dummy board is a wooden partition and it serves as a movable wall to help in reducing the size of the brood chamber so as to keep the hive air-conditioned and well protected from bee-enemies or inclement weather.

(d) **Bee Escape:** It is a device for allowing the bees to go through a self closing exit. Two types of Bee escapes are in use by the beekeepers. They are wire gauze cone and spring bee escape.

Fig. 22.15: Bee escape

✳✳✳

Practical **23**...

Aim:

(A) To study the Bee Products.

Apiculture or beekeeping is the technique of rearing honey bees for number of products like honey, wax, pollen, propolis, bee venom, royal jelly. Among these honey and bees wax are major products and rest are minor.

23.1 Honey

Honey is made from the nectar, a sugary fluid, secreted by the nectar glands (nectaries) situated at the bases of flowers of trees, shrubs and herbs. The bees draws nectar by its tongue (Proboscis) and carries it to the hive in its crop or honey stomach; where it gets mixed with the saliva and undergo certain chemical changes due to enzyme action. In the hive, it is regurgitated and deposited by the hivemates into the cells which are used for collection of nectar and its subsequent ripening into honey.

Honey is very sweet in taste and white to black in colour with variable smell depending on the juices collected from different flowers.

Chemical Composition of Honey:

Honey is a sugar rich compound and when fully ripened consists the following constituents.

Levulose (Fructose)	–	38.19%
Dextrose	–	21.28%
Maltose and other sugars	–	8.81%
Enzymes, Vitamines, A, B & C,		
Pigments etc.	–	2.21%
Ash (Minerals)	–	1.0%
Water	–	17.20%

Economic Importance of Honey:

Honey is a necessary item at puja (worship) in Hindu religion. Catholics prepare *mead* (an alcoholic drink made from honey) and in Quran there is a special chapter on uses of honey. Besides this honey has great food and medicinal value.

(i) Food value: It is estimated that 200 gm of honey provides as much nourishment as 11.5 liter of milk or 1.6 kg cream or 330 gm meat. 2.1 gm of honey provides about 67 k.cal of energy or 1 kg contains 3350 calories. The ingredients of honey like sugars; minerals, vitamins A, B and C are easily absorbed by alimentary canal. Honey is taken by healthy as well as those are ill persons. It is recommended as food for infants, the aged. It has been shown that it helps to build up haemoglobin of blood.

(ii) Medicinal value: Honey is mildly laxative, antiseptic and sedative, so it is used as an ingredient in Ayurvedic and Unani systems of medicine, just as lactose is used as carrier of Homeopathic medicines. Some tested medicinal uses of honey are its uses as laxative, blood purifier, a preventive against cold, cough and fever, curative for sores, eye ailments, ulcers on tongue, sore throat and burns. The *Chavanprash* contains honey as one of the important ingredients. It is also found that *typhoid germs* are killed by honey within 48 hrs, those of *branchio-pneumonia* in 4 days and of dysentery in 50 hours.

(iii) Other uses: Besides food and medicinal value, honey is used in number of ways for example: it is used in the preparation of bread, cake, candies and biscuits due to its preservative nature. It is also used to prepare alcoholic drinks (i.e. mead). In laboratory, honey is used to stimulate the growth of plants, the bacterial culture, in insect diet and in the preparation of poison baits for fruit flies.

23.2 Bees Wax

Bees wax is synthesised by the bees i.e. a natural secretion of the worker bees and is poured out in thin, delicate scales or flakes.

It is yellowish to greyish brown in colour and insoluble in water but completely soluble in ether solvent. It is obtained from the combs of wild hives, frame hives and cappings. The main source in India is the combs of the wild bees (*Apis dorsata*) from which several pounds of wax is produced annually. Its melting point ranges from 63.5 to 65°C and specific gravity is 1.

Chemical and Physical Properties of Bees Wax:

Following data is for pure wax it can be used to compare the adulterated sample of wax.

Chemical components		Per cent
Alkyl esters of fat and wax acids	–	72.00
Cholesteryl esters of fatty acids	–	0.8
Lactones	–	0.6
Free wax acids	–	13 – 13.5
Hydrocarbons	–	12 – 12.5
Moisture	–	1 – 2
Physical constants		**Range for bees wax**
Specific gravity at 15.5°C	–	0.955 – 0.970
Melting point °C	–	62 – 65
Setting point °C	–	61 – 62.5
Acid value	–	17 – 21
Ester value	–	70 – 80

Economic Importance of Bees Wax:

Bees wax is used in the manufacture of cosmetics (face creams, lotions, lipsticks, eyebrow pencils, rouges, pomades, haircreams, paints) and pharmaceutical use as ointments and pill coatings. It is also used in the manufacture of catholic churche and domestic candles, for the production of polishes (i.e. floor, furniture, shoe, leather dresses, car etc.). Caryons, ink, carbon paper, electrical insulation, water-proof canvas and paper, lubricants in laboratory for microtony. Bees wax has also many uses in military and atomic research.

23.3 Pollen

Pollen is main source of protein which is used by brood for growth (development) in latter stages. *Todd* & *Bretherick* showed that amount of protein content in pollen varies from 7 to 30% depending upon source from different plants. A number of vitamins also occur in various proportions in different sample of pollen.

Each microscopic grain of pollen is a complex concentration of invaluable nutritive and curative substances (Peptones, globulins, amino acid, carbohydrates, fatty substances, enzymes, minerals) and vitamins (B_1, B_2, B_6, B_{12}, A, D, E, K). Thus, these grains are a treasure chest of substances invaluable to the organisms.

Bees make bee bread from pollen. When there is no pollen in a hive the queen ceases to lay egg and the house bees stop making wax and building the cells.

In folk medicine pollen was considered an all purpose remedy and tested clinically in several illnesses and found it particularly effective mixed with honey (1 : 1) for treating hypertension, in complaints of the nervous and endocrine systems. Pollen normalizes the activity of the intestine (especially in cases of colitis or chronic constipation), improves the appetite and increases fitness for work.

23.4 Bee glue (Propolis)

The resinous exudation produced by certain plants is known as bee glue or propolis. It consists of different resins which bee collects from sticky buds of plants like horse chestnut. Pine, fir, birch, poplar, willow etc. but research has shown that it is prepared from pollen. When a bee hive is opened on a sunny summer's day, a brownish green resin-like substance can be seen sticking to the upper edge of the honey comb frame. This is propolis (Greeks – propolis – a suburb).

Bees use glue to fill in cracks in the hive, to attach the corners of frames to the grooves in the hive and to polish the cells of the honey comb. The bodies of dead lizards, snakes and mice that have entered hives are sealed into the walls with bee glue, thereby protecting the colonies against the unpleasant odour and bacterial flora of the putrefying corpses.

On an average propolis contains 55% resin and balsam, 10% scented ethereal or essential oils, 30% wax and 65% pollen. Propolis differ in colour and aroma.

In folk medicine propolis was reputed to have anti-tuberculotic properties, the Moscow Tuberculosis Institute specially tested it for bactericidal properties. During world war-II, propolis was reported to be effective in healing wounds and removing corns. (A piece of propolis was softened by heating and a thin layer smeared on the corn, which was the lightly bandaged. The corn and its root came away completely after a few days). The use of propolis ointment prevented a radiation skin reaction.

The diseases of the upper respiratory tract and the lungs (e.g. bronchitis and tuberculosis) are controlled after inhalation of propolis. (60 gm propolis and 40 g of bees wax in a bowl containing boiling water).

23.5 Bee Venom

Sting consists of acid and alkali glands. They secrete the fluid and together form venom. Bee venom is transparent, has a sharp smell reminiscent of honey, and a bitter burning taste. Its specific gravity is 1.1313. It is acidic in reaction when tested with litmus paper. It contains formic, hydrochloric and orthophosphoric acid, histamine, tryptophan, sulphur and other substances and Magnesium phosphate $Mg_3(Po_4)_2$; traces of copper and calcium. Bee venom also contains many proteins, volatile oils and enzymes - hyaluronidase and phospholipase.

In 1888 the *Viennese clinician* F. Tertsch described 173 cases of rheumatism that had been cured with bee stings. He himself suffered from the same disease. From the results obtained with *apitoxin therapy*, it may be concluded that bee venom blocks the conductivity of the sensory nerves and prevents neuralgic and rheumatic pains and dilates the finer blood vessels, thereby improving blood supply to the tissues.

In folk medicine, bee venom has been used to treat certain eye diseases – kerato-conjunctivities (inflammation of the cornea and mucous membranes) after treatment with bee stings it was completely cured. Bee venom is also used against skin diseases of face (lupus). In conclusion bee venom is being used to treat against rheumatism, eye and skin diseases.

23.6 Royal Jelly

The hypopharyngeal glands of nurse bees secrete a sticky milky fluid known as royal jelly. Nurse bees fed this substance to special grubs (throughout their development) from which developed queen.

Chemical Composition of Royal Jelly:

Royal jelly contains 18% proteins, 10 – 17% sugar, 5.5% fat, more than one per cent minerals and vitamins - B_1, B_2, B_3, B_6, B_C, PP and H but very little vitamin C, A (carotene) or D.

Vitamin – E which stimulates fertility, is also found in royal jelly. Royal jelly and extracts of drone larvae and propolis have anti-influenzal properties. The complex chemical composition of royal jelly has not yet been fully studied, but medicine has been enriched by its biostimulating properties. It is known to contain acetylcholine, which dilates the blood vessels and is therefore used to treat hypertension.

Joseph Matuszewski (1965) showed that royal jelly normalizes metabolism, has a diuretic effect and can be used to prevent obesity and emaciation, builds up resistance to infections and regulates endocrine glands and good for coronary deficiency.

***

(b) Aim:

Bee Pests, Parasites and Enemies (D).

Honey bees are attached by large number of enemies called bee pests. Everything possible should be done to keep them out of the country because they may wipe out the Indian beekeeping industry. A brief account of the bee enemies is as follows.

23.7 Wax Moths

Several moths are hazardous to honey comb and honey bees. They can be grouped into two types viz. - first are robbers and second are breeders. Most danger robber is the "Death's head hawk moth" – *Acherontia styx* (Fabr.) This the minor pest commonly called Lesser wax-moth. This moth enters the hives at night and drinks up the honey.

The breeders are the greater wax-moth - *Galleria mellonella* L. and the lesser wax moth - *Achroia grisella* L. *Galleria mellonella* is more common and more damaging. The adults are Brownish grey in colour, measures 10 to 18 mm in length and wing expanse is 25 to 40 mm from side to side. The males are smaller than the females.

Fig. 23.1: 'Death's head' moth (*Acherontia styx*)

The *Achroia grisella* L. the adults, larvae and pupae of this moth are smaller. Both the moths lay eggs in the combs, which hatch into small larvae. The larvae burrow through the wax, feeding particularly on pollen which reduces the combs into masses of webs. The first symptom of the entry of the larvae in the comb is the presence of small masses of minute particles of wax outside the holes. In severe infestation, further brood rearing is stopped and the colony deserts its home.

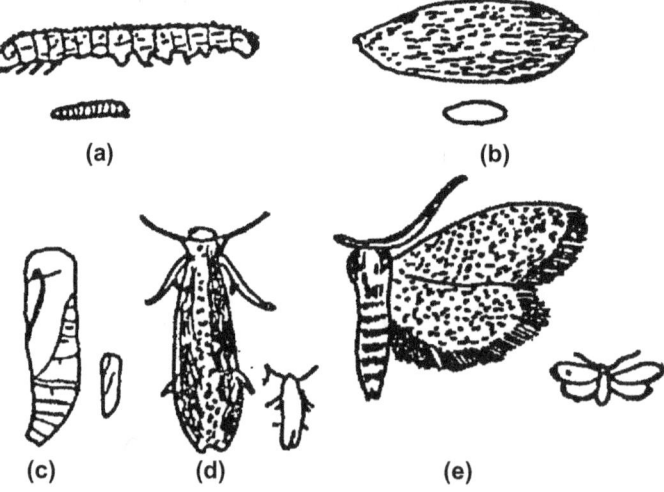

(a)   (b)

(c)   (d)   (e)

Fig. 23.2: (a) Lesser Wax-moth (*Achroia grisella*): a-caterpillar, b-cocoon covered with pellets of exereta; c-pupa; d-moth in repose; e-moth with wings spread. The figures in outline natural sizes

The larvae spin a tough cocoon from which emerges adults. Bees keep these pests under control, they catch and throw out the larvae as soon as they emerge and clean up the combs if that are slightly infested. The use of fumigant - *Paradichloro-benzene* in stored combs gives protection against these moths.

Fig. 23.3: (b) Colony affected by Wax Moth

23.8 Wax Beetles (Tenebrionidae)

Among the beetles two species are noticed as enemies of honey bees. The first Indian beetle (*Platybolium alvearium*) enter the beehive to steal honey and second the African beetle, *Aethina tunmida* enter in the hive for breeding purpose. Both are considered as minor pest of bee colonies. The female beetle lays egg in crevices of the hive. After 4-5 days of incubation period they hatch out into larvae which last for 103-120 days then transform into pupae. The pupal period is 6-7 days; after this period adults emerge. The total life-cycle is completed in 113 to 132 days.

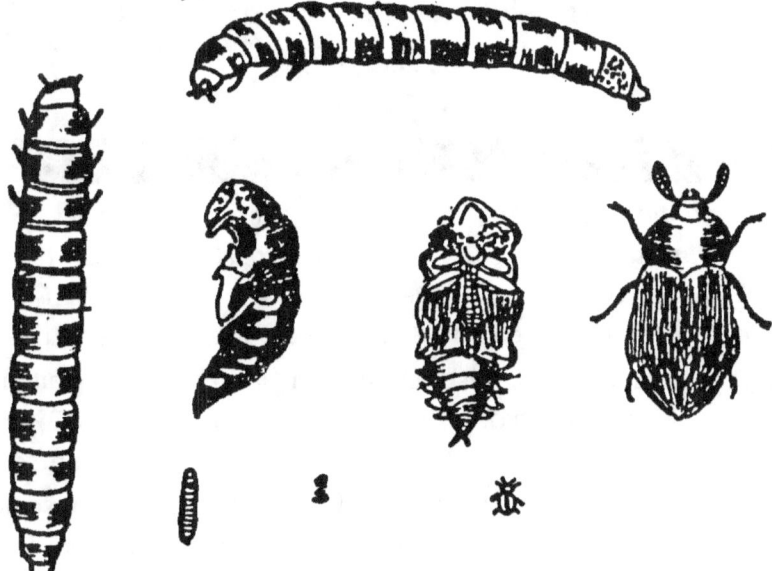

Fig. 23.4: Wax bettle (*Bradmeas sp.*): top and left. grub; centre. pupa; and right. adult. The figure in outlne show natural sizes

The grubs (Larvae) are found among the *debris* on the bottom board or nibbling pieces of an empty old comb in weak colonies. The wax beetles are responsible for unhygienic conditions in the hive, therefore, regular cleaning of the bottom boards and thorough inspection of empty comb will keep them free from these minor nuisance pests. Paradichlorobenzene (PDB) is protective for combs in storage.

23.9 Wasps

Many species of *Vespa* (*V. orientalis, V. auraria, V. magnifera,* etc.) are found on the plains and hilly regions. Wasps are social insects and build paper nests in cavities of different sites (i.e. trees, walls, cracks etc.). The wasps are predaceous in nature on the bees. They catch bees from blossoms or even at the entrance of the hive. Wasps are very bold to enter inside the hive and catch the bees directly from the comb of weak colonies; sometimes finishing off the entire colony. The wasp macerate the bees and feed their young ones (Larvae) on a paste-like material.

The method to protect the bees from wasps is to destroy their nests by burning them or spraying insecticides like 5% benzene hexachloride (BHC) emulsion or by blowing 10% DDT dust in underground nests.

(a) Yellow band wasp   **(b) Golden wasp**   **(c) Black wasp.**

Fig. 23.5

23.10 Ants

Many species of ants [carpenter ant - *Componotus compresses* (Fabr), small red household ant - *Dorylus labiatus* (shuk) and others *Monorium indicum* (Morell), *Monorium destructor* (Ters)]. Visit bee colonies and take away honey, brood, pollen, dead bodies and other debris; particularly from weak colonies. Strong colonies keep away these enemies.

(a) Control measures involved, destruction of ant nests in the vicinity of the beehives by fumigant carbondisulphide or by the use of insecticide – 0.2% BHC suspension or 0.1% calcium emulsion or sealing the underground nest of ants by mud.

(b) In the apiaries, the hives should be placed on stands whose legs should be wrapped with tapes soaked in corrosive sublimate, a good ant repellent or legs of stand should be placed in earthen pots containing water or engine oil or tar.

23.11 Lizards, Toads and Frogs

All these animals are being insectivorous feed upon bees. They often devour bees from hive entrances as well as when foragers are visiting blossoms this results in the reduction of colony strength. Protection against these animals may be keeping the hives on stands and being watchfulness.

23.12 Birds

Certain species of birds visit apiaries during particular season. The king crows - *Dicrurus macrocercus* (vielillot) and *D. ater* visit apiaries on cloudy days and prey upon bees. The bee-eater – *Merops orientalis* (Latham) and *M. superciliosus (L.)* sits on trees on telegraph wires near an apiary and picks the bees on wings.

Since, both these birds do much harm and help in keeping down insect population of a locality. No large scale measures against them can be recommended. Since, shooting them with 0.22 bore rifle is advised to beekeepers.

Fig. 23.6: Bee eater - Merops orientalis King crow – Dicrurus eater

23.13 Mammals

Some bears, badgers and ofcourse man also come in the category of bee enemies. The bears and badgers break open the hives and eat bees, brood, honey, pollen and destroy the whole colony. Man steal the honey from hives during night. Protection can be provided against the first two, who can prevent the third from depredation of the bee colonies both for honey and wax.

✷✷✷

Practical 24...

Aim:

(A) To study the life cycle of Bombyx mori (D).

Sericulture or the silk industry is a very important branch of applied zoology. It deals with production of silk yarn by artifically rearing silkworms. The five main sericulture producer and consumer countries of the world are Japan, China, South Korea, U.S.S.R. and India. The silk-fibre is a protein produced from the silkglands of silkworms. There are two main types of silks, *mulberry silk* and *non-mulberry silk*. Mulberry silk produced by silkworms which feed on mulberry leaves while the non-mulberry silkworms which feed on plant leaves other than mulberry. There are three types of non-mulberry silk, namely Tasar (Kosa) silk, Muga silk and Eri silk.

Following description is pertaining to Mulberry silk.

24.1 Systematic Position

Phylum	–	Arthropoda
Sub-phylum	–	Mandibulata
Class	–	Insecta
Sub-class	–	Pterygota
Division	–	Endopterygota
Order	–	Lepidoptera
Family	–	Bombycidae
Genus	–	*Bombyx*
Species	–	*mori*

24.2 External Characters

The adult moth of *Bombyx mori* is seldom creamy white in colour and wooly fat bodied. It is about 25 mm long with a wing-span of 40-50 mm from side to side. The body is divided into head, thorax and abdomen. The *head* possess a pair of compound eyes, a pair of bushy antennae and the mouth parts with long proboscis. The *thorax* is three segmented (pro, meso and metatoracic segments) and bears three pairs of legs and two pairs of wings. The *abdomen* of male is 8 segmented and female has 7 segments. Female has fat, larger abdomen. At the caudal end, the male moth has a pair of hooks (Harpes) whereas the female moth has a knob-like projection with sensory hair. The female is less active than male.

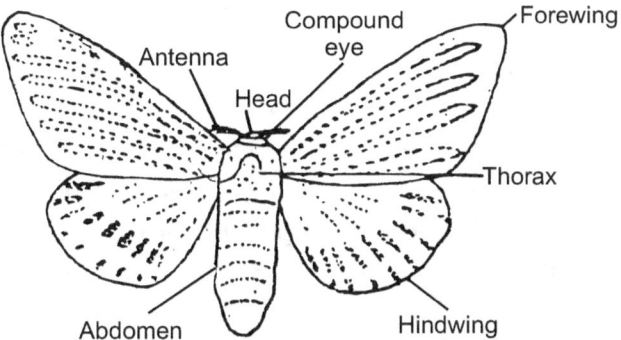

Fig. 24.1: Moth (*B. mori*)

The silkmoth is *dioecious* i.e. the sexes are separate. Fertilization is internal, preceded by copulation. Silkmoths pass through a complete metamorphosis (Holometabolous) from egg to adult stage through two intermediate stages, larva (catepillar) and pupa (cocoon).

The life cycle of *B. mori* consists of four stages, namely, egg, larva, pupa and adult.

24.3 Life Cycle of *Bombyx mori*

Egg: During sericulture, the female moth is made to lay eggs on sheets of paper. Each female can lay 300-400 small, smooth, subspherical eggs. They measure 1 to 1.3 mm in length and 0.9 to 1.2 mm in width. The eggs are kept in cold storage for about six weeks. They are then washed in water and dried indoors.

Fig. 24.2: Egg on leaves of *B. mori*

There are two types of eggs, namely,

(a) **Hibernating eggs:** Deposited in spring, which undergo diapause and hatch out only in next spring.

(b) **Non-hibernating eggs:** Derived from successive generations without any pause in a year.

Larvae: Eggs when fresh are bright yellow in colour and under suitable temperature, embryonic development takes place and colour changes from yellow to brown, then to gray and on 10th day they hatch into black coloured polypod catepillar. It has large head, the skin is rough, wrinkled and densely covered with bristles. It measures about 4-6 mm in length.

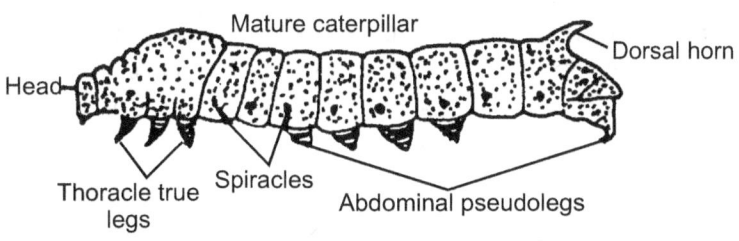

Fig. 24.3: Silk moth (*Bombyx mori*) Larva

A full grown larva is 6-8 cm in length. The body of larva is divisible into head, thorax and abdomen. The head bears a pair of short antennae, two eye spots, mouth parts and a spinnerret (silk spinning apparatus). Larva moults four times within 30-40 days and reaches to fifth instar. The fifth instar larva becomes transparent and waxy in appearance.

Pupa: Full grown larvae stops feeding and become restless and inactive. If suitable place given i.e. dried plants or bamboo mountage (chandrika), they soon begin to spin their cocoons in 3 days of constant motions of the head from side to side at the rate of 65 per minute. The cocoon is formed from a secretion of two large silk glands as a clear viscous fluid. On contact with air, this secretion becomes harden to form silk fibre. Each silk gland extrudes a fine filament of pulp material called *brin* or *fibroin* and two such brins are struck together by *sericin* or silk gum in the spinneret to form a single continuous fibre known as the *seric* bane of about 500 m long and 0.02 mm wide.

The cocoons are oval and vary in colour from white to a beautiful golden yellow. The cocoon provides protection for the developing pupa inside.

The pupal stage is generally resting, inactive stage. It is incapable of feeding and appears quiescent. During the pupal stage, internal organs undergo a compelte change and assume the new form of the adult moth.

The prominent morphological parts visible on pupa are a pair of large compound eyes, a pair of large antennae, fore and hindwings and the legs. Ten abdominal segments seen on the ventral side and only nine on dorsal side. Seven-pairs of spiracles are also seen on abdomen.

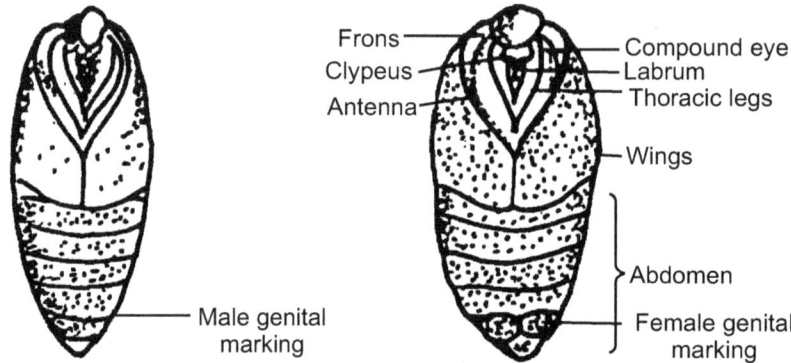

Fig. 24.4: Male and female pupa *Bombyx mori*

Adult: Within the cocoon, the pupa shrinks in length and in about 10-15 days a full-fledged moth emerges through an opening in the end of cocoon. The cocoons from which the moth emerges are called pierced cocoons. They are of low value because they cannot be reeled.

The ashy white moth has a fat body and wing expanse of about 5 cm. It takes no food and rarely attempts to fly but has high capacity for reproduction. The external features are described in external morphology of moth earlier.

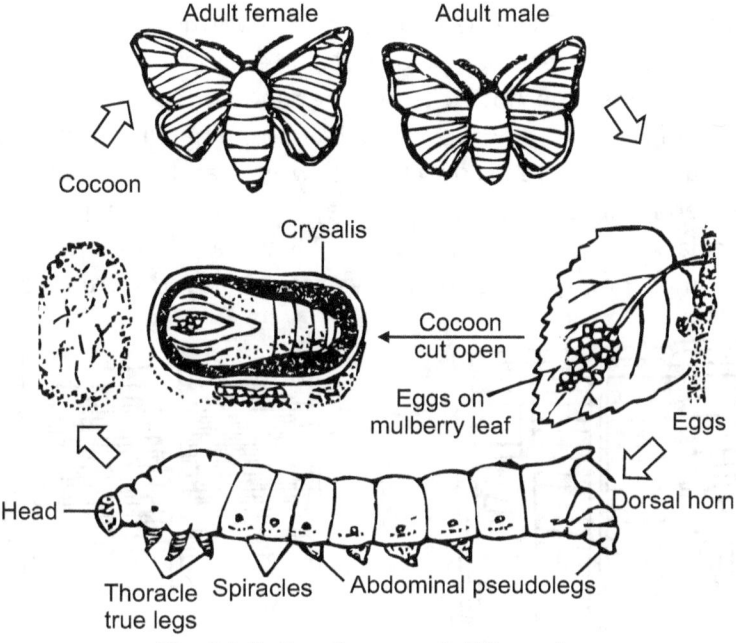

Fig. 24.5: *Bombyx mori.* Life cycle

***

Aim:

(B) Study of any five equipments of Sericulture [D].

To study any five equipments in sericulture.

Following rearing equipments are required for the proper rearing of silkworms, without which the rearing would be a partial success.

(a) Rearing stands: Rearing stands are made of wood or bamboo and are portable for transportation. A rearing stand may be constructed and have dimensions like 2.5 m high × 1.5 m long × 1 m wide and should have 10 shelves with a space of 20 cm between each shelf. The trays are arranged on the shelves and each stand can accommodate 10 rearing trays. Six stands are enough for each rearing room.

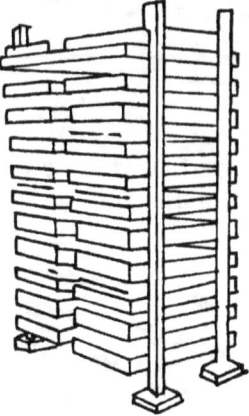

Fig. 24.6: Rearing stand with Ant wells

(b) Ant wells: Ants are a serious menace to silkworms. To protect them, the legs of the rearing stand are kept in rectangular or circular enamel or concrete bowls containing water mixed with insecticide. The Ant wells may be made of concrete or stone blocks 20 cm square and 7.5 cm high with a deep groove of 2.5 cm running all round the top (Fig. 24.6).

(c) Rearing trays: These are used to rear silkworms and are usually made up of locally available cheap material like bamboo so that they are light (in weight) and easy to handle. They are either circular (1.2 – 1.4 m diameter and 7.5 cm depth) or rectangular (0.7 – 0.9 m × 0.9 – 1.2 m). Sometimes, box type wooden trays are employed to rear early instars (I and II instar larvae).

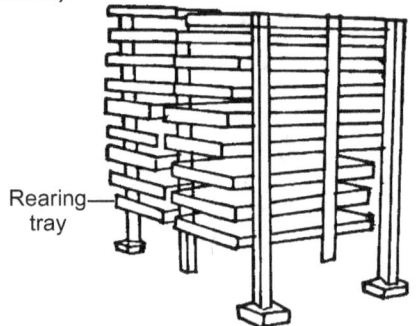 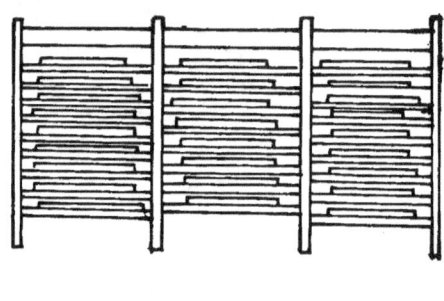

Rearing tray

(a) Rearing stand with rectangular wooden trays **(b) Rearing stand with circular trays**
Fig. 24.7

(d) Paraffin paper: Thick craft paper sheets coated with paraffin wax (M.P. 55°C) are required to cover the rearing trays to maintain the humidity in rearing beds and prevent withering of chopped leaves. It is used for rearing early stage silkworms.

(e) Foam rubber strips: Pieces (2.5 × 2.5 cm) of foam rubber soaked in water are kept all round silkworm rearing beds to maintain humidity during the first two instars. Newspaper folded strips moistened with water could be a convenient substitute.

(f) Chopsticks: Chopsticks are tapering bamboo rods meant to pick up younger stages of larvae to ensure their hygienic handling and preventing from injuries. These are made of bamboo approximately 17.5 cm to 20 cm long and tapering to one end.

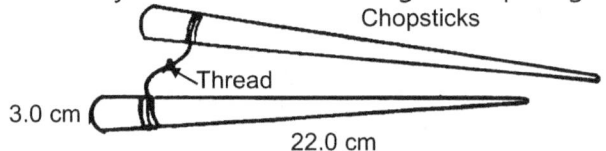

Chopsticks

Thread

3.0 cm

22.0 cm

Fig. 24.8: Chopsticks

(g) Feathers: Bird feathers, preferably white, are important items of silkworm rearing room. They are used for brushing the delicate newly hatched larvae (worms) onto the rearing bed to prevent injuries.

Feather

Fig. 24.9: Feather

(h) Leaf chamber: Mulberry leaves harvested from the field are stored and preserved fresh for feeding the worms at set intervals during the day.

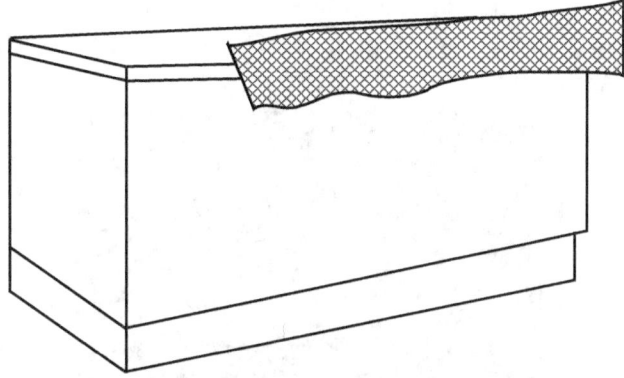

Fig. 24.10: Leaf chamber

The leaves can be stored in cool rooms or in the rooms covered with cloth or polythene sheets. They can be also stored in leaf chambers (1.5 m long, 0.9 m wide and 0.8 m deep) of wooden strips fixed some distance apart of some porous board. The chamber with leaves is covered all over with gunny bag cloth kept moist during the summer months and dry days.

(i) Chopping board: This is made of soft wood and is used for cutting the leaf to the suitable sizes required for feeding the worms in the different instars. The size of the board is 0.9 m × 0.9 m and 5 cm thick or of any convenient size.

(j) Chopping knives: Chopping knives are used for cutting the mulberry leaves. They are usually 0.3 – 0.5 m long with a broad knife blade and a wooden handle. Two sized knives, small and large for chopping small pieces for younger instars and large pieces for older instars are needed. Chopped leaves falling on the mat are better collected in an enamelled receptacle.

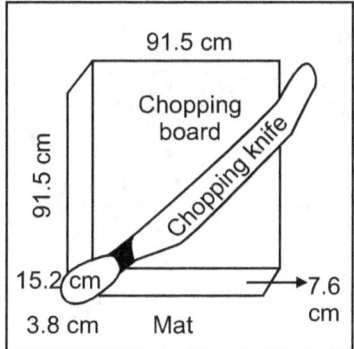

Fig. 24.11: Chopping board and knife

(k) Mats: Mats usually 1.2 × 1.8 m are used for collecting the leaves. When chopping is done on the floor, they prevent the dust and dirt on the floor getting mixed in with the leaves.

(l)   **Cleaning nets:** Nets made up of cotton or nylon of the mesh size suitable for different instars are used for changing and rearing beds so that the left over leaf pieces and litter are filtered out without the larvae being touched by hand. Mannual separation of larvae from the litter has the risk of injuring and killing many of them. Mesh sizes suitable for I, II, III, IV and V instars are 2 mm^2, 10 mm^2 and 20 mm^2 respectively.

Fig. 24.12: Cleaning net

(m) Mountages: Mountages (cocoonages) are used as supports for the silkworms to spin cocoons. They are made up of rectangular bamboo mat tied on 4 bomboo sticks and bearing on its surface spirals of bamboo tapes (1.8 m long, 1.2 m wide and 5-6 m spiral tapes leaving a gap of 5-6 cm). The ripe worms about to spin cocoons are transferred onto them. The larvae suspend themselves to the spirals and spin cocoons. The mountages are also called as *chandrikes* in India.

The advantages of chandrikes are:

1.   They are cheap and easily made.
2.   Can be easily stored/stacked.
3.   Excreta of spinning worms dry up soon due to free passages and thus prevents cocoons from getting stained.
4.   Can be easily shifted from place to place.
5.   Can be easily disinfected.

Fig. 24.13: Bamboo mountage (chandrika) with cocoons

(n) Feeding stands: These are small wooden stands 0.9 m high used for holding the trays during feeding and cleaning.

Fig. 24.14: Feeding stand

***

Practical **25**...

Aim:

Compulsory submission of atleast five photographs of insect pest/fishes/any animal corresponding to theory courses.

- The students are requested to refer theory text book for photographs of pest/fishes, and only animal, etc.
- Select any five good photographs, diagrams, figures from book and Xerox it.
- Arrange and affix the selected photographs and label it carefully.
- Submit the prepared document to your class teacher at the time of practical of your bath.

Practical **26**...

Aim:

Compulsory study tour/visit to the following Institutes:

(a) Fishery

(b) Sericulture

(c) Apiculture

(d) Agriculture University/College/Any Agricultural Farm

(e) Sea Shore.

Along with laboratory studies, field visits or visits to different institutes are equally important for effective and meaningful teaching and learning process. Students can study the animals, their life cycle in nature in their natural habitat. Therefore, such visits, excursion tours are purposefully included in the syllabus of practical course. These practicals have self-employment potential. After completion of graduation students can start their own business and generate employment for others also. Therefore, the main purpose of these visits is to acquire the knowledge of these applied branches of Zoology and also generate the self-employment.

Before you visit to a particular institute follow the important tips given as follows:

(1) Collect the information, postal addresses, telephone numbers, e-mail address and website of the institution to which you want to visit.

(2) Seek the permission from the Head or Director of the institution through proper channel i.e. either through College Principal or Head, Department of Zoology.

(3) Fix the date and time of your visit to the institute.

(4) Do not visit the institute without prior permission of the concern authority. Many times sudden visits are not entertained.

(5) Observe the discipline and silence during visit.

(6) Request the concern authority for giving detailed information, guidance through film show, slides or lecture.

(7) Ask the questions, queries, doubts to the guide.

(8) Request for more and additional information.

(9) If allowed, try to take important photographs of the animals or site.

(10) Prepare the tour/visit or report in your own words and write in the journal.

26.1 Visit to Fishery or Fish Farm

For each district, District Fishery Department has been set up by Government of Maharashtra under the District Fisheries Officer. This Office has got fish farms near dam areas. Fish farm is located at Hadapsar which is one of the well set up fishery farm.

During the visit, study the following important aspects of fish farm:

(1) Study the nature of soil where fish tanks are developed.

(2) Collect the information of tank size, water level, physio-chemical characteristic of water in the tanks.

(3) Study the different types of tanks, breeding happa, nursery ponds, rearing ponds, production and stocking ponds.

(4) Study the types of cultiviable fishes and their food and feeding habits.

(5) Collect the information regarding induced breeding by hypophysation.

(6) Observe the eggs, egg stripes, finger lings small and large fishes.

(7) Study the different types of weeds and predators which grow in fish tanks and their methods of eradication.

(8) Study the different methods of fish harvesting and get the information regarding Economics.

(9) Try to take photographs of fish tanks and different types of fishes.

(10) Write the visit report.

Hadapsar Fish Breeding Centre, Pune; Manar Fish Breeding Centre Barul; Tal-Khandar, District Nanded; Dhanegaon Fish Breeding Centre, Dhanegaon, District Latur, Nasik and many centres are located in different districts. Students can visit nearby centre and study the fish farms.

26.2 Visit to Sericulture Institute

A very old and well maintained sericulture located in Pune near *Mariaai Gate*. Observe and study the following things:

(1) Observe the different species of silkworms.

(2) Study the life cycle of *Bombyx mori* with eggs, larva, pupa or cocoon and adults.

(3) Study the mulberry plant and its leaves.

(4) Study the rearing house.

(5) Observe the rearing stands, ant wells, rearing trays, paraffin paper, foam rubber strips, chopsticks, feathers, leaf chamber chopping board, knives, mats, cleaning nets, mountages, feeding stands and other miscellaneous appliances.

(6) Study the rearing technique.

(7) Observe the important diseases and pests of silkworm.

(8) Observe the different types of silk.

(9) Prepare the visit report. Add your comments.

26.3 Visit to Apiculture Institute

Central Bee Research Institute is established at Pune, (opposite to Agriculture College) by Central Government of India and Apiculture Institute of Mahableshwar by State Government. Both the institutes are involved in research, extention, training and development, etc. activities of bee keeping.

During the visit, study the following important aspects of apiculture:

(1) Observe the different types of honey bees. *Apis mellifera, Apis, florea, Apis indica* and *A. dorsata* with their caste system i.e. queen, workers and drones.

(2) See the honey comb and observe the different types of cells as per caste.

(3) Study the life cycle of honey bee. *Apis mellifera.*

(4) Study the various types of bee disease and parasite.

(5) Observe the bee enemies.

(6) Study the bee-keeping equipments i.e. bee box, honey extractor, smoker, bee veil, queen cages, knife etc.

(7) Study and observe the various bee products like Honey, Wax, Bee glue, Bee venom, Royal jelly and Pollen.

(8) Make photographs of honey comb, honey bees, beekeeping equipments etc. with the permission of Director of Apiculture Institute.

(9) Write the visit report.

26.4 Visit to Agriculture University/College/Farm

There are well set up six Agricultural Universities in Maharashtra State viz.: Mahatma Phule Agriculture University, Rahuri; Konkan Krishi Vidyapeeth, Dapoli, Panjabrao Krishi Vidyapeeth, Marathwada Krishi Vidyapeeth Parbhani etc. Visit the entomology department of your nearest Agriculture University of your area and observe the following:

1. Different types of insect pests.

2. Time of infestation of pest according to the crops or vegetables.

3. The stage of development of insect life causing damage to crops/vegetables.

4. Nature of damage.

5. Control measures undertaken to check the pest population.

6. Types of insect protection appliance used to control the pest.

7. Take the photographs of pests, type of damage to crops etc. for you study tour record.

26.5 Visit to Sea Shore

The Maharashtra state is having 720 km sea shore/coastal line (Konkan Kinarpatti). Visit the any sea shore (i.e. Alibaug, Ratnagiri, Murud jangira, etc.) in early morning and afternoon i.e. while tide and after tide.

Collect the various marine animals i.e. different fishes, starfishes, crabs, prawns, worms, shelled animals etc. Preserve them in diluted formalene. Brought to your laboratory and try to identify their common and biological names.

Practical Skeleton Paper

Max. Marks: 100

Q.1 Dissect Starfish/Scoliodon so as to expose its ......system.   **(16)**

Q.2 Make a stained temporary preparation of ......from Honey bee/Starfish/Scoliodon **(10)**

Q.3 Identification (Non-chordates and Chordates)   **(21)**

    (a) Identify and classify giving reasons (Arthropoda)

    (b) Identify and classify giving reasons (Mollusca/Echinodermata)

    (c) Identify and classify giving reasons (Cyclostomata/Reptiles)

    (d) Identify and classify giving reasons (Aves/Mammals)

    (e) Identify and describe the types of mouthparts of insect

    (f) Identify and describe (Shell/Foot of mollusca/Poisonous/Non-poisonous snake)

    (g) Identify and comment on its modifications (Beak/feet modifications in birds)

Q.4 Identification (Applied Zoology)   **(18)**

    (a) Identify and give its economic importance (Any fish)

    (b) Identify and describe (Any gear/craft)

    (c) Identify and give its application (Plant protection appliance)

    (d) Identify and describe (One stage of life cycle of honeybee/silkworm)

    (e) Identify and describe (Sericulture equipment)

    (f) Identify and describe (Bee keeping equipment/Bee product)

Q.5 (a) Tour report and Certified Journal   **(05)**

    (b) Viva- voce   **(05)**

Q.6 Submission of field visit report along with five photographs/sketches of insect pest/fishes/any animal   **(05)**

✱✱✱

(P.1)